Hello?

LIZA WIEMER

Spencer Hill Contemporary / Spencer Hill Press

This book is a work of fiction. Names, characters, places, and incidents are products of the author's imagination or are used fictitiously. Any resemblance to actual events, locales, or persons, living or dead, is entirely coincidental.

Contact: Spencer Hill Press,
27 West 20th Street, Suite 1102, New York, NY 10011

Please visit our website at www.spencerhillpress.com

First Edition: October 2015
Liza Wiemer
Hello?/ by Liza Wiemer – 1st ed.
p. cm.
Summary: Linked by one phone call, Hello? combines five teens' stories in a narrative of friendship, loss, love, heartbreak, and hope.

The author acknowledges the copyrighted or trademarked status and trademark owners of the following wordmarks mentioned in this fiction: Aaron Rodgers, Absolut, Academy Award, Alfred Hitchcock, Alicia Keys, AP, Baby Ruth, B.B. King, Berol, Big Mac, Camaro, Camry, *Carrie*, Chevy Tahoe, Coke, Converse, *CSI*, Culver's, Death's Door vodka, Dom Pérignon, Emmy Award, *Entertainment Weekly*, Facebook, Ford Expedition, Ford Explorer, Frisbee, Google, Grateful Dead, Green Bay Packers, Happy Meal, Hello Kitty, *Henry and Mudge*, iPod, Jeep, *Law & Order: Special Victims Unit*, Led Zeppelin, *The Lord of the Rings: The Two Towers*, M&Ms, MasterCard, Minnesota Vikings, MTV, NYU, PayPal, *People*, Remington, Sith, Six Flags Great America, *Sports Illustrated*, Starbucks, Super Ball, Super Bowl, Syfy, Tabasco, Taylor Swift, *Teen Mom*, Thermos, *Thrasher* magazine, Tic Tacs, Tiffany, Tony Award, *Where's Waldo*, Wrangler, Xbox, Zenith, Zest

Cover design by Kate Kaynak and Jim Wiemer
Cover layout and element contributions by Jenny Zemanek
Cover photo by Steve Waldron
Drawings by Jim Wiemer
Door County Map © 1997 : Used with permission from the Door County Visitor Bureau
Interior layout by Jenny Perinovic
Author Photo © Jim Wiemer

ISBN 978-1-63392-037-8 (paperback)
ISBN 978-1-63392-038-5 ((e-book)

Printed in the United States of America

To these incredible women, who for decades
have been a positive force in my life.

Lena Goldberg, OBM
Barbara McCray, OBM
Barbara Wiemer, OBM

Eileen Graves
Betsy Kaplan
Lynn Wiese Sneyd

Benay Browne Katz
Shirlee Doft
Barbara Goldberg

PRAISE FOR *HELLO?*

Authors:

"During the 1960's, Carole King released an album entitled *Tapestry*—a masterful weaving of story and song. A half-century later, author Liza Wiemer has mirrored that blend by wonderfully stringing together several forms of narration, one specific to each of her characters. *Hello?* is a truly remarkable and memorable story communicated in a superbly envisioned way."
–Paul Volponi, award-winning author of *The Final Four, Game Seven,* and *Black and White.*

"A triumph of writing and humanity. The characters stayed with me long after I read the book."
—Huntley Fitzpatrick, author of *The Boy Most Likely To, What I Thought Was True,* and *My Life Next Door*

"Brave, beautiful, and wholly original, this story about tantalizing connections and heartbreaking relationships will haunt you, fill you with hope, and leave you smiling."
—Martina Boone, author of *Compulsion* and the *Heirs of Watson Island* series

"Liza Wiemer's *Hello?* is a poignant tale of friendship, love, loss, and resilience. Told from multiple points of view, the richly drawn characters offer a powerful example of how connected we all truly are. This book will compel readers to consider the existence of destiny. *Hello?* grabbed me from the first page and pulled me right through to the gorgeous ending."
—Kristina McBride, author of *One Moment* and *The Tension of Opposites*

"In *Hello?*, Liza Wiemer beautifully weaves together a moving story told by authentic characters, tackling important subjects that will deeply touch the reader."
—Elizabeth Eulberg, author of *Better Off Friends* and *Lonely Hearts Club*

"A sensitive and deeply drawn portrait of five teenagers whose lives intersect in ways both obvious and surprising. Liza Wiemer's characters are so real they leap off the page."
—Leah Cypess, author of the *Death Sworn* series

"Heartfelt and honest, *Hello?* will have you rooting for its characters until the very last page."
—Heather Demetrios, author of *I'll Meet You There* and *Something Real*

"Tendrils of destiny and healing weave through this fearless exploration of interconnected grief and guilt within the overlapping spheres of love, friendship and family. Deeply moving!"
—Tammara Webber, author of NYT Bestsellers *Easy* and *Breakable*

Bloggers:

"In her YA debut, Liza Wiemer has officially launched herself on the map with grace. *Hello?* is a powerful and brilliantly woven story of love, loss, and human connection that makes you believe in the world again. It owned my heart from the first page to the last. One of the most original books EVER."
—Hannah McBride, *The Irish Banana*

"Liza Wiemer's words evoke the heart of the Door County, Wisconsin setting and allow the story's honest portrayal of five teens to resonate far beyond. Through the intertwining formats and perspectives, elements of family, grief, faith, memories, friendship, love, fear, and hope seem destined to combine in a profound way. A remarkable YA debut."
—Jillian Heise, NBCT, *Heise Reads & Recommends*

"HELLO? is a captivating story about fractured families, authentic friendships, and the way lives connect, impact, and transform each other. This book is so originally crafted and beautifully executed it will stay with you for a long time."
—Andye Epps, *Reading Teen*

"Heart-stopping, real, and a breath of fresh air, Liza Wiemer's debut is the kind of story that captivates and sticks with you long after you turn the last page. Poignant relationships between family and friends will grab your attention while stunning writing and authentic characters will leave you unable to stop reading until the very end. *Hello?* is an absolute must read."
—Meg Caristi, *Swoony Boys Podcast*

"A beautifully written and uniquely told story about love, loss, learning how to let go, and finding hope again."
—Jen Cooke Fisher, *Jenuine Cupcakes*

"Through love and friendship, choice and fate, the mundane and the divine, Liza Wiemer expertly weaves together five incredibly relatable teen stories. As the characters struggle to reconcile the past and the present, readers take a journey of both heartbreak and hope. With its authentic voice and lyrical writing style, *Hello? is* a strong addition to the genre of contemporary YA. I absolutely loved it!"
—Heidi Zweifel, *YA Bibliophile*

"A uniquely written story about the beauty of human connections told through incredibly vivid characters. It's one contemporary YA fans shouldn't miss."
—Kathy Coe, *A Glass of Wine Book Reviews*

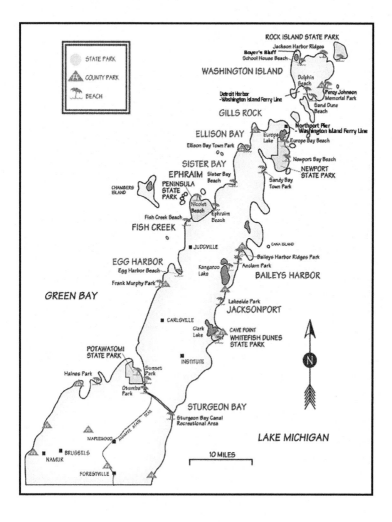

ONE

"It is not length of life, but depth of life."
Ralph Waldo Emerson

TRICIA
WASHINGTON ISLAND, WISCONSIN   SUNDAY, 11:49 P.M.

SOMETIMES I WISH I were a robot. Get a wrench, tighten a bolt. Fix me. Yeah, right. What's wrong with me?

I move my cheek to a dry spot on my tear-dampened pillow and focus on the dim glow coming from the nightlight in the hallway. My hand slips from Brian's as my mind drifts from my darkened bedroom to three doors away—my grandma's room.

In my head, I relive that last night I had with her five months ago today. I climb into her bed and snuggle into her bony body, inhaling the faint smell of her homemade lavender soap and the sour coming from her shallow breaths. She tries to talk, but she's too weak.

Sitting up, I choke out, "I love you so much, Grandma." Her eyes flicker open, then close. I watch her chapped lips move. "Love you," they say. With a heavy sigh and a peaceful smile on her face, she slips into death.

For hours or maybe minutes, I cuddle next to her, hold her hand, and try to comprehend how I will live without her. The person who raised me, loved me, cherished me. Gone. My only family. I can't stop crying. At some point, Brian walks in, the hospice nurse close behind. She must have called him. Sobbing and shaking, I shift away from Grandma. I'm not ready for good-bye. *I'm not ready.* Brian gathers me into his arms and leads me to my own bed. Dr. Wellington gives me two pills and I sleep and sleep and sleep.

I wish I could sleep now.

I glance over at Brian. His bare, broad shoulders gently rise and fall with each breath as he sleeps on his stomach. His closest arm is stretched toward me, but I remain out of reach. A thousand miles away. So alone. *C'mon Tricia. Think about something positive. Think about Brian. One happy memory.*

It should be easy.

It's not.

Breathing deeply, I forget about Brian and begin to play the memory game. Something my grandma and I did when I was little. Because of her rheumy eyes, instead of reading bedtime stories, we'd snuggle in pj's and she'd tell me about a special moment from my childhood. She'd share. I'd share until I could picture every detail. After years of this, I had a stockpile of memories. Somehow, I think she knew I'd need a stash of them.

Looking around my room, I search for an object that will trigger a happy memory. My gaze lands on my dad's dog tags, dangling from the bookshelf above my desk. A breeze from my open window causes them to sway. Almost like they're dancing.

Dancing. Wonderful images fill my mind, and I smile. I'm at the kitchen table eating breakfast with Dad and Grandma. Mom walks in and Dad's attention shifts from his crossword puzzle to her. His face lights up. He drops his pencil, dances over to her, body swaying, hands posed ready to waltz with her. He takes her into his embrace, twirls her around. Even clad in jeans and T-shirts, they're as beautiful as any dance partners I've seen on TV. Perfect for each other. Dad's dog tags swing from Mom's neck. She tucks them into her collar and wraps her arms around Dad's shoulders. I laugh. Grandma laughs. Without missing a beat, Dad bends over, picks me up. They sandwich me between them, and we slide and spin to the sound of Frank Sinatra, Grandma's favorite singer, crooning from the old radio sitting on the counter.

After a few more dizzying twirls, Dad sets me down on my chair, grabs Mom around the waist, dips her low, then gives her a noisy kiss. Winking at me, Dad says, "I'm the luckiest man in the world to have the three best girls."

Dressed in her usual purple velour housecoat and warm smile, Grandma clears our cereal bowls and says, "Enough of the moony-eyes and sweet-talk. Let's get our girl to school for her first day of kindergarten."

Dad scoops me under his arm like a football, does his Green Bay Packers wide receiver imitation. He sprints, ducks, and dives, dodging invisible players around the kitchen. I giggle as he brings me to the sink to wash my hands and face. He gives me a gentle noogie and says, "Pack a lot of knowledge into this brain."

Before we leave, Grandma hugs me close, and I inhale her lavender scent. "How is it possible you've grown up so fast?" she asks.

Little did we know how fast I'd have to grow up.

The memory of Dad's tear-stained face looms in front of me.

Brian shifts closer, yanking me back to the present. His eyes open. I brush the hair off his scruffy cheek, then quickly drop my hand to my side. Watching me, he skims a palm over my leg. With his free hand, he laces his fingers with mine, holding tightly. The feel of his unbreakable grip takes me back to that dancing day with my parents, that first day of kindergarten, before my life changed forever.

My mind wanders to the moment our teacher Mrs. Ehrlich sat Brian and me next to each other during circle time. To when Brian and I read the *Henry and Mudge* chapter book. To holding his hand for a game of charades. Brian whispers, "Don't let go."

"I won't," I say. "Never." And I turn to stare down our first opponent.

Linnea Johannson barrels toward us, and Brian tightens his grip. She bounces off us like a Super Ball. Turn after turn, Brian and I stay locked together. The last one up is Hunter Gunnlaugsson, the biggest and strongest in our class, who runs at us full-force. Brian squeezes my hand, and though it hurts, I don't complain. I grip his as hard as possible. Not even Hunter can break us apart. Prophetically, by the end of the day I know, out of all my friends, Brian will be my best.

Is he still?

His free hand drifts to my inner thigh, and I quiver, but not because it feels good. I tell myself that I should love this. I don't. My head and heart and everything between are engulfed in a pain-filled, miserable fog.

My stomach aches as he continues to caress my body. He lifts my tank top up and over my head. His lips trail over my breasts to my neck until they reach mine. His fingers tangle in my knotty hair. His tongue teases and entices and I try to respond, to give him a part of me. I should want to. I know I should. I used to love his kisses, his touch. He wraps an arm underneath my waist, presses his hips into me. Firm, hard, wood...

Wood.

Once again, like a kite slipping through my fingers and sailing away, my thoughts leave him. Us. My bedroom. My lighthouse. Boyer's Bluff.

I'm leaning against the trunk of a barren beach tree at the edge of the Boyer family plot. I watch Grandma's pine coffin being lowered into the snow-speckled ground. Brian comes over to me, wraps his arm around my waist, and supports me so I won't collapse. The sea of islanders—some sniffling, some stone-faced—fan around the grave; the smell of freshly turned soil lingers in the winter mist. Hardened earth clunks against her casket. One of the worst sounds in the world.

And at this moment, I am one of the most detestable, morbid, messed-up girlfriends in the world.

Brian stops. He shifts his weight onto his forearms, opens his brown eyes, and stares at me. I look away, ashamed at my rejection and the dejection written across his brow. Without a word, he grabs and puts on the Grateful Dead T-shirt I gave him six months ago for his eighteenth birthday. I cower under my grandma's patched quilt—too numb to cry, too lost to be found.

Brian stands. I brace myself for an argument.

He hands me my top. "I'll be downstairs," he mumbles and heads for the door.

"I'm sorry," I whisper. *So sorry.*

The day my grandmother died, Brian stayed over. "I don't want you to be alone," he had said. A part of me recognized that he didn't ask. If he had, I probably would have told him to go home. I needed time to think, to mourn without his vigil. He was here the next night, and the next night, and the next, until his sports equipment filled shelves in the shed, his running shoes were in my closet, and his boxers and T-shirts and jeans were folded neatly in my three bottom dresser drawers. Without ever a formal discussion about him moving into my lighthouse, we were suddenly living together.

I know he worries about me. But this arrangement has strained our relationship. I wish I were strong enough to tell him to leave. I'm consumed by guilt each time I wake and find him asleep on the den couch with the TV on low and an infomercial for an acne product or colon cleanse playing because I've asked him to "give me space."

There are times when he copes with my worst moods—anger, resentment, despair—by walking away. Because it's too damn much to handle. But sometimes—okay, most of the time—his reactions fuel my frustration. Especially when he fiddles around with his cell phone when I'm trying to talk to him about how much I miss my grandma. I want to scream, "Listen to me!" and hurl his phone against a wall and tell him to stop ignoring my pain and deal with it, deal with me.

The few times we did talk about it he said, "Tricia, you think for a half-second I could forget your grandma's gone? I miss her too. What else do you want me to say?" Or "Whatever I do or say is wrong, so give me a damn manual and maybe I can figure it out." Or, "I'm here for you, I love you. Can't you see that? Maybe if we got married now, it would be easier for you."

I don't have answers. Or at least not the answers he wants to hear. I don't want to be married at eighteen.

And I definitely don't want to get married when I'm a mixed-up mess.

I've tried to explain, telling him that I need time to cope with the deep, cutting losses, the emptiness inside me. To work things out in my head and figure out what I want for my life. I know I shoulder plenty of blame for the tension between us and I've said so. Inevitably, I apologize.

He gets this forlorn, distressed look in his eyes like he doesn't have a clue what to do with me. He'll stand there, tightlipped, letting me know he's being extra patient. Like he knows that I'll eventually snap out of this funk and return to the person I was *before.*

I've come close to blurting out, "I want you to move back home." But I've managed to cage and swallow the words. There's too great a risk it might end us. It's not what I want—I love him—and I'm terrified that if I push too hard, I'll lose him too.

Two weeks ago, I thought maybe he had reached his end. Brian was downstairs finishing the laundry while I headed upstairs to bed. Instead, I wandered into Grandma's bedroom. The need to be close to her, to feel her presence, overwhelmed me. I opened her closet, took her purple velour housecoat, and put it on over my clothes. It smelled like her, but it wasn't enough. On her dresser, she had a bottle of lavender oil. I dabbed it on my neck, leaned against the wall, hugged her housecoat close, and breathed in her scent.

Brian walked in, scrunched his nose, and said, "What are you doing?" He eyed Grandma's threadbare housecoat, dotted with bacon grease stains from one of the last breakfasts she cooked. Disgust was written all over his face.

"I just...needed to be close to her."

"By wearing *that*?"

I clung to the sleeves. "Yes. What difference does it make? I wear my dad's Army sweatshirt all the time."

"Yeah, but you wash it." He let out an exasperated breath. "It's clean if you want me to go get it."

I shook my head, frustrated my explanation wasn't enough. Frustrated he didn't understand that Grandma's lavender scent comforted me. How that ratty housecoat was more valuable than gold. I sat on Grandma's bed and started to cry.

"Tricia—" The inflection he added to my name included the unspoken words of *"Oh great, not again."*

I cut him off. "Don't."

He turned his attention to the window overlooking the front of the house and stared out for a long time. Then he shoved his hands in his pockets and refocused on me. I heard the *clack* of his car keys as he fingered them, followed by more silence, then mournful resignation. "I'm going to sleep."

"Okay." I dried my eyes on Grandma's soft sleeve. "I'll be there in a minute."

He turned, hesitated, then said, "Do me a favor, please? Take a shower before you do. It's kinda creepy having you smell like your grandma, ya know?"

Embarrassed, humiliated, ashamed, I nodded, then removed her housecoat and returned it to her closet. I took one of the longest showers of my life. I even stayed after the water turned cold.

I wish I were better for him. I wish I knew how to fix me, fix *us*. It's bad enough that for the past five months Brian has seen the worst of me, that I don't know how to love him the way he needs anymore. That I *can't*.

Under the circumstances, I do what I can to insulate myself from others. Not easy in a community where almost everyone is in everybody's business. There are plenty of islanders who like to be in mine. No point fighting it. It's the way it is here. So, I try to avoid the places I'll see people and choose off-peak times to buy supplies at Mann's Grocery Store. Occasionally, when I can't cope with another well-meaning person checking up on me, I won't answer the doorbell.

I think about my friends, especially Linnea, Jeremiah's daughter and a fellow senior. She doesn't get on my case or invite herself over. She gives me the space I need. On occasion, she'll text and I'll text back. It's enough.

I haven't walked into school for months. All my courses are online, and being a part of the smallest school district in the state of Wisconsin allows Principal Schuster to be flexible. We have an agreement. As long as I do the work and keep my grades at As and Bs, studying from home isn't a problem. Brian hates that Principal Schuster "caved in." But I calmly explained that I wanted and needed to be away from all the normal, non-grieving students. I couldn't handle the constant reminders that I'm different from everyone else. Everyone else has at least one brother or sister or cousin attending the school. Family permeates our community and is the center of everyone's activities. Birthdays, holidays, baseball, trips off island, church, community center. Every business is family. It's too much.

Principal Schuster understands. Brian doesn't. "I'm your family," he argued. "My parents, my sister, this community *is* your family." No matter how many times I try to explain, he just doesn't get it. We have two different definitions for family.

THE DIP OF the mattress wakes me up. I open my eyes to Brian, who's sitting close to the edge, not touching me. Dim light from the hallway casts a halo around his head and shoulders. His face remains shadowed and I can't decipher his expression. I'm not even sure he's looking at me.

To see him better, I shift onto my side, fold and shove my pillow under my head. It doesn't make much of a difference other than to let Brian know I'm now awake.

A long, heavy sigh escapes from his mouth, weighing me down with dread. It hangs in the air like a question I'm supposed to answer. "What am I to do with you?" it asks.

I don't know.

He slips one of my hands into his and absently traces my fingers and palm. I hug my legs into my chest. He flinches at my retreat and I'm instantly sorry. I release my grip, scoot closer to him, and rest a hand on his knee to prove I'm making an effort. I'm trying. Of course, it's not enough. We both know it. But I don't have anything more than this to give. He deserves someone who's happy, carefree, unburdened from loss. I can't be that Tricia Boyer. What was left of her disappeared five months ago.

Brian stands, leans down, and gives me a brotherly kiss on the cheek. He rests his forehead against mine. His warm breath shudders over my closed eyelids. Tension radiates from his body as the muscles I know so well stiffen against my torso.

"I can't do this anymore," he says.

My eyes fly open.

"You need help, Tricia." Concern spreads across his face as he waits for a reaction, *any* reaction from me. My heartbeat picks up as I dig my fingertips into the bottom sheet and brace myself. Brian has said this before, and every time we've argued about it. I don't want to fight. I'm worn to the bone from fighting with him.

"I'm done, Tricia. *We're* done."

His words slam into me. The room spins and I grip the sheet tighter. *What? He's what?* Every coherent thought vanishes in a puff of exhaled air.

When he reaches the door, he glances back at me. Hesitates. "Call me if—" But he doesn't finish. As reality rushes in, I open my mouth to speak, then close it. The protestation is trapped behind my ribcage in my hollowed-out heart. Brian shakes his head. Misery I'm responsible for distorts his features.

His footsteps plod against the wood stairs. I swing my legs over the side of the bed and am forced to close my eyes to regain equilibrium. Before I stand, the front door creaks open, then bangs shut.

I dash to the window facing the driveway. Under the stark moonlight, Brian halts in front of his pickup truck. A small voice yells at me to go after him. But I'm temporarily paralyzed.

He sinks onto his knees and cradles his head against his knuckles. Seeing him like this jumpstarts my legs and I race through the hallway and down the stairs. My mind is jumbled with confusion and panic. Just as I open the front door, I'm greeted with the roar of the truck engine and the putrid smell of exhaust and burning rubber. By the time my bare feet hit gravel, Brian's gone.

Numbly, I stare past the lawn to the dirt road cutting through Boyer's Bluff's forest and wait for Brian to return.

He doesn't.

I'm done, Tricia. We're done. Over and over I hear him say it, not quite believing it's true. Through a silent flow of tears, I wait and watch, watch and wait until all that's left is cold.

I turn to go inside. The dark, empty place that used to be home. I can't bring myself to take one more step toward it.

Without much thought, I walk to the cliffs behind the lighthouse. The limestone reflects into the mirrored surface of Lake Michigan. Layer by layer by layer of jagged edges and jutting embankments. From where I stand, the drop is breathtaking. The roots of towering white cedars dig into stone crevices, wrapping around them like desperate children clinging to their mothers' legs. I stretch my arms between two trees and grab hold of their spindly branches. The limbs flex like a slingshot ready to fling me back as I peer into the abyss. I imagine catapulting myself off, banging and bouncing along nature's balconies until my body smashes into Lake Michigan's freezing water.

Horrified, I jump back. Something soft caresses my calf. I shriek. It's only the arcing leaves of a maidenhair fern. Boyer's Bluff's flora and fauna have never spooked me...until now. I look around. The forest's silhouette, the cliffs are as foreign as Mars.

I can't stay out here a second longer. My joints creak and ache from the cold as I hustle toward the lighthouse. A sharp pain shoots into my left foot, but I don't slow down.

Limping through the foyer, I leave a smudged trail of blood that follows me to the den. My heartbeat harmonizes with the *tick* of the antique grandfather clock standing proud and oblivious against the wall near the parlor entrance. *It'll outlive the Boyers*, I think.

I turn on a floor lamp in the den, walk to the TV cabinet, and run my fingers along the trim until they connect with the key for my father's gun cabinet.

An image of Brian's frowning face fills my head. For a moment, all I want to do is call him. But if I did, would he come back? What would I say? *I know I'm wretched, but I need you?*

It's hard to believe we planned to marry someday in the Stavkirke here on the island. It's hard to believe he ever loved me. How many times did he walk away and come back? But not this time. Deep inside, I know it.

It's my fault.

Looking around, I take in the room and the view of Boyer's Bluff through the window. What I see is a shell of miserable memories.

I want to go home to my mother and father and grandmother. How naïve I was to think Boyer's Bluff was heaven. It's only meaningless space. Meaningless earth.

I unlock my father's gun cabinet and take out the Remington 12-gauge shotgun he used for deer hunting, load a shell, and carry the rifle to my bedroom. Carefully, I set it down on my bed. Shuffling to the desk, I open up a new document file on my laptop. I'll leave a note to be found after I'm gone, most likely by our chief of police, Jeremiah Johannson.

For a few breaths, I allow myself to imagine Jeremiah searching the lighthouse for me and finding my brains sprayed across the shower wall. His mouth will purse, his brow will deepen the craggy, hard lines that never disappear. Maybe his eyes will tear up as he reports my death over the police radio. At least the clean-up will be minimal, simple.

Unsure what to write, I stare at the blank screen. The last thing I want is for Brian to feel guilty. How can I absolve him? NO. I can't think about Brian. It's my turn to do something just for me. I need to be with family.

I adjust the font size and center the cursor. I believe...Brian will understand.

I'VE GONE HOME.

I pick up the shotgun, walk into the bathroom, and prop it against the tub. Without looking in the mirror, I remove the gold heart necklace Brian gave me for our year anniversary, twelve years as best friends, and set it on the chipped counter. Sitting on the toilet seat, I eye the shotgun. I'm not afraid. But I want and need to get it right. One shell, and it has to count.

I think about my grandma. We were so close and she loved me fiercely. She promised to watch over me from heaven. She promised to be my guardian angel. She promised to witness my high school and college graduations. She promised to attend my wedding and the births of my children. In her last conscious moment, she promised to help me from the other side. No matter what, she'd be here.

Once again, the crushing pain of loss grips my body. I cry.

And cry. Tears drip down my nose, my sunken cheeks, the curve of my chin, and they stain my loose-fitting pink tank top.

Snot splatters the cream-colored tile floor. I'm shivering. A blood-curdling wail escapes between my chattering teeth. I want the suffering to end. I want my grandma to hug me one more time and tell me it will be okay. I want to know if she can hear me.

I grow still and listen, hoping she'll send me a sign. Just this once. Because up until now there hasn't been any evidence that she's watching over me. An empty promise. No pennies from heaven, no *chirp-burr* song or sighting of her favorite bird, the scarlet tanager, and no crooning of Frank Sinatra on the radio, which she said would be a reminder to me of her presence.

I wait. And wait.

And then...I think maybe I hear my cell phone. "New York, New York," the Sinatra song I used for Grandma's ringtone. I bolt out of the bathroom, run to my bedroom, and grab my phone off the nightstand.

Just my imagination. It's highly probable I'm delusional—until I look at the time. 3:08 A.M. 3:08. March eighth. March eighth was her birthday. Was this her sign to me?

I sit on the edge of my bed, drape her quilt over my bare legs, and stare until the time changes to 3:09. "If you're here, Grandma," I say in a choked whisper, "then prove it."

I dial her old phone number and hope, hope, hope for someone to answer.

TWO

"What he did, he did because he must; it was the most natural thing in the world, and grew out of the circumstances of the moment."
Ralph Waldo Emerson

EMERSON

STURGEON BAY, WISCONSIN   MONDAY, 2:49 A.M.

FREEZING WATER POUNDS my head and streaks down my neck and back. I take a deep breath and allow the stinging cold to spread to my lungs as I brace myself against the marble shower. I glance down. The evidence of the incredibly arousing incredibly arousing wake-up call Angie gave me a few minutes ago shriveled to normal. Dammit, two seconds of her purring like a stripper and I was hard. Some guys would be grateful to be woken up by their drunken girlfriend for fantasy ball-play. I'm not one of them.

Practically every guy at Sturgeon Bay High says I'm the luckiest dude on the planet. I must be the dumbest four-point-o male on this planet, because I don't get it. Shouldn't there be more than the physical? A week doesn't go by without at least one guy mentioning Angie's fine assets. A few have jokingly offered to take her off my hands. Tempting, if they weren't such pompous tools using their screwdrivers more than their brains. Angie deserves better.

But maybe I do too?

I nudge the handle to warm, then hot, and even with the exhaust fan on the space fills with steam. I write on the glass, "What am I supposed to do about Angie?" like the answer will magically appear. No such luck.

I'm struggling to understand why things have changed between us over the past months. What's changed with *her?* Drinking more, studying less. Angry. Insecure. Doesn't matter how many times I ask what's going on, what she's thinking, she shuts down, goes radio silent, or changes the subject.

I don't even remember why I wanted to be with her anymore. No. That's not true. The truth is the girl I once knew was vivacious, playful, creative, bold, and daring—so opposite me—and I wanted her. Wanted to be more like her and, despite our differences, we worked.

Two years ago, the last Saturday before our sophomore year, one of my best friends Matt Busby had a party when his parents were out of town. (Stupid or ingenious for a guy whose dad is a cop.) I was a designated driver. Angie's best friend, Brenda, wanted to stay, and Angie didn't. So she asked me if I'd take her home. We detoured to Grant Park. Sitting on the break wall, our feet dangled toward the bay. Angie trailed her fingers down my chest and kept going until they circled the top button of my cargos. I cuffed her wrist and watched her face split with a mischievous grin.

I learned then what's most predictable about Angie is her unpredictability. She stripped to her black underwear and dove into the mica-colored bay.

Every rippled reflection played tricks on my eyes as I frantically searched for her. I shouted her name. No Angie. I shed my T-shirt and sneakers and jumped in, panicking more and more until finally...

"Up here." She waved from the Oregon Street drawbridge, several stories above me. In a second, she climbed over the railing. With awe and fear, I watched her push off and jump. She emerged quickly, swam over, and before I could chew her out for scaring the crap out of me, we were kissing. Despite a foot of height difference between us, her incredible body molded to mine like we were custom designed for each other.

We clicked. But something major's changed. I'm tired of getting called to pick her up whenever, wherever. I'm sick of her unfounded accusations every time another girl looks at me. I'm sick of her resenting me for studying instead of blowing off the last three months of our senior year. I *need* my AP credits. I have plans for medical school.

Our latest fight was probably the worst, and it was my fault. We'd been fooling around in her bedroom—third base stuff—and while Angie finished getting dressed, I picked up her poetry journal and started flipping through it. She snatched it away, ripping the cover. She said that I was invading her privacy, that the journal was like her diary, and that I had no right to touch it. She was so upset that she was on the brink of tears. Stunned by her emotional reaction, I apologized over and over again. Promised never to look at it without her permission. I haven't seen or heard a poem of hers since. A few weeks ago, I asked her about it. She said she's not interested in writing poetry anymore.

Is that my fault too? The shower cools. I twist the hot water handle to its max and step back so the spray hits my chest. Suddenly, the scar slashed across my pecs begins to throb. I rub the raised line, but it does nothing to relieve the pressure, the deep ache banding my repaired heart. It drags me back to a time I wish I could forget, to the five-year-old boy who cheated death not once, but twice in twenty-four hours. *Don't go there.*

The shower sputters cold, and thankfully yanks me out of the past. I shut off the water, tuck a towel around my waist, and wipe the condensation off the mirror with my hand. I'm not sure I like the guy scowling back at me. Disgusted, I smack my palm against the image.

My phone blares, startling me. Angie calling back? Instantly I'm annoyed, which morphs into guilt. I was an idiot for ending our call so abruptly. I fortify myself to deal with her tears, her need for reassurance. God, I need to break up with her. I race into my room, yank off my bedding in search of the phone. On the fifth ring, I find it between the mattress and headboard. "Hello?"

"Oh. Hi."

Not Angie. The voice is soft, a little shaky. I look at caller ID. Private.

"Hey, what's up?" I say quietly, pretending I have a clue who's calling at—I look at the clock—3:09 A.M.

"I'm sorry if I woke you." Her voice is familiar and there's something in the tone that makes me uneasy. Desperation? A plea?

"You didn't. I was—Never mind. Can you hold on a sec? Promise to be right back."

I scramble into clean boxers, grab last year's yearbook off my top bookshelf. "Hey, I'm here. What's going on?" I throw my bed into order and hop in. Propping the yearbook against my knees, I scan my grade's photos, hoping to connect the voice to a face and name.

She sniffles. *Who is she?* I flip to the sophomores, this year's juniors. "Are you...crying?"

"Not really. You don't know me, so maybe—"

"I don't?" I close the yearbook, toss it. "Then why—" She cuts me off with a moan-whimper, a sound so raw, so vulnerable that my heart temporarily goes A-Fib. "What's wrong?"

"Oh God. This is going to sound crazy."

Crazy like crank call? ET phone home? Exhaling I say, "Don't care. Talk to me." Maybe I'm the one who's crazy. Why am I talking to a stranger?

"You have my grandmother's old phone number. She died five months ago today. I-I miss her. We were really close, and...I-I hoped someone would answer."

My throat constricts, temporarily barricading my ability to speak. When I do, my voice is strained. "I'm sorry. It's rough losing someone you love."

"Have you...lost someone too?"

I glance at my scar. "Um, well...no, not really. Not anyone I knew personally."

"Oh."

"But you don't have to lose someone you love to be touched by death. To understand the impact." I close my eyes and wonder what the hell I'm saying.

Silence fills the space with thick intangible dread. I rack my brain trying to remember if anyone at school mentioned losing a grandmother. No one comes to mind. It's hard to peg her age. Could be sixteen or twenty-five. "What's your name?" I ask.

"F-F-Frank. Frankie."

"Frank, Frankie?" I register the lie like a polygraph machine. "What's your *real* name?"

A breath of a laugh comes through. "You're right. It's a nom de plume that I'm...taking on for the night. You know Frank Sinatra?"

"Sure. The famous singer." I leave out "dead." If I didn't know Sinatra it'd be a slap to my Italian heritage and my nonna. He's her all-time favorite crooner.

"My grandmother loved listening to his music."

"Ah, that explains choice of name." I stretch out, cradle the phone between my shoulder and ear. My area code is 920, which means Frankie's grandma could have lived somewhere in this area. I'm playing detective. "So, Frank-Frankie, since we're talking at this ungodly hour and are now clearly on the way to becoming good friends, tell me about yourself. Like... oh I don't know. Age, favorite food, social security number?"

"Um, I don't know if I..." Her voice trails off.

"I'm Emerson. Real name, just so you know I'm not some creeper who has your grandmother's phone number. I live—"

She cuts me off. "Wait. No details, okay?"

"Because why?" I drag the words out, emphasizing how whacked this is.

"Have you ever been on an airplane and talked to a stranger without giving your name, just because the person was there?"

"Sure. So that's what this is?"

"Actually, we can hang up now. I have my answer."

"Your answer? What was the question?"

"I don't think you really want to know."

"Yeah, I do. Besides, we're strangers on an airplane. This conversation can't end here. No airplane ride would ever be this short. Oh, and since the cabin is dark and I can't make out your face, you might as well reveal your deepest secrets."

"I'm pretty sure you're teasing, right?"

I laugh. "Yes."

She chuckles. "Emerson, that's different. I've never met an Emerson."

"Really? Where did you say you're from?"

"Nice try, Emerson."

"Thank you." I smile. "Okay, so I was named for my mother's favorite poet, Ralph Waldo Emerson, who just happens to share the same birthday as me, May twenty-fifth, in case that isn't a trivia fact you have stored in your brain. She decided not to name me Ralph, thank God, because it's hideously dorky, plus she said some author named Blume ruined it for her. I was fifteen when I asked one of my four sisters what that meant. Trust me, it was one of my most embarrassing moments of my life. And thankfully my mother spared me a lifetime of *Where's Waldo* jokes. Thus, the name Emerson."

"I like it," she says. "And don't knock *Where's Waldo*. I'm a huge fan of all kinds of puzzles."

"Hmm, I'll add that to my long list of 'What I know about Frankie.' I'm keeping one, you know."

"You are, huh?"

"Yup." I pick up my towel, rub down my wet hair.

Her tone softens. "Well then, I'm eighteen, my favorite food is banana chocolate-chip cherry muffins, and my social security number begins with a three and ends with nine. Satisfied?"

"Hardly. Especially now that you've made my stomach grumble. I wouldn't mind one of those muffins."

"Me too," she says wistfully.

Something sweet, intoxicating drifts into the air, and it isn't homemade muffins. It smells like the array of bath products my sister Isabelle brought back after her semester in France. I'm pretty sure she said it was lavender? The whole house reeked of it. I sit up, inhale.

I whisper, "Hold on a sec. I need to check something out." I sniff my towel, then toss it aside.

The scent grows stronger, overwhelming like I'm standing in a field of flowers. I stop in front of my closed door, grip the handle ready to spring it open and catch Mia, my youngest and only sister still living at home, eavesdropping on the other side, which she's been known to do. But the hallway is empty and odor free. Stumped, I check my windows. Shut tight. The scent weakens and the bloodhound in me gives up. All righty then, that was...strange.

I hop back into bed and pick up the phone. "You still there, Frankie?"

"Yup. Everything okay?"

"Yeah, tell me more about you. I need to fill this notebook."

"'To different minds, the same world is a hell, and a heaven.'"

"What?"

"It's an Emerson quote."

"Ah, brilliant. Sorry to shatter my wise persona, but I haven't memorized every poem, essay, and quote by my namesake. Shocking, I know."

"I'm crushed. How about, 'Hitch your wagon to a star?'"

I snort. "Got my lasso right here babe. Care to do some roping with me?"

"You're a dork." She laughs, and I admit, I kind of like the sound of it. I like the banter.

"Sincerity is the highest compliment you can pay."

"That's Emerson."

"It is. I am."

She chuckles, bittersweet. "Wow, I haven't laughed in a long time. It feels..."

"...amazing?"

"Wrong. It feels wrong."

How can laughing be wrong? I'm about to ask when it occurs to me that maybe the first Emerson quote was a clue. Do I want to know? I trace my scar and cross the line. "So, 'To different minds, the same world is a hell, and a heaven.' Which is it for you?"

"Hell."

I flinch. "Because of your grandma?"

"You sure you want to hear this? It really *is* okay if we hang up now, call it a night. Or technically morning."

"Frankie, I'm fully awake and more curious than George. If we hang up I'll lie here formulating a million reasons for your call, none of them your truth, and that would drive me crazy. You wouldn't do that to the guy who has your grandmother's old phone number, would you? Trust me, you can tell me anything."

"Trust you?"

"It's the foundation to all relationships."

"Another Emerson quote?"

"I don't think so. It's true enough, though." Based on her voice, I try imagining what Frankie might look like. That only leaves a billion possibilities.

"Okay then." She pauses. "You're sure?"

"Frankie—"

"I—Well—Before—" I wait. Seconds feel like an eternity. I check to see if we've been disconnected. Nope. Finally, she releases her breath, and starts again. "I am *only* telling you this because once we hang up, we'll never talk again."

"Your secrets are safe."

"My boyfriend broke up with me tonight, and it was my fault. After my grandma died, he stayed with me. The first few days it was good to have him around, to have him with me all the time. But as more days passed, I felt like I was suffocating. We hadn't even talked about him moving in. It just...happened." She lets out a heavy sigh. "From the day we buried my grandma everything started to change between us. I've been miserable, and I've dragged him down, made him miserable too. I can't even say I love him the way I used to, and he deserves that and so much more. But it still hurts that he left, you know?" She sniffles. "Oh God, why am I telling you all this?"

"Because we're such great friends?"

"Right."

"And I'm a good listener. It's in my blood." When you grow up in a house filled with sisters, you learn the art of listening. You learn when words are fight bait, when to ask questions, and when it's best to say "yeah," or nod because they don't want your opinion—they have their own opinions. What they want is sympathy. Ninety percent of the time I get it right. The last ten break all the rules.

"Well, friend. Brace yourself. It's not...pretty."

Apprehension pumps into my veins. Any normal person would have hung up shortly after hello, but for some inexplicable reason, I'm drawn in. Drawn to her. Couldn't walk away even if I wanted to.

Frankie can't be from around here. Since we're the same age, I'm certain some part of her story would have been shared through the grapevine. None of it is familiar.

She lets out a soft whistle. Her voice is barely audible. Increasing the volume, I press the receiver hard against my ear.

"Have you ever felt empty? So empty that..."

Oh God. "That what?"

"If you hadn't answered, I might have—I would have—"

Despite the frisson of fear coursing through my body, I keep my tone gentle, reassuring. "You would have what?"

"I have my father's shotgun."

My bones snap as I kick off the blankets, lunge for my keys on the desk. I reach my door and break, teetering forward. "Whoa. Frankie, no. That's messed up. Seriously messed up. You can't do that. You can't kill yourself!"

I shift to the window, lay my forehead against the cold pane. The pre-dawn moon casts an eerie glow over the trees and illuminates a sliver of the empty street. Backing away, my face leaves a damp impression that fades to nothing.

"Tell me where you are. I'll come to you," I say, jamming my arms into a T-shirt.

"No. A car wouldn't help you. So unless you have your own plane—"

A plane? She could be in Paris or San Francisco or Timbuktu. "Then promise me right now you won't hurt yourself."

"It's just—I'm so alone." I'm pretty sure she's crying again. "Thank you for answering."

What if I hadn't? I can't think about that. My pulse continues to race and the band around my heart constricts even tighter. "I'm—I don't even know what to say, other than you're welcome. But—" I hesitate, then say, "Why would you have to call a stranger? What about your family?"

"When I said I'm alone, I meant I have no family. My grandma was my last blood relative. She raised me. When I was five, m-my mother was killed, and what I remember the most about that time was my father falling apart. After the trial, after my mom's killer went to prison, my dad re-enlisted. He went overseas, and during his third tour, when I was ten, he was killed by friendly fire. And Gran—My gran—" She lets out a muffled sob.

"She was your world."

"Yes," she says like she's amazed I understand. "Most of my memories of my parents are based on photographs or stories my grandma told me. It's hard for me to trust that any of them are one hundred percent my own."

"And this guy? Your ex? He *knew* about this?"

"We've known each other pretty much my whole life. So yes. But it doesn't matter, because honestly, I don't blame him for leaving." She's sobbing now. "I let him down. He asked me to try, and I did. But it wasn't nearly enough. I'm not what he needs, what he deserves."

"Frankie, maybe *he* was the one who didn't give you what *you* need, what *you* deserve. Have you thought about that? What was it that you needed from him?"

"I-I don't know. When he was here all the time, I couldn't think." Her voice hitches. "I wanted to be alone to figure out my mess of a life and piece it together again. I wanted my own space. Now that I have it, now that we're over, I'm scared. I'm scared to be alone. So you see? I'm confused." Her breath shudders. "Why are you talking with me?"

"Maybe that's what you need? Someone to listen. Just listen. It's okay to be confused. To be upset. It takes time to work things out." An arrow of heat shoots into my heart. I massage the scar. I think about how long it took me to recover—the years—and say, "Five months isn't a long time. Not for grieving. Maybe he..." *was a selfish prick.* But I don't say it. Some whisper of a voice tells me not to. My conscience?

"He did what he could. He tried. I don't want you to think that he's an awful person. He's not." Practically every word breaks with her tears.

I feel utterly helpless. I wish I knew how to comfort her. I've turned every card over, and they're blank. No conversation with my sisters about girls prepared me for this. Not even my sessions with Dr. Shale prepared me for this. After an eternity, her torrent slows, her breathing steadies. She blows her nose.

"I'm sorry," I say, regretting how insignificant, feeble, pathetic those two words are for what she's endured. I look around at my room. The basketball trophies, the books, signed Packers paraphernalia. All meaningless.

She doesn't say anything. I drag a key across my thigh. Lines form and fade against my skin. I wait for her to speak. She doesn't, and it makes me uneasy.

"Frankie, you know what I think? I think—"

"You think *what*?"

"I think you want to live. I know that's what your grandma would want you to do. From everything you said, I can tell she really loved you, that you were close. She would want the best for you, and maybe this guy? Maybe he wasn't it? Maybe you have to find your own way? I don't know how to explain it, but I get this sense that if she were here, that's what she would say. I know you feel alone. But there are people who care. *I* care. You matter." I sound a little like Dr. Shale, not that I would tell Frankie.

She sighs again. "You don't understand. I'm over*whelmed* with people who care. People think that should be enough. It's not. And why should you care? You don't know me."

I look around my room, desperate. Begging, praying, *Help?!* I rattle off, "I have your grandmother's number. That counts for a lot. Imagine who could have ended up with it—a scuzzbag, drug-dealing pedophile. But no, you got me. Super stud, genius dude with no police record. That counts for everything." My fingers curl into my damp neck. I tilt my head side to side to work out the kinks.

"Super stud?"

I allow a grin. "Well, yeah. You didn't think I'd be an eighteen-year-old butt-scratching, nose-picking, hairy-chested, portly ignoramus street sweeper named Emerson, did you?"

She groans. "No. That wasn't quite how I envisioned you."

"Well that's a huge weight off my shoulders." I laugh. She doesn't.

Suddenly, a blurred image flashes in my head, an image of a girl. *Frankie?*

"Let me guess," I begin, giving in to curiosity. "Your hair is long and brown, chestnut brown. Am I right?"

"My hair is not brown."

"Wait, I'm not finished. It's naturally brown, but you dyed it blonde. And you're pretty." I feel a nudge, a tug to say, "I was wrong. You're not pretty. You're beautiful. More beautiful than Ava Gardner."

She sucks in a loud breath.

Who the heck is Ava Gardner? The words sprang from my mouth like a ventriloquist controlling a puppet. Definitely freaking.

"How did you—My grandma—She always—" Frankie pauses. "My grandma *loved* Ava Gardner."

"I...don't know. I have no idea why I just said that. The name just...popped out? Who is she?"

"You really don't know?"

"No." I sandwich my skull between my sweaty palms and press, like that'll prevent me from becoming the male version of *Carrie*.

"She was one of Frank Sinatra's four wives. Are you—?"

We both say "psychic?" at the same time.

"No. Definitely not. Nothing like this has ever happened to me before. It was a coincidence, a lucky guess?"

"You're a freak of nature, Emerson."

Before I formulate a rational response, I bluster out, "I'm an answer, Frankie. Maybe you're an answer for me, too." *What? Why did I say that?* I clamp my hand over my mouth, afraid of what I'll say next. Freak of nature? More like the start of a new series for the Syfy Network. "Ignore me. I don't know what I'm saying. My brain's foggy and I'm getting tired. But not too tired that I'm tired of talking with you," I clarify. "Tired, tired. My girlfriend called before you did. That's why I was up." *Geezus, Emerson. You're rambling, and why would you mention Angie?*"

"Oh. So you have a girlfriend?"

"I—Yes, but I—" I close my eyes, worn out and wanting an out. But I don't want to hang up, either. Can I tell Frankie that I want to break up with my girlfriend after what she went through with her boyfriend?

"We're anonymous friends, remember?" she says, softly. "You helped me. Maybe I can help you? What about your girlfriend?"

I groan, torn over what to say.

"You don't have to tell me. But I'd like you to."

I swallow hard. "We've been together for over two years. But for the past few months, I've been thinking about breaking up with her."

"But you haven't," she says. "So maybe there's a chance you could work it out? Do you want to?"

I'm bowled down with the realization that it's been easier to talk with Frankie than it's been with Angie. Maybe because we're strangers? But still, it makes me wonder if Angie has ever been a true friend. Someone I can confide in?

"You and I, we're being honest with each other, right?"

"Definitely," she says.

"I'm going away to college in August and she isn't. So I hope we'll just…drift apart. Or she'll find someone else when I'm not around. I know it sounds like the easy way out, but hurting her—" I rub my aching scar. "It's too much to deal with right now. Do you know what I mean?"

"Yeah, I do." Her voice drips with misery.

"I'm sorry. I didn't mean to upset you."

"You didn't. It's life in general that sucks. And Emerson?"

"Yeah?"

"Please don't say you're sorry. None of this is your fault. I called you, remember?" She makes a breathy noise like she's chastising herself.

"I'm really glad you did."

"Me too," she says. "Look, a minute ago you said I might be your answer, right? So, I have a question. You ready?"

I glance toward my window. The sky is more blue slate than black. "No. Not really. But go ahead if you must," I say with a hint of humor.

"Do you love her?"

I don't hesitate. "No."

"There's your answer. Break up with her."

"I can't. Not yet."

"You *can*. Just pull the plug and get on with your life."

"Under the circumstances, 'pull the plug' does not seem appropriate."

"Smart-ass."

"Promise me you won't kill yourself."

"You have my word. I'm not going to hurt myself. This wasn't planned. It was more...a spur-of-the-moment idea after my boyfriend left. I promise not to kill myself and *you* have to promise to break up with your girlfriend. Today."

"And if I don't?"

"I keep my promises, so trust me and I'll trust you, especially since we will never speak again. Besides, I'm doing you a huge favor. It's a win-win for both of us. You seem to be the kind of guy who keeps promises. Am I right?" I hear a smile tickle her voice and I relish her better mood. Still, that isn't a reason for me to give in. "C'mon, you can do this."

There's something about Frankie; I want to believe her.

I sputter out, "I-I promise to break up with my girlfriend. Today. But how..." *How in the world am I going to do this?*

"You'll be fine," she says.

I can't believe, after everything she's been though, she's reassuring me. "Give me your phone number. I'll call you tonight and tell you all about it."

"No. I don't think—Emerson, I need one last favor. It's really important."

I'm definitely leery, clearly getting trapped into another promise. "What?"

"Change your phone number."

"*Arrrrrg!* Are you kidding?"

"I know I don't have any right to ask, but I need you to. Please? Because two minutes after we hang up I'll want to call you back. I like you. There's something uniquely special and unbelievably sweet and kind and completely unexpected about you."

Despite my initial annoyance, I can't help but smile, tease. "It was the super-stud comment. You can't resist my good looks and incredible charm."

"Ha-ha. Exactly."

"Frankie, I like you too. A lot." *God, what am I saying? I don't even know Frankie's real name.* "I know this sounds crazy. But I've never—" I cut myself off. *Should I say what I'm thinking?* I briefly close my eyes, then glance at my alarm clock. "I've never spent anywhere near this amount of time talking with anyone the way I've talked with you. I want to talk with you again. So I don't see why it's a problem."

She groans. "It's a problem because it's not what I need. And knowing it makes this so much harder. I haven't been able to talk to anyone the way I've talked with you since my grandma died. But it has to end here. I-I have so much to figure out. To decide what I want to do with my life. If you don't change your number, I'll want to call you. I'll rely on you when I need to rely on myself. It wouldn't be fair to either of us. That's not what this call was supposed to be." Her ragged exhale causes goose bumps to rise along my neck.

"I *will* call again. Tonight at five o'clock. And if you answer, if you keep my grandma's number, it'll be the most unfair, hurtful thing you could do to me. To us."

Unfair? Hurtful? I dig a fist into my pillow. "You have a warped concept of what's unfair."

"I know it seems like I'm being selfish. But it's the complete opposite. Please, Emerson?"

The rational part of me wants to tell her she's being unreasonable, ridiculous. We could be friends. *Maybe even more than friends?* The thought catches me off-guard. *Now who's the one being ridiculous?* Yet I don't want to end this conversation without being able to get in touch with her.

"This is the way it's supposed to be," she says. "I asked for a sign from my grandma. That's why I called her old number. I knew if someone picked up, then it would *prove* she's watching over me. She's still with me." She pauses. "Logically, how else could you have known about my dyed hair or Ava Gardner?"

"I don't know. I just—God Frankie, talking with you..." I'm struck with a feeling of loss. Like she's taking something important away from me. In the span of this conversation, I've come to like her. To care about her. She doesn't seem like a stranger. More like a new friend. Someone I really want to get to know better. Much better. But how do I explain to her why or what that means when I can't explain it to myself? "Frankie, I meant it when I said I care about you. Tonight, tomorrow, next week, a *month* from now, I'll want to know you're okay."

"I'll be better than okay. I promise. So please, promise to change your number."

"It's that important to you?"

"Yes."

I gnash my teeth. If only I could come up with one persuasive argument to get out of this absurd plea. But my sleep-deprived brain's worthless, and my resolve dissolves faster than sugar in coffee. "All right. Under extreme protest and duress, I promise to change my number."

"Thank you. And perhaps some day, like years from now, if I meet an Emerson, I'll—"

I interrupt her. "I'll ask for your real name and phone number."

"Perfect. If Providence knocks and we meet. Good night, Emerson. And thank you, again."

I hesitate, then say, "Pleasant dreams, Frank-Frankie, and a long, happy life."

She hangs up.

The silence is shocking. I've never felt this cut off, lost.

Even with the heavy fatigue and my burning eyes begging to close, I fight it. Because I'm afraid if I sleep, I'll forget the sound of Frankie's voice, the image of her sketched in my mind. How was that possible?

Starting from hello, I recount details—the smell of lavender, our banter, her loss, her tears, the strange way I blurted out Ava Gardner, and our promises. The most incomprehensible idea plagues me with what ifs. What if I hadn't picked up the phone? Would Frankie have killed herself? I can't think she would have gone through with it.

For what seems like the millionth time since Frankie's call, I rub my scar. It's been years since it ached this much. Not since I last saw Dr. Shale.

A red-orange glow of sunrise tints the sky. I whisper, "If anyone's listening, please watch over Frankie."

7:20 A.M.

GET UP.

I moan. Maybe I'm dreaming. Turns out Mia's shoving me hard enough to roll me over. I peek at the clock. "Ten more minutes."

"No," she says, shaking me again. I grab her wrists before one of us gets hurt, most likely me, since she knows I won't fight back. Mia may be tiny, but she could wrestle me to the ground.

"You told me that a half-hour ago. Mom and Dad left and Betsy's mom is going to be here any second and—"

I release her and wave her away.

She stamps her foot. "Fine, I'm going, but don't blame me if you're late for school." My door slams.

7:58 A.M.

RINGING NUDGES ME AWAKE. I scramble around for my phone with the hope that it's Frankie.

But no. It's Angie.

THREE

"Insist on yourself; never imitate."
Ralph Waldo Emerson

ANGIE

STURGEON BAY, WISCONSIN   MONDAY, 7:48 A.M.

Emerson
is late.
And he's never
late. A pet
peeve of his.

I tap
my boot on a broken
flower pot at the edge
of our driveway, look
toward Hudson and Maple
for his '68 Camaro
to turn
the corner.

Are the three
drawbridges
up?
Is a barge
motoring

d
   o
w
n
the waterway,
holding up
       Emerson from crossing over
to the other side,
the west side
of Sturgeon Bay?

Or maybe
he's hugging
the toilet, moaning,
miserable? His cell
too   far away
to answer my four
text messages?

Car crash?
No.
Emerson's driving
rivals the geriatric crowd.
Unless a tired trucker
crossed over yellow lines,
slamming into his car.
Gawd, I'm morbid. Still,
it could happen.

⌒⌒

7:55 A.M.

Fifteen minutes
late.
Fifteen minutes.

No text.

Flashback five
hours to my
stup-end-ous
2:45 A.M.
call to Emerson.
Not my idea,
but Brenda's.

Don't think
about that
nightmare
now.

Speed-dial Emerson.
Again.
One, two, three,
four rings. Finally.
he answers.

Groggy, he says,
"Hey Angie."

"You overslept?"
The words fly
razor sharp, bitchy.
Not the way
I want to be.
I blanket
my tone.
"I've been worried.
Are you sick?"

"I'm fine. Sorry, I shut off
my alarm. Can you get a ride
from Brenda?"

Blanket slips.
"If I have to. Can't you
pick me up?"

"Then we'd both be late.
Why don't you ride
your bike?"

"My bike?"
Does he think
I'm getting
fat?

Stomach
cramps. Acid burns
my throat. I pop
an antacid into
my mouth.

Chewy.
Chalky.
Cherry.

Across the street,
Jordan's green bomber's
parked in his driveway.

Over two years ago
Jordan kissed me.
Once.
It meant nothing.
Still...Emerson could use
a dose of competition.

"Jordan's home. I'm sure
he'll give me a ride."

Hello?

"Good.
Thank him for me."

Ugh. Is he that oblivious?

"See you in homeroom?"
I ask, hopeful.

"Won't make it."

"Then lunch. Oh,
and I don't need
a ride after school.
Brenda's helping
me shop for a dress."

Hint. Prom.

One beat. Two.

"Emerson?"

"Yeah. Meet me at 11:30.
Main entrance. We'll go
off campus for lunch.
Just us two."

My promposal?!

"Really? Can't wait!
"Love you," I say
to a dial tone.

He hung up on me? Again?

No sign
of Jordan.
Swallow.   .

Liza Wiemer

Hold it
to-ge-th-er.

Fear
is for wimps.

Should I walk
across the street
and knock?
Five minutes,
then I'll knock.
School doesn't
start for ten.

I fantasize
about prom, a slow
dance with Emerson.
My cheek against
his chest,
girls watching,
envious.

Sigh.

From the track meet
yesterday, Travis Davis
texted me a pic of Emerson
talking to a super hot girl.
Fourth one this month.
Girls from Sevastopol, Gibraltar,
Southern Door, the other
Door County high schools.
Rumors he's been hooking
up behind my back. Not true.
Why do people tell
lies
lies
lies

lies

lies?

Emerson would NEVER
cheat. Then why
do I worry?
Because girls flirt
with him
A   L   L   T   H   E   T   I   M   E.

If I mention it he laughs.
Says I'm being ridiculous, no
need to be

JEALOUS.

Who wouldn't be?
It's been months since
he said: ~~I LOVE YOU.~~

Last night, I swiped
my mother's Absolut
and called Brenda. "Did
you see Sophia's car
with Jesse's promposal
on her windshield?
The dozen pink
roses? I wish Emerson
would give me roses."

Brenda sighed. Tired
of hearing
about prom?
NOT my fault
she's NEVER
had a boyfriend.
I tried to set

her up with Matt,
Emerson's best friend.
But NO.

She said,
"You know you're going, so what does it matter?
Besides, you know Emerson. He's preoccupied
with track meets and AP exams and graduation."

Emerson's
val-e-DIC-torian.

"You think he's bored with me?"

"You, boring? Taylor Swift,
Kate Middleton, compared to you,
they're boring."

Her cheer-you-up lies,
a temporary fix to sulking.

"I should do something wild,
like sneak into his room."

She laughed. "You're
going to do that, how?"

"We'll strap
a ladder on top
of your SUV."

She harrumphed.
"I don't think so."

"You have a better idea?"

A minute passed.

"Yeah, how about a
performance
he'll remember?"

Brenda's the actress.
She helped me practice
the late-night TV promo:
Guy seeks sexy, seductive girl.
Oh yeah, I'd give Emerson
a reason to love me.

Several more shots for a fortified
buzzzzzzzzzzzZZ.
I called, roused him from sleep.

He was breathing hard—husky, deep
—bolstering my courage, encouraging
flirtatious words and *mooooooooooans.*

U N T I L...

Emerson cut
me off,
said he needed sleep
for his AP Spanish
practice exam.
Click. Emerson? Dial tone.

I've never been so humiliated.
Embarrassed.
  Mortified.

Jordan's front door slams.
"Hey Jordan?" I wave.
He nods, walks to the green jalopy.
"Can I catch a ride with you?"
He stops, stares. Will he refuse?

Liza Wiemer

"Sure."

The rusty passenger
door squeaks when he
holds it open, expecting
me to climb in. I scoff.

"You want me
to sit on *that*?"

"Haven't you gone
mudding?
But hey,
princess,
if a little
dirt scares you—"

"Where's the thrill
in spinning wheels
in a farm field,
spraying mud
everywhere?"

He chuckles—
low, throaty.
I remember
that laugh.
I've missed
that laugh.
Damn him.

"To each their own,
your highness."

He offers a hand.
I accept and climb in.

Damp, wavy blond hair
cascades into his eyes.

Aftershave—musky, earthy.
Different from Emerson's
Zest mountain fresh soap.
Jordan's lean body moves
gracefully as he rounds
the hood, looks dorky in
beige chinos,
blue button-down shirt,
brown loafers. Not
his usual casual self.

Light spikes
through the corroded
floorboard.
I crisscross my legs
under me.

"Jordan, seriously,
is this thing safe?"

He pats the dashboard, rubs
the tiny conch shell hanging
from the rearview mirror.

                              "Hey, no disparaging JJ."

Ignition g r r r i n d s,
one, two, three times.
Gray smoke farts
from the exhaust pipe.
Jordan grins like he knows
a secret. Should I ask?

One beat. Two.

I give in.
"What's with the goofy grin?"

Liza Wiemer

The Jeep jerks as he pulls
over to the curb,
shifts into park,
shuts off the engine.

"What's wrong?
Why are you stopping?"

Sparks in his eyes
rekindle candles
he extinguished
years ago.
They flicker, burn, melt
my heart of wax, drip
into my stomach,
soothing the storm.

UNTIL...

                              "Do you believe
                          in omens? Because
                              I do. I couldn't
                                   sleep, cause
                                  I was thinking
                                    about you.

                                    "I've missed
                   our late night conversations.
                                     I've missed
                     our sunset walks to the park.
                                      I've missed
                   our late night chocolate sundaes
                                      I've missed
                                              you.

                 "So I said, 'Hey if anyone's listening, I need
                               to speak with Angie.
                                   It's been so

Hello?

long, too
long.
Give me a sign.'
You asked for the ride."
He shrugs.
"Guess there's an angel on my side."
He smiles.

Angel: His old nickname for me.

I shake my head,
hurt,
angry,
confused.

"You blew your chance,
Jordan. Two years ago.
Emerson and I are practically
engaged. Dump him for you?
No way."

I bite my tongue,
glance at Jordan, expect red
to flash in his hazel eyes.
Nope.

Amused, he says,
"Get over yourself, Angie."

With my hand on the door handle,
I'm tempted to bolt.
I don't.
Fury boils
in my stomach.
I hate Jordan Jacob Lieberman.
His stupid proclamation.
Smug superiority.
As if.

Liza Wiemer

Tears prick
my lids,
sting
my throat.

His gaze skims
my black scoop-necked shirt,
skin-tight skirt, high-heeled boots.

"This..."
He points to my
shirt as if he knows
what's really inside
my pushup bra.
"...is not you."

"The real you wears ratty tops,
frayed jeans, flip-flops.
The real you shines without all
that hairspray and makeup.
The real you sings when you
think no one is listening.
The real you loves to write kick-
ass poetry. Do you still?

"I've seen you stumble and crawl
through your window,
drunk, miserable. I've heard you
make up stories about
your family to fit in. You eat carrots
when you hate carrots.
You attend basketball games
when you hate basketball."

Jaw clenched,
I fight the urge
to scratch
out his eyes.

"You're *jealous*
of Emerson
and to cover
it up you're being
cruel, hateful, mean.
I hate you."

Quickly, I blot
the tear
before it spills.

He laughs.
Derisive, scathing.
"You don't hate
me, you hate
yourself for becoming
exactly the type
of person we used
to make fun of.
And yeah, I *am*
jealous. Jealous
of Emerson
because he's the
reason you betrayed
me. I was gone
ten miserable weeks,
and you couldn't
wait for me?"

"Wrong.
Wrong. Wrong."

Jordan unbuckles
his seatbelt,
unbuckles mine.
Leaning over,
strokes my hair
tenderly.
Like he used to.
For a moment,
I'm engulfed in
childhood.

"Angie—"

I slap his hand away.
"Don't touch me!
You have no right
to touch me!"

Retreating,
he reaches
for the ignition.
I snatch
the keys, hold
them in my fist,
and **RAGE.**

"You're the one who forgot about me!
  Not   one   word!"

Suck

in a breath.
Buffalo wings
with Tabasco sauce
pack less heat than this heartburn.

I choke out,
"I didn't know
if you caught
a horrible disease.
I didn't know
if you were missing
or dead.
I emailed you (nearly)
every day,
thought of you
every day,
worried about you
every day.
You promised me—

"But not ONE WORD. No email. No text.

"Because...
you were too busy being a hero in Haiti,
        delivering medical supplies, school supplies.
                Rebuilding homes and orphanages.
And then,
you came home.

"I was so happy,
relieved to see you
alive.
I walked over.
You ducked
into the house.
Pretended
not to see me.
Three whole frickin'

weeks. You avoided
me."

Pre-Haiti memory cuts
my last thread
of composure.
The good-bye kiss shared
in our climbing tree.
Tender, sweet, brush of lips,
tongues explored, fingers trailed,
leaving an invisible tattoo.

                Tears
            t r i c k l e
                d   d
                   o
                w   w
                n   n
                my
            cheeks.

"You abandoned
me. You're
the one
who changed."

Suddenly,
window gazing
is Jordan's
new specialty.

UNTIL...

                        He clears
                his throat, faces me.
            "I-I wanted to email you.
                I had promised to *try*.
                    But I...couldn't.

Hello?

I mean I could have,
I just—

"What my parents
and I saw in Haiti
broke my heart.
Massive graves,
malnourished babies,
sickness,
filth,
poverty.
For every person
we helped,
there were hundreds,
thousands,
we couldn't.

"Even
now, there
are unfathomable
things I can't talk about.
Images I want to forget. Memories
I wish I could destroy. Coming home
where everything was normal, the same. It
was hard to readjust. I couldn't
cope." He shakes his
head.
"I had hoped
you'd figure it out.
We always seemed to know
what the other needed and thought. I
messed up. It took a while to find my footing.
I would have called. But by then, you were with
Emerson."

My hand clamps
over my mouth,
prevents the cry

Liza Wiemer

from escaping.

All
these
years...
gone.

> "You need to know,
> when I was in Haiti,
> I thought of you
> every day.
> *Missed* you
> every day."

His
fingers trail
d
o
w
n
my cheek,
neck,
shoulders.

> "I'm sorry I blamed you.
> I'm sorry I hurt you.
> I've missed the *old* you.
> I've missed my friend."

That's all I am to him?

I grab his shirt,
pull him to me,
set my lips on his,
and kiss him.

One beat. Two.

Jordan breaks away.
What the hell's wrong
with me? He didn't kiss back.

Desperate
to escape,
I yank
the handle.
Stuck.
Smack.
Doesn't open.
Jordan traps
my wrist
with his grip.
The more
I resist,
the firmer
his hold.

He slips the keys
from my palm
like Houdini.

Engine r r r u m b l e s.

Four agonizing minutes
later, Jordan parks
in front our school's
main entrance.

I can't look at him.
Won't look at him.

>"I've cared about you for a long
time and I'm not willing to settle for a piece
of you. You're with Emerson. No games, Angie.
I respect myself too much. When you figure out
who you are and what you want, let me know.

I'll be here to listen."

He reaches over, grazes
my thigh, wiggles the handle.
Pop! Sprung from my prison.

As he drives toward
the parking lot, I see
him looking at me
through the rearview
mirror. My middle fingers
rise. Jordan shakes
his head and smiles.

I despise Jordan.

I love Emerson!

DON'T
think
about
Jordan.

I text Emerson: Can't wait 4 lunch.

Strrrrretch out neck of tee.
CLICK. Add picture: SEND
Text: Here's dessert. xoxo

What
did I just do? Why?

FOUR

"It is easy to live for others; everybody does. I call on you to live for yourselves..."
Ralph Waldo Emerson

EMERSON

STURGEON BAY, WISCONSIN   MONDAY, 9:22 A.M.

I JERK AWAKE. Shaking, breathless. My head throbs with the sounds of crushing metal, shattering glass, splintering wood, and above all else the screams. Oh God the screams! As piercing as they were thirteen years ago when the truck barreled onto the sidewalk and crashed into the building. It carves into me, guts my insides, and leaves me with nothing but an overwhelming sense of despair. Moisture pricks the back of my eyelids. I blink, but tears leak anyway. I press my palms against my ears, then cover my eyes unable to take myself out of this holographic nightmare.

I'm on my knees, a foot or so from the woman sprawled on the ground. Her lower half is under the truck bed. Her auburn hair fans around her face and blood trickles from her nose. One of her legs is bent in the most unnatural way. Her bright eyes stare at me, then dull, empty. I look down at my hand in hers.

Then I'm grabbed from behind, torn away. Her palm left scraped, filthy.

Nooooo! Help her!

Breathe Emerson. Breathe.

I picture a giant eraser and begin wiping away the scene, a technique Dr. Shale taught me years ago. First her battered face, twisted body, broken leg until there's a blank screen, which I fill with sand dunes and blue sky. Try as I may, shards of the hellish image cut through.

My scar burns across my chest, searing and raw as if I were just sliced with a knife. I press my palm against it. Wet and slick, I turn it over, almost expecting blood on my fingers, but it's sweat.

I know, *I know,* I remind myself, that Dr. Shale would tell me that this nightmare was caused by my subconscious, that something pulled the trigger. None of this is real.

But it *was* real.

He taught me another technique to regain control, and my body automatically reacts. A good thing since I'm close to a full meltdown. I scoot against the headboard, set the pillow between my bent knees, and drop my face onto it with plenty of space to take in air. Sweat soaks the pillowcase as I concentrate on counting backward from one hundred, slowing my breathing and diminishing the flashes of light rocketing underneath my closed lids. By the time I reach fifty-five, I'm able to lift my head. My erratic pulse is back to normal.

Normal. I wish I were normal. Whatever the hell that means.

Two years without sleeping pills. Two years of the illusion that I had conquered my fears and could sleep through the night without being terrorized.

Why did the nightmare return?

Frankie.

No doubt, the conversation with Frankie caused it. *I might have—I would have—I have my father's shotgun.* She was the trigger, a reminder that life is fragile.

Did I save her life? I shiver with the idea that maybe I'm alive today because I needed to be there for Frankie.

Yeah right. I dig the heel of my palm into my throbbing scar, then drop my hand into my lap. If anyone in my family sees me rubbing this spot, red flags will go up. They'll ask if I'm having nightmares again. Mom will worry. Everyone will worry, and I won't be able to lie my way out of it. How could I begin to explain Frankie? I can't imagine saying, "Some girl called me in the middle of the night. She was going to kill herself, but because I picked up, because we talked, because of Ava Gardner, because I promised to break up with Angie..." There would be millions of questions I wouldn't be able to answer. For sure Mom would call Dr. Shale.

I'd love to laugh off the phone call, say it meant nothing. But I can't. What's crazy is talking with Frankie was so easy. I liked it. I liked her. I wanted to get to know her. Which *is* crazy. Ridiculous, ludicrous to believe we had a...a what? A *connection*? Just because I had her grandmother's old phone number?

I grab my phone from my nightstand, stare at the screen, and check call history. Private caller.

Who are you Frankie?

I want to talk to you again. To hear you laugh.

I will my phone to ring.

It doesn't. Of course not.

And then...two missed text messages. For one glorious moment I actually believe, hope.

Messages from Angie: Photo: Top view of black lace bra and some serious skin. Delete. *"Here's dessert. xoxo."* Delete.

I sigh in disgust over my own ridiculousness. Like Frankie would text? *Change your phone number.*

The breakup is one promise to Frankie I'll keep, but why should I do it today? Tomorrow. Next week. After prom? I don't know what to do, and maybe that's the biggest reason why I *should* break up with Angie today. Get it over with. *Pull the plug.* Not so easy after two years.

< NOTES

BREAKING UP W ANGIE NOW?

Pros:
1. Won't disappoint her by not having the most romantic promposal ever still don't know what to do.
2. No more ridiculous accusations about wanting to be with another girl, tho she'll think it's true if I break up w her. Pro or Con?
3. 2 sec. MOOD swings, WTH?
4. No more kissing medicated lip balm.
5. If I don't do it now, I'll be thinking about it all the time.
6. I promised Frankie.

CONS:
1. I'll have to actually break up w her
2. How??

Then there are the other questions I've been turning over in my head. Should I change my number? Destroy the only chance I have to reconnect with Frankie?

It irks me that she got under my skin. That I care.

Why should I when Frankie's a phantom? A voice. A pseudonym for nobody. Why should I change my phone number? Still...if she calls at five o'clock and I answer, is there a chance she might actually be happy? Would she forgive me for breaking the promise? Is it worth the risk?

Maybe I could ask around? See if someone knows a girl whose grandma died? But that could lead to questions. Think, Emerson. Is there another way?

There must be some way to uncover her number, some way to get in through a back door like a hacker hacking into a secure site. I start searching. My carrier nets zero—no access to info on private callers. I do a Google search, read site after site, and discover that yes, there is a paid app I could download, which promises to reveal blocked and private numbers. I watch their promo video and am disappointed to learn it only works on new, incoming calls.

I continue to search. Despite twinges of guilt, I try two suggestions—hitting redial for her private number and *69 Talk. Surprise, surprise, neither works.

One more text from Angie. "<3." Delete.

Can I really go through with this? Yeah. Because I'm not doing this for Frankie. I'm not. *Promise or no promise,* I need to break up with Angie for me. I have no idea what I'm going to say. *After you woke me up this morning...* Yeah right. I won't be revealing Frankie to anyone, especially Angie.

I wonder what Frankie's doing right now, what she's thinking about. Is she thinking about me? In my mind I hear her plea: *Please change your number...* I type my cell phone carrier's website into the address bar, review the instructions. *Okay, Frankie. You win. After school, I'm changing my number for you.*

FIVE

"The world belongs to the energetic."
Ralph Waldo Emerson

TRICIA

WASHINGTON ISLAND, WISCONSIN   MONDAY, 10:57 A.M.

LIGHT SLASHES ACROSS my face, waking me from a deep, peaceful slumber. I stretch, take in the early spring flowing through the open window—a warm breeze, the mating calls of redwing blackbirds, and the faint smell of daffodils, tulips, hyacinths, and lily of the valley.

I get out of bed and walk to the window. For several wonderful seconds I have this notion that Grandma's outside working in one of her gardens. A flicker of movement catches my attention, drawing my eyes to the lawn. I almost call out for Grandma, but reality catches up.

Without a care in the world, a white-tailed doe and her fawn saunter away from the lighthouse toward the forest and stop to graze on Pennsylvania sedge. The fawn nuzzles against her mother's belly. A buck and another fawn emerge between two beech trees and stroll closer to the other pair. I watch, mesmerized by this family, and in an irrational way I'm envious.

High-pitched squawking shifts my attention to the east side of Boyer's Bluff. Hundreds of migrating broad-wing hawks circle and search for prey above the canopy of trees. Grandma would have loved this spectacular airshow.

I slam my window shut and walk to my door and, even though I know it's absurd, I call out, "Brian?" He isn't here. Even on a normal day, he wouldn't be here. He'd be at school. I glance at the clock. 11:15 A.M. Will he come home—here—like he always does for lunch, his afternoon online classes, then stay overnight?

I'm dizzy from the idea of Brian not being in my life. *My best friend.* From that first day of kindergarten until my grandma's death, our relationship was simple, uncomplicated. We've fought more in the last five months than we had in the thirteen years before. Brian once described our relationship as the perfect team—two people sitting side by side, rowing together through life. But I see now that it's not true. He did most of the rowing, and I was content to occasionally paddle. The moment a storm brewed and the waves kicked up and got rough, he took over for me, and I let him. Did I decide or did he persuade me? Did I agree or give in, give up?

I think back to the many conversations freshman year that we had about us, when Brian said friendship wasn't enough. He loved me, wanted me, wanted *us*. Forever. Ten months I held back. Ten months it took until I finally agreed, because other than my grandma, I loved him the most.

The day I said yes we were watching the sunrise from the Jackson Harbor dock. Draped in a blanket,

I leaned back against his chest, cradled between his runner's legs. His fingers traced circles over my neck. My arms rested against his thighs. His free hand was on top of mine, stroking, urging me to reciprocate, to touch him. He grew hard against the base of my back. I froze as he pulled me closer. Brian slid the spaghetti strap off my shoulder, pressed a kiss to my tingling skin, and used a fingertip to spell out *I L-O-V—*

"Brian," I said, panic rising. "I don't want this to change us. You're my best friend. I can't lose you." I had voiced this same concern at least a dozen times in a dozen different ways. I was worried. He wasn't.

It's hard to explain, but I felt a dread that left me scared and desperate for reassurance. I twisted the tiny ruby and diamond promise ring my dad had given my mom in high school, which I wore on my right ring finger. He noticed. Lifting my hand to his lips, he kissed the ring.

He brushed the hair off my neck and whispered, "No matter what, you will *never* lose me. I love you. Friends first, forever." A promise made as solemnly as any marriage vow in the presence of God. I wanted to hold on, hold him as tightly as possible. I turned around, straddled his lap. We sealed his promise with a kiss that left me breathless and wanting, needing more. *How could I feel so much, be so turned on by him, if we weren't supposed to be together?*

He smiled against my neck and said, "See, I told you we'd be perfect together." With another long, amazing kiss I released the last lingering wisps of doubt.

Maybe I shouldn't have.

After all this time, I lost him anyway. I lost my best friend.

I crawl into bed, slip under the covers, and sweep my hand over Brian's cold side. I hug his pillow to my chest, and breathe deeply. The smell—a combo of smoked hickory and grease from cooking at his parent's bar and grill—isn't quite him. What's missing is potter's clay, another difference between before and after Grandma's death.

Turning my head, I spot Dad's shotgun propped against my desk. The remnants of my mental fog lift and I'm reminded of how deeply I've plunged. Shame hits me in my chest. An angry tear rolls down my cheek and I swipe it away. I want to scream, hide. I'm so glad I didn't tell Emerson my real name. It would only have added to my humiliation, agony.

I scan the room for evidence that Brian hasn't left completely. His Islanders baseball cap is hooked on the doorknob and the bottom dresser drawer is cracked open, stuffed with his T-shirts. He'll have to come back for his things. Should I ask him to stay?

I check my phone. No text or voice messages from him. More evidence of *I'm done, Tricia. We're done.* Underneath the spike of pain, there's something bigger. Stronger. Determined. A chance to start a new life, fresh as a blanket of snow burying old footprints, ready for new ones.

I sink into memories of last night's conversation with Emerson. I smiled. I laughed. I can't remember the last time I did any of those things. *She'd want the best for you,* he said. Who wouldn't want the best for someone they love? But what I didn't tell Emerson is that Grandma used to say that. A lot. Was it another sign? I want to call him, talk to him. Or just hear his hello. One more time. My finger hovers over Grandma's old number, *Emerson's* number. *Call him.* I draw my hand back. I *can't*. Not now. At five o'clock, I'll call, and I hope he kept his promise and changed his number. Then Fate will decide, just like we agreed.

Drawing Grandma's quilt over my head, I close my eyes. I'm so tired. There's time for fresh starts. Later.

SIX

"There are moods in which we court suffering, in the hope that here, at least, we shall find reality, sharp peaks and edges of truth."
Ralph Waldo Emerson

EMERSON
STURGEON BAY HIGH SCHOOL
MAIN ENTRANCE PARKING LOT

MONDAY, 11:26 A.M.

WHAT MY FOUR sisters' ex-boyfriends have taught me about breakups:

Don't:

1. Compare her kissing to a carp. 2. Cut up a photograph of the two of you and tape it to her locker. 3. Confess that you're more attracted to and have more fun with her best friend. 4. Deny ever loving her when you said that you did. 5. Box up the things she gave you and leave them on the doorstep with a note that says, "I'd like my stuff back." 6. Tell her, "My mom doesn't like you." 7. Break up at a cemetery.

Do:

Well, that's the problem. Their ex-boyfriends have always screwed up. I don't know the right way, the *nice* way to break up with Angie, and there's no way I'm going to ask for my sisters' advice.

I pull out my phone and read through my list:

< NOTES

THINGS TO SAY TO ANGIE?

1. I think we need to talk about us.
2. We've been fighting a lot.
3. I'm not making you happy. You should be w someone who makes you happy.
4. I care about you, but I can't see us staying together after I leave for college.
5. I don't want to go to prom w you or anyone.
6. I think we should break up.
7. I'm sorry.

SEVEN

"Life is a series of surprises, and would not be worth taking or
keeping, if it were not."
Ralph Waldo Emerson

ANGIE
STURGEON BAY HIGH SCHOOL
MAIN ENTRANCE PARKING LOT   MONDAY, 11:30 A.M.

Emerson leans
against his Camaro,
focused on his phone.
Is he looking
at my pic?

The thrill
of what's
to come
shimmies
d
o
w
n
  my
s
p
i
n
e.

72

He's irresistible
in worn boots,
stonewashed jeans,
and the T-shirt
I bought him to match
his sky-blue eyes.

"Hey," I say.

"Hi."

Quick hug.
Before I can plant
a kiss on his scruffy
chin, he backs away.
No time to shave?

As usual,
his wavy black hair's
mussed, his cowlick
sticks up. Once,
for Homecoming
I convinced him to use
hair gel. He hated it.

Jordan doesn't need hair gel.
Stop thinking about Jordan!!!

Engine rumbles.

"Where are we going?"
He turns right
onto Michigan,
toward the center
of town.

"Sunset Park.
I thought it'd be a great place
to...talk."

Liza Wiemer

"What about lunch?"

Hitchhike thumb
sweeps over his shoulder
to the backseat.

A flannel blanket, mini-cooler, wicker basket.

I grin.
"A picnic?"
So romantic.

He nods, turns
on the radio,
surfs stations,
stops on
a Frank Sinatra song.

"Seriously?" Before
I reach the dial,
he covers it and sings
along. The lyrics
are about two lonely
strangers in the night
B O R I N G! Lame.
A lopsided grin blooms
on his face as he looks off
into the distance.

"What (who) are you thinking about?" I ask.

One beat. Two.

"My nonno serenading
Nonna with Sinatra.
It's her favorite song."

His smile grows. Mine

74

does too, remembering
the time we danced
to Sinatra at his sister
Isabelle's wedding.

UNTIL...

Another memory. Ouch.
His nonno patted my cheek,
bellowed, "Emerson, feed
this girl. She's skin and bones.
Get her pasta and a cannoli."

Know how many calories
are in pasta and a cannoli?
Carbs. Fried food. No thank you.

BB King's
"Three O'Clock Blues"
begins. Emerson taps out
the beat on his knee
oblivious to my misery.
Sometimes, I don't get him.

He has too many rules like:
No touching his radio knobs.
(He says they're temperamental.)
No PDA.
No alcohol EVER. No exceptions.
Not even to toast Isabelle.

At a party, Travis
spiked Emerson's Coke.
Emerson went ballistic,
cuffed him on his head,
shouted, "What the hell,
Travis? I'm the DD. You
trying to kill us?"

Liza Wiemer

Emerson poured the vodka

d

o

w

n

the drain.

"Overreact much?" I said.

Emerson grabbed
his jacket,
announced
we were leaving.

Brenda stepped in,
said she'd take me home.
He glared at her, then me,
knocked over a beer can
pyramid, and stormed out.

Later, twelve hours later,
he called, contrite.
Said he was out of line
and was sorry he left.

I asked, "Someone in your family
an alcoholic or addict? You can
tell me, any secret's safe with me."

Emerson said no and changed
the subject. I still wonder why
he
shut me
d
o
w
n.

Left turn into Sunset Park.
He drives past
the baseball field,
basketball courts,
disc golf course,
and parks in the beach lot.

He hands me the blanket,
takes the cooler and basket,
walks toward Little Lake.

<u>SILENCE is a THICK, INVISIBLE WALL.</u>

I follow him, step
over geese turds
to a semi-secluded
spot under a weeping
willow tree. Pretty.

Dozens of honking
geese and goslings
waddle away.
A breeze off the bay
cools my bare arms,
making me shhhi**ver.**
Emerson doesn't notice.
He seems...nervous?

Inhaling the damp
earthy smell reminds
me of Jordan's cologne.
Ugh. Sensory overload
as I remember his
fingers skimming
my hair, the sparks
when my lips pressed
against his. Rejection.
Stop thinking about Jordan!!

Liza Wiemer

Emerson spreads the blanket,
opens the cooler, the basket.
I crane my neck, look, hope
for flowers, chocolates?

But NO.

Ick. PB&J sandwiches,
sliced apples,
two bags of chips.

"This is nice."

Why didn't he remember
I only eat whole grain? I bite
into the apple, probably
not organic,
and track Emerson's gaze
to two mallards bobbing
near an uprooted birch tree.

"So." I dig up
courage. "I know how shy
you can be. I'll save you
from the agony. "Yes, I'll go
to prom with you." I laugh.

He grimaces. Shakes his head.

Oh. No. No. No. No.

I've earned my PhD
in humiliation. How
is it I've been so blind?

"Is there...
someone else?"

He shakes his head again.
Liar. Liar. Liar. Liar. Liar. **Liar.**

"Then what?"

Mist off the lake
reflects in his blue
eyes like rain clouds.

                                    "I-I—"

His gaze drifts
over the water,
trees, grass, geese,
and finally lands
on me. He looks
angry? Irritated?

                        "Really, Angie. Tell me,
                        'cause I'd like to know.
                        What was last night
                                    about?"

Puzzled, I draw a blank.

                        "The drunken call?
                        The performance?"

Oh.
I sputter, "Brenda said
you'd like it."

Looking at his face,
I clearly made a mistake.

                        "Why in the world would
                        you listen to Brenda?"

Is this a trick question?

                                                    79

Liza Wiemer

"Umm, because she's my best friend?"

He tilts his head, laughs, like
it's a joke, confusing me more.

                    "Yeah? Well, I hardly think
                            she qualifies
                to give you relationship advice."

I don't appreciate
his tone.
"W-what's that
supposed to mean?"

                    His forehead scrunches.
                "You think that's what I want
                from you when you're drunk?
                    Maybe that's what
                        Brenda wants."

What?

                "You told me yourself ages ago you
                thought she was gay. No boyfriends?"

My eyes
grow w i **d** **e.**

"I-I- said that in jest."

                        "Well, I'm pretty sure
                        she's in love with you."

My mouth
F
A
L
L
S
open.

"Geez, Ang. You haven't noticed how
she needs to know where you are,
what you're doing all the time?
She gets upset if you don't check in.
It's...excessive for just a friend."

S L O W L Y
it sinks in
and I start to
comprehend.
Brenda gay?
Wanting me?
Not my BFF?!

Wish
I could fry
the memory
of last night's phone
performance Brenda
scripted. The perfect
screenplay. I practiced
for her before Emerson.
She gave me tips.
Maybe that's how she
got into NYU's Tisch?
Gawd, I sound like a
board-certified bitch.

Mortifying.

I've taken all her advice on clothes and makeup.
She helped me shop for bras, thongs, swimsuits.
I've undressed in front of her, slept in the same bed.
Drunk, she kissed me on the lips, said it was an
accident. (Maybe it wasn't?)

How many of her
I love you's

were *more?*

"Are you sure? You really
think she's gay?"
~~It can't be~~ true.

Shrug.
"Why would it matter?
Two years ago,
six months ago,
last week,
today. Nothing's
changed. She's still
Brenda.
She's your best friend,
a great friend."

Best friend? Great
friend? How did
I not know?

"So that's why
she said no to Matt?"

"Ang, can we stop
talking about Brenda?
After
last night, I
realized that I—"

One beat. Two.

"I've been thinking that..."

"What?"

"We should break up."

My world

      c r

        u

      m b

        l

        e s.

But I won't. I look
around. *Here?* He broke
up with me *here!*
One beat. Two.

I curse him out
knowing how much
swearing annoys
him. There's no
satisfaction, not even
a pea. Legs shake
with the quake under
my feet as I stand.
He stands.

                          "I'm sorry."

Fist. Punch. Block.
I yank my hand away.

"LEAVE, asshole. I NEVER
want to see you again."

What a fool I've been
wasting my heart on him.

Emerson doesn't move.
I scoop up apples, whip   by a mile.
them at his head. He
doesn't flinch 'cause

          I miss

Liza Wiemer

I smash-crack,
        smash-crack
the wicker basket.
Spl-in-ter-ed wood flies s s.
He watches,
blank-faced.

I swoop down, grab
the blanket, drag
it across the grass,
to dump it into
Little Lake.

        Slick sludge.

  Slide.   Slip.

        FLAIL.

    Splashhhhhh.

Soaked skirt. Soaked shirt.

Emerson rushes
over, offers help.

"Leave me alone!"

His hands fly
up, conciliatory
as he backs away.

Muddy mess. I snatch
my purse, pull out
my phone, unsure
whom to call.
Not Brenda. Heck no.
Scrolling my contacts

84

list. A, B, C, D, E, F, G,
H, I, J, K, Lieberman.

Asshole Emerson's still
here, continues his doe-eyed
stare, until I yell, "Go, dickhead."

Great. Just my luck.
Travis Davis drives
by in his pickup.
Huge grin.
Waves to me.
Waves to *him*.

Emerson
looks awfully grim.
Slouched, he walks
to the Camaro,
hesitates at the door,
pivots on his heels.

"Are you *sure* I can't
give you a ride?"

Still the gentleman.

"Go to hell, Emerson."
And I dial Jordan.

EIGHT

"Every violation of truth is not only a sort of suicide in the liar,
but is a stab at the health of human society."
Ralph Waldo Emerson

EMERSON
STURGEON BAY   MONDAY, 12:08 P.M.

THAT WENT WELL. I laugh, miserable, as I take one
more glance back at Angie, drenched and talking on
the phone. Hopefully, she called Brenda to pick her
up. I climb into my car. There's no way I'll leave her
completely behind until I know she has a ride. But for
both our sakes, I'm giving her the illusion of leaving.
I drive toward the only entrance/exit for Sunset Park
and pull onto the grass, just far enough for cars to pass
on both sides.

I watch for Brenda's Ford Explorer feeling relieved
it's over between Angie and me. But also guilty. What
a disaster, literally and figuratively. I'll come back after
Angie leaves and clean up the mess she made. The
hurt, shock, dismay on her face when she realized I
wasn't asking her to prom might haunt me for weeks.
Great, another nightmare. My only consolation is
there are probably ten guys lined up ready and willing
to take her.

I know she's not my responsibility. But I can't help but worry. There's something inside me that is tempted to turn around and go back to her. Try and make things right. Apologize for bringing her here. I thought it would be quiet, neutral territory, far enough from school, close enough to get back in time for classes. I saw her excitement. How she looked around expectantly. I deserve her wrath. Who's the jerk now?

Speaking of. Through my rearview mirror, I spot Travis Davis's truck slowly rounding the bend by the baseball field. Didn't he just pass me by the lake? He must be circling around doing who knows what, and that's cause for concern. What if he harasses Angie?

There aren't many people I don't like. Travis is one of them. He's a splinter, getting under everyone's skin to the point he's so deeply embedded that there's no way to extract him without major pain. He just happens to be our team's best varsity basketball player and one of the reasons why we're Division II champions, so we tolerate him. Barely. He's got a mouth dirtier than an outhouse latrine and I'd love to shove him in it.

Last year, Travis got me in a boatload of trouble at home. His father works for my dad's shipping company and apparently Travis's dad reenacted a blowjob that Angie definitely did not give me at Graham Park. There was lots of hooting and hollering that made its way from the men's locker room to my dad's office. When Dad confronted Mr. Davis, they had two different ideas on what constitutes family pride and joy.

I vehemently denied the PDA, and my parents believed me. But when our family's reputation within the community is at stake, there's no reasoning with Dad. I received the privilege of scrubbing the shipyard's locker rooms every night for a month. Six months later, Mr. Davis was transferred to the graveyard shift.

Truth is, Angie and I had been at Graham Park with a bunch of our friends. Travis was there too. He saw Angie and me kissing—we weren't the only ones—when Angie slid her fingers into my waistband. I stopped her and Travis noticed. He laughed, made some obscene hand motions and suggested Angie hook up with a real dude—him. I answered by tossing him into the bay. When he came up for air, I swept Angie into my arms and carried her to the Camaro to the wild applause of her girlfriends. I made a big show of it, but inside I was a little pissed. Angie knew I wasn't into that brand of PDA.

When I got to the car, I set her down, opened her door. She climbed in, and I watched her slip her already short skirt up until red lace peeked out. I groaned—a frustrated, lustful groan that gave Angie a message I didn't intentionally want to encourage in the parking lot. It did. She gave me an eyeful of her matching strapless bra as she leaned over and unlocked my door for me.

After several blocks, she asked, "Where are we going?" Her hand was on my thigh, stroking toward dangerous territory and almost stroking me out.

I pulled over; the front tire scraped against the curb. "We need to talk," I said a little too sharply. She deflated faster than our basketball team's pride after a major loss.

I leaned in, kissed her bare shoulder, and said, "Of course I want you, want to be with you, but not while I'm driving and never with people around. Our reputations mean something to me."

With all the crying my sisters have done over my lifetime, you'd think I could deal with Angie's tears. Definitely not, no. I struggled to figure out what it was she needed from me and why she took offense to what

I said. I asked. She didn't like my tone, so I tried again. It took some convincing, but Angie finally understood when I took her to an old hunter's shack at the end of an abandoned road and showed her very specifically and satisfactorily what I meant by wanting to be with her in private.

We returned to the park and to our friends, holding hands and smiling. Travis ended up getting tossed into the bay again, not by me this time, but by a bunch of other basketball players who were sick of his mouth. Some guys just never learn, and he's a blowhard, especially in front of his dad. I wasn't going to tell my parents any of this.

Besides cleaning the locker rooms, my parents sent me to Father John, not for confession—since I had nothing to confess—but for a priestly lecture on the sins of premarital sex. I would rather have jumped from the Oregon Street bridge into the bay.

Trust me, no lecture was needed. If a condom failed, if I'd gotten Angie pregnant, not only would I face my parents' immense disappointment, they'd expect me to man up. All my promises to myself, to Dr. Shale to make something out of my third chance at life would have gone up in flames for a girl I only thought I had loved. Just thinking about it makes me shudder.

I'm still watching Travis, who's taking his sweet time. Can't be going more than two miles per hour, and he's not even looking at the road. I think he's texting.

A minute passes, maybe two before his hands are on the steering wheel. Much to my relief, he doesn't make a left to loop around the park again—because I would have followed him—but continues for the exit. When Travis approaches my car, he slows, stops. Rolls down his window. I do the same.

I acknowledge him with a chin-lift-nod. He has a grin on his face. "Well done, Caruso." His smile morphs into malice as he waves his phone, then guns the engine, tires spinning on the gravel. He peels onto Sixth Street nearly colliding with a dilapidated Jeep Wrangler.

Jordan Lieberman.

Angie called Jordan? I feel like Hercules after he no longer carried the sky on his shoulders. Thank you Jordan.

Jordan's Jeep stalls. The engine grinds and sputters until it kicks back into life with enough soot and smoke to haze his entire car. When the cloud clears, his eyes lock with mine. Weird, for a few seconds, he doesn't move. Maybe I was wrong. Maybe Angie didn't call him? But he turns in, eyes forward, clearly ignoring my existence. I stick my arm out like a roadblock. Though he could pass easily, he doesn't. I crank my fist, indicating that I want him to roll down his window. He does.

"Angie called you," I say as a statement, hoping it's true.

Barely glancing at me, he nods. His fingers tap against the doorframe. *What's with him?*

"I'm glad. I didn't want to leave her alone after breaking up with her. She refused to get in my car."

Jordan's head snaps whiplash-fast to look at me. Confusion, then recognition transforms his face to stone. It catches me off-guard. Is he...angry?

He lets out an almost imperceptible sigh. His cold expression's replaced with resignation? Which makes me think he knows Angie a little bit better than I thought. I mean, sure, I know they've lived across the street from each other forever and we've all gone to school together. But this—the way he can't look at me—seems out of character. It bothers me. Before he shifts gears, I need to ask, "What did Angie tell you?"

I have his full attention. Frowning, he says, "She said she broke up with you, that *you* left her stranded." Now I'm the one who can't speak. He drags a hand over his face, rubs his eyes, then drops it back onto the doorframe. "Just Angie being Angie." He chuckles, but it's bitter, jarring.

From his tone, I can tell my hunch was right. He does know Angie. How well, how close, I'm not sure. "Don't tell her I told you the truth. I don't care if that's the story she wants to tell, all right? Well, not the stranded part, but that she broke up with me. It's fine. I screwed the whole thing up anyway."

He gives me a sideward glance, and I don't care if he thinks I've lost my mind. What do I care if Angie needs to save face? Graduation's only seven weeks away. "You'll take care of her, right?"

His shoulders practically touch his ears with his exaggerated shrug.

"Thanks." I pour a ton of gratitude into it, disregarding his solemn, pissed attitude. Don't care. Problem solved. I'm done. Much to my relief, the burning ache that bands around my heart finally, finally, finally eases.

He lifts his hand in a half-wave good-bye. I'm tempted to wish him good luck, but he takes off without another word between us. I watch him until his junkyard special is out of sight, then I pull into the road and park down the street. A few minutes later, when he leaves, I return to Little Lake. It takes me ten minutes to gather the strewed pieces of the basket, collect a plastic baggy that drifted into the water, gather the other garbage, and drag and wring out the blanket.

BY THE TIME I park and get a tardy slip from the office, I'm twenty-five minutes late for AP Calc. As I approach Mr. Bordon, he turns around from the board, peers over his reading glasses, and says, "Emerson?" There's concern in his voice, but my smile relieves it. I've had Mr. Bordon for math three years in a row and have never been late. He takes the slip from my outstretched hand, crumples it in his, throws it across the room and into the wastepaper basket. The room cheers. Mr. Bordon's our basketball coach and he hasn't missed a shot once this year. He takes a small bow, then refocuses on me as the classroom quiets down. "See me after class for your test grade," he says and goes back to the lesson.

As I make my way to my seat, everyone's looking at me, except Avery, who's drawing in her textbook. A lot of the other girls nail me with death stares. Like I committed some horrific crime? I stare back. Everything goes a bit fuzzy as I try not to cringe. My only hypothesis is that Angie texted someone about the breakup and it's spread faster than weeds. But if she's telling everyone she broke up with me like she did with Jordan, then I don't get it. Why would I get ostracized over it?

I grit my teeth, glance over at Matt, and use my eyes to ask what's up. He holds up his hands, pushes them out, and shrugs. Whatever that means. When I reach my seat, Marina Martinez leans forward, yawns loudly, and pretends to stretch. She extends her arms across my desk, preventing me from sitting down. Without looking away from the board, she slaps her wrist. Like she's trying to shame me, embarrass me.

Okay. I shake my head as much to clear it as to express my annoyance. Then I turn my attention to the lesson on integrals and derivatives.

When the bell rings for the next block, I pass on getting my test grade to catch up with Matt, who was the first one out. I'm greeted in the hallway with more razor-sharp stares. All around me, cell phones ping and more and more people look at me like I'm the incarnation of Brutus. Matt confirms my suspicions that this is about the breakup when he says, "Disastrous picnic, eh?" But before I can respond, the crowd swallows him.

Only a few guys make eye contact. Those who do, smirk. I get a couple heavy-handed pats on the back. It seems like the entire female SBHS population despises me. Whatever Angie said must have hit a nuclear reactor because I've never seen *this* huge of a reaction over a breakup, not even when Marcus cheated on Theresa and dumped her on Facebook.

I try and ignore it, hold my head high with as much dignity as I can muster. Still, it's hard to concentrate on the AP Spanish practice exam. By the time I finish, I have a smashing headache.

✎

3:16 PM

THE MOMENT I enter the hallway, people stop talking. Even the guys. Almost like someone organized it to humiliate me. The air buzzes from their glares. A few mumble *asshole, douche, prick.* But for the most part,

I'm hit with a wall of silence. There's so much hatred beamed at me that it chills me to the bone.

Screw this bull. No way will I acknowledge that they're getting to me. I am so, so over Angie. When I reach my locker, the hallway noise returns to normal.

Someone nearby says, "Dude, check your texts," but I can't be sure he's talking to me.

I grab my backpack, close my locker, and walk into Mrs. Fensman's room. She teaches computer science, part-time mornings, and in the afternoon we use the space for online classes.

After a quick check to make sure I'm alone, I pull out my phone and turn it on. Two texts from one of the guys on our basketball team. "*WTH?*" is the first. The second is a gif. Off in the distance, Angie's sprawled out, soaking wet, glaring up at me. I'm standing at the water's edge. My body bends forward and down while my hands reach for Angie. The way the gif plays, my movement is completely the opposite of what took place. Hands flying down and up, down and up making it look like I pushed her in. The image is blurry and far enough away that it looks like I touched her. I never laid a hand on her!

Travis.

Every swear word I can imagine, and even some in Italian, rattles in my brain. I've kicked his ass before and I'll do it again.

I'm screwed. No idea how I'm going to clear my reputation of this unless I can get Angie and Travis to admit it's fake. Yeah, right.

Not in a million years will I be sorry for breaking up with Angie. But I am sorry I did it in a public place. I'm sorry I took her to Sunset Park.

An incoming call blinks onto my screen. It's Brenda. She can be cold and annoying, but for the most part we've gotten along okay. With some luck, she'll hear me out and help me clean up my second disaster of the day.

NINE

"I do not wish to treat friendships daintily, but with roughest courage. When they are real, they're not glass threads or frostwork, but the solidest thing we know."
Ralph Waldo Emerson

BRENDA
STURGEON BAY   MONDAY, 3:19 P.M.

FADE IN:

INT. STURGEON BAY HIGH SCHOOL SENIOR
HALLWAY - DAY

The hallway is filled with students
getting ready to leave for the day.
A cacophony of CLATTERING BOOKS,
BANGING LOCKER DOORS, VOICES, grows
louder, then dissipates as students
begin to file out.

BRENDA (18), visibly upset, hoists
her backpack onto her shoulder, shuts
her locker, and pulls out her phone.

INSERT - BRENDA'S PHONE
A series of texts to Angie:

12:19 What did Emerson do to u?
1:06 WTH? Are u okay?
1:09 Where r u?
2:18 Call me!!!!
3:16 Why haven't u returned my calls?
STRESSING OUT! If I get zits,
it's yr fault! CALL ME!

No response from Angie. She rechecks
her phone messages and missed calls.
There are none.

She scrolls through her contact list,
finds Emerson's number and hits TALK.

> BRENDA
> (into phone)
> Emerson?

> Emerson (V.O.)
> (over phone, filtered)
> Hey. Where are you?

> BRENDA
> (into phone)
> At my locker. Where are
> you? What the hell happened
> between you and Angie?

Brenda glances anxiously across the
hall at Angie's locker DECORATED
with GOOD LUCK SIGNS for a SBHS swim
team meet. A few students walk by,
talking, smiling.

                    EMERSON (V.O.)
          It's not what you think, what
          everyone   thinks.   Angie's
          fine. I'm in Mrs. Fensman's
          room. Come   in   and   I'll
          explain.

Brenda   starts   walking   toward   the
classroom.

                    BRENDA
                 (into phone)
          So you two really broke
          up?

                    Emerson (V.O.)
                 (beat)
          Yeah.

                    BRENDA
                 (into phone)
          I've tried to reach her
          a hundred times and she
          hasn't answered.

                    Emerson (V.O.)
          Maybe her battery's dead?
          You know how she sometimes
          forgets to charge it.

INT.   STURGEON   BAY   HIGH   SCHOOL
CLASSROOM - DAY - CONTINUOUS

Brenda steps into the room, spots
EMERSON (18) who's sitting at a

desk. Emerson ends the call, sets his phone down, and stands. Brenda plants herself in front of him, drops her backpack at his feet.

She clicks onto her text messages, holds her phone up to his face. He winces.

> BRENDA
> So, you want to explain?

Emerson steps back until he knocks into the computer table.

> EMERSON
> (beat)
> I took Angie to the park so that we'd be able to talk without anyone else around. I just—I thought it would be easier if I...
> broke up with her over lunch.

He scrubs his face with his hands.

> EMERSON (CONT.)
> She got upset, rightfully so. But then she went ballistic. She smashed the picnic basket, and when she dragged the blanket to the lake, she slipped on the muddy edge, and fell

in. I tried to help her up, but she refused. I swear, I never touched her. You know I would never hurt her like that.

BRENDA
(sympathetic)
Travis flooded every social media site. I doubt you'll be able to make this go away.

Emerson scowls and reaches for his phone. Opens the gif.

EMERSON
If I had pushed her, wouldn't it show her falling? He must have shot the video from afar because I didn't see him until I was almost at my car.

BRENDA
You left Angie?

EMERSON
No! I mean I was going to take her home, but she told me to go. I waited by the exit thinking she called you to come get her. I wasn't going to leave until I was sure she

had a ride. Jordan showed
up. She called him.

                    BRENDA
          Jordan?

Her face morphs from confusion to
hurt.

                    BRENDA (CONT.)
          Why would she call Jordan?
          She despises him.

Emerson leans against the table,
picks up a pencil, twirls it between
his fingers. He focuses on his feet.

                    EMERSON
          Well...

Brenda snatches the pencil from his
hand, forcing him to look at her.
Emerson shoves his hands into his
pockets.

                    EMERSON (CONT.)
          This may or may not be the
          reason. So, don't freak
          out, okay?

                    BRENDA
          Just tell me.

                    EMERSON
        I thought Angie knew you
        were gay. But she didn't.
        Honestly, it's no big deal.
        I'm certain she'll get over
        it. She was surprised,
        that's all, and probably
        upset she pushed Matt on
        you for a prom date. You
        know Angie, she'll work
        through it. You're best
        friends. It doesn't change
        anything.

                    BRENDA
        What the hell are you
        talking about?

Emerson flinches.

                    BRENDA (CONT.)
        Why would you think I'm
        gay? I'm not gay.
                (beat)
        This is a joke, right?

She walks around, scans the ceiling
for hidden cameras and microphones
and checks the computer monitors to
see if the built-in cameras are on.
As she does that, she says:

                    BRENDA (CONT.)
        Okay, I get it. This is
        an audition for a reality

TV show. Angie joked about it last night. She thought it would be funny if I did MTV's *Teen Mom*. Except I'm a—

Her face turns bright red and she recoils, then straightens her spine, puts her hands on her hips.

> BRENDA (CONT.)
> (annoyed)
> Angie, you can come out now. This isn't funny.

Emerson shakes his head.

> EMERSON
> Brenda, she's not here. This isn't an audition. I'm…sorry.

She glares at him.

> BRENDA
> You actually told her I'm gay? Why? You don't know me. You know nothing about me!

> EMERSON
> I've always thought— With the way you look at her, check up on her. Last night's performance? And

the kiss? She told me about it in another drunk midnight call.

BRENDA
(growing angrier and angrier)
So that's it? That's your evidence? You think it's okay to jump to conclusions and spread lies about me? To my best friend? Just because I care about her? Want the best for her?

EMERSON
No! I—

BRENDA
(lowered voice)
Oh my God. On everything holy tell me you didn't say anything to anyone else, did you? Because if you did I swear—

EMERSON
No! Of course not! You and I are friends.

BRENDA
Friends? This is how you treat a friend? Or anyone? You had no right to talk about me, about my life

behind my back. You had no right to make assumptions! You have no right to discuss my business with anyone!

Emerson reaches out to Brenda, but she backs away.

> EMERSON
> It...We...You're right. I-I'm sorry.

> BRENDA
> You're sorry? A lot late for that.

She picks up a piece of paper, tears it in two, then balls the halves in her fists. Distraught, she lets out a soft moan.

> BRENDA (CONT.)
> Angie must hate me!

> EMERSON
> Of course she doesn't hate you.

> BRENDA
> You don't know that.
>   (beat)
> Do you have any idea what you've done? Do you know

what I've had to do to
protect her?

Brenda fights back frustrated tears.

          EMERSON
          Protect her? What are you
          talking about? Protect her
          from what?

          BRENDA
          From assholes like you!

He stares at her, trying to figure
out exactly what she means.

Brenda heads to the door, yanks it
open, and storms into the hallway.

INT. STURGEON BAY HIGH SCHOOL SENIOR
HALLWAY - CONTINUOUS - DAY

Emerson catches up. Touches her
shoulder. Brenda wrenches away and
spins around.

          EMERSON
          You're overreacting. Just
          tell her it's not true.

Brenda lifts a combat boot, kicks out
toward Emerson. He jumps back quickly
enough that she misses contact.

BRENDA
Overreacting? How dare you! Angie didn't call me! Her best friend. How would you feel if our situations were reversed, huh? My life, my relationship with Angie has nothing to do with you. Even if I were gay, it's none of your damn business.

EMERSON
I know. I'm sorry.

BRENDA
You should have thought about it before you opened your mouth.

Emerson motions for Brenda to calm down. Points to himself.

EMERSON
I'll talk to her, okay? My mistake. I'll take all the blame, accept full responsibility, and tell her I misinterpreted and misunderstood the situation.

BRENDA
She won't believe it.

                    EMERSON
          Yes. She will. I'll fix
          it. I'm sorry.

Brenda sweeps toward Emerson, slaps
him hard across his face.

                    BRENDA
          You're sorry? A hundred of
          those and then maybe we're
          even.

INT. BRENDA'S FORD EXPLORER - LATE
AFTERNOON

Brenda sits in her SUV in front
of Jordan's house looking toward
Angie's. Her hand rests on the door
handle as she glances back and forth
between the homes.

EXT. JORDAN'S HOME - CONTINUOUS

JORDAN (18) opens his front door.
ANGIE (18) stands at the threshold
and smiles at him. They hug. Angie
turns, freezes when she spots Brenda.
She says something to Jordan. He
looks at Brenda, nods, and shuts the
door.

Angie starts walking toward Brenda's
vehicle.

INT/EXT. BRENDA'S FORD EXPLORER -
CONTINUOUS

Brenda rolls down the passenger
window as Angie approaches. Angie
opens the passenger door, climbs in.

> BRENDA (CONT.)
> Jordan, huh? After all
> this time?

Brenda sees Angie's lips tremble,
resists reaching out to touch her.

> BRENDA (CONT.)
> Oh Ang. You're going to be
> okay.

> ANGIE
> I've never been so
> humiliated. Embarrassed.
> Everyone must be laughing
> at me. I don't ever want
> to go back to school.

Angie folds her arms against the
dashboard and drops her head onto
her crossed wrists.

> BRENDA
> Actually, Emerson's the
> one who's been humiliated,
> and he should be. The
> whole school's rallying
> behind you. Most of the

girls gave him the biggest
stare-down. Believe me, it
made SBHS history.

Angie lifts her head.

                    ANGIE
          Really? Why?

                    BRENDA
          Hello? You saw the gif?

                    ANGIE
          Yeah, but…he didn't do
          it— I'm the one who acted
          like—

Angie's phone beeps. She pulls it
out of her pocket, scrolls through
the massive number of sympathetic
text messages, and cringes. After a
few more seconds, she puts it away.

                    ANGIE (CONT.)
               (mournfully)
          I haven't had a chance to
          respond. But I will. It's
          my fault. I—

                    BRENDA
          Don't say a thing.
          Emerson's getting exactly
          what he deserves. He was
          an asshole, so who cares
          how much was true? Let him

suffer. At least for a few days.

Angie's face brightens a little.

                    ANGIE
          Did you really slap him?

                    BRENDA
                (surprised)
          You talked to him?

                    ANGIE
          Yeah, he came over after
          school. That's how I
          heard about the gif. He
          apologized for a lot of
          things. Mainly for being
          an idiot.

Angie flashes a quick grin. Brenda has a hard time looking at Angie.

                    ANGIE (CONT.)
          He even brought me yellow
          roses. Why does he have to
          be so nice?

                    BRENDA
                (hesitant)
          Does this mean you two are
          back together?

Angie shakes her head. Brenda looks relieved, then waves toward Angie's door.

                    BRENDA (CONT.)
          I better go. Homework.

Angie looks point-blank at Brenda. Brenda seems to know what's coming and reaches for the key in the ignition. Before she can start the car, Angie speaks.

                    ANGIE
          Emerson told me he made a
          mistake. About, um, you
          being gay. But I've had
          some time to think about
          it, and it's hard for me
          to believe it's not true.
             (beat)
          I want you to know it's
          okay. You're my best
          friend and I love you. I
          will always love you, but
          not in that way. I hope you
          still want to be my best
          friend, because I don't
          know what I'd do without
          you.

Brenda gapes at her.

                    BRENDA
          I'm not gay! I'm telling
          you and I told Emerson. And
          yes, we're best friends,
          purely platonic friends,
          okay? So just drop it. I
          don't want to discuss this
          anymore.

                    ANGIE
          Why not? Best friends—

Brenda cuts Angie off.

                    BRENDA
          Angie, there's no issue.
          Everything is fine. We're
          fine. End of discussion.

Brenda's eyes dart to Angie's house,
then to Angie.

                    ANGIE
          Do you want to come in?
          We could order pizza? I'm
          starving.

                    BRENDA
          I should go. I wouldn't
          even be here if you'd
          answered my texts.

She turns the ignition, shifts the
car into drive, waits for Angie to
get out, but she doesn't.

                    ANGIE
          I shut off my phone. I
          needed to think. Jordan and
          I talked, and it helped.

                    BRENDA
          You didn't tell him any of
          this, did you?

Angie looks down at her lap.

                    BRENDA (CONT.)
          Dammit to hell, Angie. How
          could you?

                    ANGIE
          It's no big deal.

                    BRENDA
          Are you out of your mind?
          This is how rumors get
          started.

                    ANGIE
          He won't say anything to
          anyone. He told me to
          discuss it with you.

                    BRENDA
          You seriously couldn't
          figure that out on your
          own? Geezus, you could
          have called me! You
          could have asked me. I'm
          supposed to be your best

friend. And you know what? I don't understand why you believed Emerson in the first place. Don't you think I would have told you if I had other feelings for you?

ANGIE
Truthfully? I don't know. Sometimes you're hard to read. There are times when I feel like I don't know you at all. I've been thinking about it a lot. Trying to figure you out. Figure out our relationship. In seventh grade, after the burglary, you avoided doing things with me. Then everything was okay. Except you never come over.

BRENDA
I'm here now. And may I remind you that for the past two years you've had a boyfriend. Now please get out of my car. I have homework to do. You should try it, instead of the booze.

Angie holds onto the edge of the seat.

                    ANGIE
          Whenever I want to talk
          about anything serious,
          you change the subject.
          Hell, you're so good at
          deflecting, I wouldn't
          be surprised if you saw
          someone else's reflection
          in the mirror.

                    BRENDA
          This from the girl who
          didn't notice that her
          boyfriend had lost interest
          a long time ago. Who do
          you see when you look in
          the mirror?

Hurt flashes across Angie's face.

                    ANGIE
          You know what I think? I
          think you're a master at
          not facing your problems.
          I think you love acting
          and writing screenplays
          so much because you can
          forget about yourself and
          morph into the characters.
          When you're acting, you
          know who you are. You're
          confident and strong and

command that stage. You
own it.

Brenda folds her arms across her
chest.

> BRENDA
> That's what every good
> actress or writer does.
> And be honest, you've
> done a fantastic job of
> pretending to be someone
> you're not. You're far
> from perfect, Angel.

Angie laughs. It's filled with pain.

> ANGIE
> Yeah, you're right. But
> we're not talking about me
> right now. You know what
> I figured out? I don't
> know who you really are.
> I'm supposed to be your
> best friend. I thought we
> shared everything. But you
> always have an explanation
> or an excuse whenever I
> want to
> talk about you. You're not
> gay? Fine, then why not go
> to prom with Matt? Go with
> him as friends.

Frustrated, Brenda chokes back tears. She starts the car.

ANGIE (CONT.)
>I don't understand. Talk to me. Tell me what's going on between us. Emerson said you—

Brenda cuts Angie off.

BRENDA
>After he publicly humiliated you, after he broke up with you, you'd listen to him? There's nothing wrong with me except you're frustrating the hell out of me. Now, for the second time, get the hell out of my car!

ANGIE
>Brenda, c'mon. Please? Why are we fighting? Just…talk to me.

BRENDA
>Isn't that why you have your old best friend Jordan back? Talk with him.

Angie opens her mouth to protest, but Brenda starts the car, points at Angie's door. Angie climbs out.

Brenda drives away leaving Angie standing on the curb staring after her.

INT. BRENDA'S APARTMENT BEDROOM -EARLY EVENING

Brenda is in her bedroom, which is decorated with MOVIE PROPS, POSTERS, WIGS, and FRAMED NYU-TISCH ACCEPTANCE LETTER. She walks to her bedroom door and twists and re-twists the lock to make sure she's safe. Then she checks the window, twists and re-twists the safety latch. She goes back and forth between the door and the window checking and rechecking three more times. Then three more. Once satisfied, she collapses onto her bed, reaches for her phone.

INSERT - PHONE

Brenda opens her "favorites" list, scrolls to "Brian" and taps his name.

BACK TO SCENE

She flips onto her back. The phone rings four times.

> BRIAN (V.O.)
> Hello, gorgeous. How's my favorite cousin?

> FADE OUT.

TEN

"Nothing can bring you peace but yourself."
Ralph Waldo Emerson

BRIAN

WASHINGTON ISLAND

MONDAY, 5:15 P.M.

WALKING OUT ON Tricia at two-thirty this morning was the most wretched, painful choice I've ever made. But I can't live in this nightmare anymore. I've watched her disappear before my eyes. Losing weight. Talking less and less. Trekking into the woods around the island alone, sometimes during the middle of the night, without a note or her phone. Inevitably, I'd end up on a search mission.

On numerous occasions, I found her lying across her family's graves, sometimes prone like she wanted to crawl or claw her way in. At first, she let me hold her while she trembled and sobbed. But then she started to push me away, asking me to wait in the truck, to give her space, or to leave her alone all together.

A few weeks ago, during another search, I found a brand-new engraved stone at the base of her grandma's grave. It left me red-eyed. Feeling so damn helpless and hopeless. *If Tears Could Build A Stairway,*

And Memories A Lane, I'd Walk Right Up To Heaven And Bring You Home Again. What more could I do to console her? Yet I hoped somehow she'd make her way back to the living. Back to me.

Was I being unreasonable? Not patient enough? I dunno.

She says I don't listen. But how much misery can a person take, huh? Sometimes I need to chill in front of the TV or concentrate on something else without having to rehash the past. I can't bring her grandmother back. I wanted her to see and acknowledge that I was there. For *her*. That shoulda meant something.

When her grandma died, I told my parents I wanted to stay with Tricia. That I couldn't let her face an empty house alone. They were supportive. Before I knew it, I'd moved in. Maybe that was part of the problem. I thought staying with her, loving her would be enough to help fill some of the void. It wasn't.

On her worst days, there was such a thick, black cloud surrounding her that she barely noticed me. I used to be able to joke with her, get her mind focused on other things. We were like two clocks going through life in sync with each other. Even on the rare occasion when we disagreed, argued, we always figured it out. I knew she loved me, wanted me, wanted *us*. We were planning our future. I was important to her. And now...

The abyss.

Nothing I've said or done has made one bit of difference. I tried to go about my daily activities and pretend everything between us was status quo—concentrating on school, filling in when I absolutely needed to at my parents' pub and grill, and cooking and cleaning for the two of us when she wasn't in the mood, which admittedly wasn't *that* often. In the end, all I did was take up space in her house and her bed.

I called our pastor, hoping he'd have another heart-to-heart with her. Tricia wouldn't let him in the house. She stood on the porch with him and told him she wasn't interested in talking about God. She said God had forsaken her.

Could I blame her? Guess not.

Last night, sitting alone in her den, I realized we were done. A few hours before, I had started to make love to her. It was the most affection she had allowed in a long time, and I could tell she wasn't there. A blank, brittle book with the pages ripped out. The lighthouse had transformed into a decrepit tomb of misery and memories. And if I stayed, I was gonna be buried alive with Tricia.

I couldn't take another second of it.

I'm done, Tricia. We're done.

At two-thirty in the morning, I left. I left her and went home.

I parked behind the old horse stable—my pottery studio—because the last thing I wanted was for someone to spot my truck and begin to speculate why I was home and not at Tricia's, grapevine-worthy news over coffee at the Red Cup. Then the entire island would weigh in. Within five minutes someone would volunteer to drive over to Tricia's, most likely Jeremiah. Not because he's police chief, but because he was her dad's best friend. I guess he sees himself as a surrogate father. Not that Tricia would ever allow that. She finds his visits irritating and intrusive. But then again, that's how she feels about everyone on the island. I had thought I was an exception. Yeah right.

Getting into my childhood bed brought on a loneliness and sorrow so overwhelming I screamed into the pillow until exhaustion lulled me into a deep, black sleep. A few hours later, I woke up disoriented and grumpy thanks to my sister's alarm clock blaring through the thin wall separating our rooms. Savanna and my parents walked into the kitchen as I poured a cup of coffee and buttered a piece of toast. I'm grateful they didn't ask why I was home. No way I coulda held it together. Savanna ate her yogurt, chatted about dissecting a cow's eye for biology, then sprinted out the door to catch a ride to school with her boyfriend Oliver. Mom kissed my cheek, wished me a good day. Dad said he'd see me later at the pub.

When I climbed into the truck, I lost it—coulda filled a trough with the buckets I dumped. Reaching empty wasn't such a bad thing. It kept me numb long enough to pull myself together and hold steady for the day.

Every minute throughout the day was filled with guilt, worry, and fear. I wanted to leave school and go to Tricia. I typed-deleted, typed-deleted "R u ok?" at least ten times. I never hit SEND. During lunch, I sat in the truck and considered driving over to the lighthouse, but I couldn't turn the key. *We're over,* I reminded myself. For my mental health, I resisted the tug-o-war to go see her. Instead, I went back into school and ate lunch with our friends.

I have loved Tricia Boyer most of my life.

And now I resent her.

Sometimes, even though it's nearly impossible, I guess you have to move on.

Move on. That's what I tell myself after I stop at Mann's Grocery Store for an ice-cold soda. Except what kinda guy dumps his grieving girlfriend? An awful, beastly, contemptible, despicable dick. Oh hell.

I glance to my right. I could drive up Main Road toward Boyer's Bluff, the place I called home for the past five months. But if I'm honest with myself it really wasn't my home—just space I occupied since Tricia's grandma died. Going left means my real family, Charlie's Pub and Grill, my neglected pottery studio— the stable I gutted, wired, dry-walled, painted, heated, and shingled over the last five years with help from the community. I turn left. Left is my future.

My future is the studio and the art gallery I hope someday will feature local Door County artists. Not Tricia. I gotta remember this. Using my hands and imagination to shape, to mold, to create art is as necessary to me as breathing.

With Tricia, I stopped living. It's been months since I sketched out an idea or dirtied my hands kneading clay, mixed a slurry, threw a pot on the wheel, experimented with glazes, fired up the kiln. I miss the scratching sound the Berol pencil makes against a blank page as I transform it into a drawing. I miss the clay smell in my studio—earth after a rainstorm. Tricia never asked me not to create. I just felt like I couldn't. Too much joy in it. Somehow, I allowed myself to get swept away in her grief. Time for a change.

I turn into Charlie's Pub and Grill, and just as I shut off the engine my phone rings. Okay, for one crazy second I thought, hoped it would be Tricia.

5:22 P.M.

IT'S BRENDA. HER picture fills the screen—purple-streaked hair falls over her shoulders. A sassy smile shows she's a force to be reckoned with and her sapphire eyes sparkle with mischief. She can be a demanding pain in the ass. Still, she's one of my most favorite people in my world.

Brenda's drama might be exactly what I need to take my mind off Tricia. I answer, "Hello, gorgeous. How's my favorite cousin?"

"Still your only cousin."

"Well, that's a relief. So, what wild drama do you have to share with me today? Our mothers fighting again?"

It seems like every other week, her mom—my aunt Linda—and my mom are fighting. After nearly twenty-one years, my dad is still the center of it. Linda used to be my father's girlfriend until she cheated. Six months after they broke up, my dad started dating my mom. They fell in love and married. Linda can't get past it. Drama.

"No, no drama, just a favor," she says.

"Anything for you. What do you need?"

"Can I stay with you and Tricia for a few days? I need to get away. I'm sick of school, sick of Sturg."

I suck in an audible breath.

"What's the matter?"

"I...ah—" I mutter a few choice swearwords under my breath. This is much harder than I coulda ever imagined. The finality smacks me in the face. I manage to spit out "broke up with Tricia." It leaves a vile aftertaste that's still on my tongue even after downing the rest of the Coke.

"You did *what*? Did you just say you broke up with *Tricia*?"

What have I done? I open the glove box for the pack of cigarettes I nabbed from my father's car, so tempted to start smoking again. "Bren, I can't—I don't wanna talk about it. But please come up. My parents will love it. You can stay in Savanna's room. She won't mind."

"You sure?"

"Believe me, having you around'll be the perfect distraction." *And the perfect excuse for why I'm not with Tricia.* I toy with the cellophane wrapper, then toss the pack aside. "So, are you gonna tell me why you need to run away for a few days?"

"Maybe when I see you."

I look at the time on my phone. "The last ferry left a half-hour ago."

"I'll take the eight o'clock tomorrow morning. You'll skip school to hang out with me?"

"I could use a day off. We can hike and kayak. But do me a favor. Meet me at the visiting center. If you come to the house my mom will want the latest details on your mom and we'll never get on the water. I'm pretty sure they're back to not talking."

"Because she told Uncle Charlie he only married your mom as revenge for her sleeping with my father."

"So what else is new?"

"New York University, Tisch School of the Arts. I am so sick of school productions. I can't wait to share my screenplays with professionals."

"Lucky you."

"You'll visit, won't you?"

"Yeah, of course." I sigh, a little envious she's going to college. I wish we could afford art school. "Tomorrow, do me a favor. Since you have the annoying habit of turning your phone off to avoid people, if you're gonna miss the ferry, call so I won't wonder what the hell happened to you."

"Yes, worrywart. I'm hanging up now." And she does.

THIS IS THE longest Tricia and I have gone without talking or texting or seeing each other since seventh grade.

~

I SINK ONTO my pottery studio's floor. I think I'm in shock. I'm not sure what I'm supposed to do. I coulda made the biggest mistake of my life because...I thought I needed to leave Tricia to survive. I'm barely breathing. I thought she'd realize she needs me, loves me, and I thought once she did, she'd call or text. She hasn't.

~

I PICK UP my sketchpad and a Berol pencil. They feel so perfect in my hand, and I can't believe I deprived myself of this, that in some warped way I thought it was a good idea to give this up for a while and be fully present for Tricia. No matter how much doodling I did on my textbooks and notebooks and napkins, that could never match the thrill I get from transforming a blank page into something I wanna shape in clay.

I pull out my box of photographs of favorite island locations and begin to plan a new pottery series titled *Island Beauty*. Drawing helps ease a little of the doubt, fear, misery. My first rendering is of Schoolhouse Beach, a magnificent natural wonder of smooth, rounded limestone rocks along the crystal-clear waters of Lake Michigan.

By the time I finish another drawing—a historical building on Jens Jacobsen's land—it's nearly 4:30 A.M.

8:14 A.M.

STEPPING ONTO THE porch of the Red Cup, I'm greeted by a new sign on the door. "Friends don't let friends drink Starbucks." I laugh. Given that there aren't any Starbucks on the island, I doubt my friends will be drinking any in the near future. But I get it. The point is that we support and look out for our own. Except that brand of support can also mean occasionally receiving unsolicited advice and opinions, and I definitely don't need that right now. I enter with caution, praying the breakup is still a secret.

After saying hello to the group of morning regulars, I hand Caroline two Thermoses and dig out a crumpled five from my wallet. Thankfully, today's topics are the latest sightings of the pileated woodpecker and a pine snake that curled up next to Mrs. Jessen in her nice, cozy bed.

"How's Tricia?" a deep voice asks from behind.

I turn around to Mr. Welsby, one of our local real estate agents, and hope he doesn't see through my fake smile. "Great," I say. "Keeping busy."

"I'd like to stop by, talk with both of you. Maybe four o'clock, if that's all right?"

"I uh, sorry. Can't." The Red Cup suddenly grows quieter, warmer as if everyone inched closer and tuned their ears to our conversation. Sure enough, a half-dozen pairs of eyes are on me, some curious, some filled with affection, some concerned. "My cousin Brenda took the eight o'clock. We're spending the day together, hiking and stuff, so I'm not sure what time I'll see Tricia." I hold up the Thermoses like evidence.

"Skipping school," Mrs. Cornell says, dripping with disapproval.

"I'm a senior," I say, as if that explains everything. And I guess it does because she nods.

Mr. Welsby's shoulders relax with his smile. "Oh," he says. "Well, that's fine. I'll just drive on over and see Tricia. She can fill you in whenever you get home."

I nod, the word "home" buzzes in my head like a jackhammer breaking up concrete. Just that half-second pause and it seemed like everyone was checking for signs of potential Tricia and Brian discord. Or it could be that I'm paranoid. Sleep deprivation, broken heart. Yeah, that would do it.

⌒⌒ ⌒

8:38 A.M.

BRENDA PARKS HER SUV next to my truck and comes bouncing out with her duffle bag slung over her shoulder, her now pink-streaked ponytail caught in the strap. She opens my door, steps onto the running board, and nuzzles me in a neck-bracing hug.

"Boy have I missed you," she says, holding me at arm's length. Her smile disappears as she takes full inventory of my appearance. "Are you growing a beard to match those bags under your eyes?"

I touch her raccoon circles. "Minus the stubble, we're a match-set."

She laughs. "Speaking of match-sets." She tugs my unbuttoned blue lumberjack flannel, then unzips her duffle and removes the red plaid shirt I had bought for her. She slips it on over her white tank top.

"Guess you only wear that for me, huh?" I ask.

"This hideous thing? I wouldn't be caught dead wearing it anywhere *but* here. Fashion police would arrest me and burn this flannel in a bonfire for censored apparel. But I love it." She pulls it tight against her, rubs the collar like a blanket. "The best birthday gift anyone ever gave me. Thank you."

"You're such a liar. Your car was the best gift."

"It would have been if my father delivered it himself. So no." Her frown is replaced with her sassy smile. "This shirt is the best present *eva*!"

I smirk. "Good, I know what to buy you next year."

"Don't you dare." She pokes me. "Oh, I almost forgot." She goes back to her SUV, grabs a greasy white paper bag from the back seat, and carries it over, holding it in her palm like a model hawking perfume at a department store. Except what's in the bag smells a thousand times better—Door County cherry crullers from DC's Best Bakery. My favorite. She waves the bag in front of my nose. "You love me?" she asks, with an impish smile.

"Hell yeah." I snatch it outta her hand and take out a cruller. The sweet and sour cherries make my taste buds sing with gratitude. A moan of pure ecstasy slips from my lips. It's seems like forever since I've enjoyed anything so basic as a donut.

An image of Tricia curled like a wilted flower onto her bed invades my bliss. I swallow, take a huge gulp of hot coffee, letting the earthy flavor wash away the sweetness. "Thanks. Here's to us," I say, lifting my cup in a toast.

"You're welcome," she says with her mouth full, spraying donut onto my shirt. She giggles. I brush it off, start laughing too. Pretty soon we're cracking each other up with obnoxious faces and grotesque burping sounds. It's the most I've laughed in months, and it punctuates the misery lingering beneath the surface.

I turn away from Brenda and watch as the Washington Island ferry prepares for its next trip to the mainland. She touches my shoulder. "You all right?" she asks, raising her pierced brow.

"Definitely," I say. "Let's hike Mountain Park Trail. I need to stretch my legs before we kayak."

❧

A HAZY SUN filters through the canopy casting pale shadows on the spongy ground. Blooming gaywings, bloodroot, and forget-me-nots dot the forest floor. The smell of musky lichen and decaying leaves fills me with excitement for a day of adventure, and also a twinge of guilt.

When we were kids, Tricia's grandma was the one who taught us about the island's flora and fauna, creating themed nature scavenger hunts for us. We'd search for mushrooms—oyster, puffballs, shaggy mane, bears-head tooth—or birds to photograph like a horned lark, tuft titmouse, or sage thrasher.

On one of our outings, we wandered deep in the woods to find a red-bellied woodpecker. I climbed into an overgrown deer blind that hadn't been used by hunters for at least a century. When my foot stepped onto the mildewed platform, the board cracked beneath me. As I fell, my binocular strap hooked onto a branch, jerking my neck. Tricia moved lightning fast, grabbed me around the knees, and held me up. When it was over, and I was flat on my back catching my breath, Tricia collapsed into my side. She kept repeating, "I've never been so scared in my life!" She planted several quick kisses over my bruised neck. And that's when I fell in a completely different way.

I waited two long, agonizing years to tell Tricia I wanted more between us.

Feeling a bit lost, I look around, searching. Tricia should be here with me.

Brenda twirls, brushes her fingers over the rough bark of maple and white pine. She prances off the trail, skittering like a squirrel through the underbrush and ferns. Glancing over her shoulder, she calls, "C'mon slowpoke."

I catch up to her in a small clearing. She flops onto the ground, pillows her neck with her hands, and stares up at the pale blue sky. I join her. Moisture seeps from the earth through my shirt and dampens my skin. We track a hawk flying with what might be a whitefish in its grip until it swoops outta sight.

Brenda takes a deep breath and lets it out in a heavy sigh.

I study her. "So, you gonna tell me what's on your mind? Why you needed to escape to the island?"

She stands, shakes her head. "It's not important."

I get to my feet too. "If something's bothering you, then it's important." Bending down, I pick up a stick and run it over lichen growing on an uprooted beech at the edge of the clearing. Brenda turns, but before she can shut me out with her silence, I step in front of her. "C'mon, Bren, just tell me." Nudging my shoulder, she moves into a thicket of trees. "Guess I'm an asshole for being concerned," I call after her.

Spinning around, she says, "I'm not in the mood to talk about it now, okay? Just let it drop."

"Fine." I slap the branch above. "Sue me for caring."

"Why do you have to push? Just leave me alone!"

Brenda takes off, running deeper into the woods. I can barely believe it. Stand with my mouth open like a mute moron.

She wants to be left alone? Done. I'm done being an effing punching bag. Screw Brenda. Screw Tricia. Why the hell should I care? I don't.

I lean against a storm-torn birch, tilt my head back, and breathe.

Guess this isn't the day to enjoy the great outdoors like I had hoped. What I need to do is lock myself in my studio and plow elbow-deep into clay. I stomp through the forest. With every step I imagine trampling Tricia and Brenda's melodramas into the ground. What a pair those two make. I hop into my truck and start the engine.

That's when my phone rings. Brenda.

I know not answering makes me a selfish bastard. But guess what? I. Don't. Care. My studio's calling and Brenda can walk the mile home when she's done with her temper tantrum.

ELEVEN

"That mood into which a friend can bring us is
his dominion over us."
"...we boil at different degrees."
Ralph Waldo Emerson

BRENDA

WASHINGTON ISLAND   TUESDAY, 9:36 A.M.

FADE IN:

EXT. MOUNTAIN PARK PARKING LOT - DAY

Brenda hobbles with the aid of a
WALKING STICK down the steps leading
to the parking lot. In her other
hand, she holds her PHONE, which is
on speaker.

>   BRIAN (V.O.)
>   Hi, you've reached Brian's
>   phone. If you like talking
>   to machines, leave a
>   message.

Brenda holds her phone out in front
of her.

                    BRENDA
               (talking loudly)
          Brian,   pick   up   your
          frickin' phone.

She hangs up, hits redial. Brian's
voice message picks up again. She
continues to hang up and redial
until:

INT. BRIAN'S TRUCK - DAY - TRAVELING

                    BRIAN
               (into phone, pissed)
          What?

INTERCUT with Brenda in Washington
Park.

                    BRENDA
               (into phone)
          You left.

She gingerly lowers herself onto a
step.

                    BRIAN
               (into phone)
          Maybe because I got the
          impression you wanted to
          be left alone.

                    BRENDA
               (into phone)

> Well, you didn't have to
> leave. What if something
> happened to me?

Brian briefly lifts his hands from
the steering wheel, pretends to choke
an invisible Brenda.

> BRENDA (CONT.)
> (into phone)
> Where did you go?

He turns the truck around, heads back
to Mountain Park.

> BRIAN
> (into phone)
> I'll be there in a minute.
> (beat)
> But—and I say this with deep
> affection—if you ever pull
> that running away crap on
> me again, I'll leave you
> to the mountain lions. I'm
> sure you'll make a tasty
> Happy Meal.

Brenda looks over her shoulder.

> BRENDA
> (into phone)
> There aren't any mountain
> lions in Mountain Park.

                    BRIAN
                (into phone)
            Yeah, well. Lucky for you.
                (beat)
            Look, either talk to me
            about whatever it is
            you're running away from,
            or don't. I can't and won't
            be your wall to punch down.
            After the last few months,
            Tricia pretty much left me
            a pile of rubble.

                    BRENDA
                (into phone)
            I'm sorry.

She places the phone on the step
next to her, turns on speaker. Then
she examines a few of her cuts and
bruises.

                    BRIAN (V.O.)
                (over phone, filtered)
            Forget about it. Just talk
            to me. I'm not the effing
            enemy. Face whatever it is
            that's bothering you and
            let me help.

Brenda picks up her phone again and
takes it off speaker. She stretches
out her legs, visibly in pain.

BRENDA
(into phone)
What about you? Are you dealing with your problem? Do you want to tell me what happened between you and Tricia? Maybe I can help you?

BRIAN
(into phone)
Nice. Just so you know, I finally faced reality and made a choice to leave after months and months of trying to work through issues with Tricia. And just because I don't wanna talk about it doesn't mean I'm avoiding it. I'm dealing and moving forward.

BRENDA
(into phone)
You can't give up on Tricia. You two are like the classic fairy tale couple. If you don't have your happily ever after, there's no hope for the rest of us.

BRIAN
(into phone)

Then I guess I'm a disappointment. You can't write a script for this. My life's not a two-hour movie.

                    BRENDA
              (into phone)
          But you love her.

                    BRIAN
              (into phone)
          Maybe not enough. Maybe too much. I don't know anymore. I do, unfortunately, know she doesn't love me, at least not enough to want me around or even to call.
              (beat)
          I just pulled into the parking lot. So I haven't given up on you, if that's what you're worried about. Where are you?

                    BRENDA
              (into phone)
          Over by the path on the steps. Resting up for kayaking.

Brian parks. Spots Brenda, who's bleeding from cuts and scratches. He jumps out, goes to her.

                    BRIAN
          Geez,   what   the   hell
          happened to you?

Brenda half-grimaces, half-smiles.

                    BRENDA
          I was attacked by an Ent.

                    BRIAN
          What?

                    BRENDA
          One   of   those   tree-like
          creatures   from   *Lord   of
          the Rings: The Two Towers?*
          First, its roots tripped
          me up, then like five of
          its twiggy arms grabbed
          me. It was an epic battle.
          I barely escaped.

Brian fingers the fabric on Brenda's
RED LUMBERJACK SHIRT.

                    BRIAN
          You tore your shirt.

                    BRENDA
          Vast   improvement.   The
          fashion police approve.

                    BRIAN
          Uh-huh.

Brenda extends a hand to Brian. He helps her up, then walks with her to the passenger door and lifts Brenda into the cab. He removes a FIRST AID KIT from under the seat. Standing outside, Brian cleans and bandages Brenda's scrapes.

> BRENDA
> Okay, so I have an important question. It's kind of why I'm here. Do you find me attractive?

> BRIAN
> Shit. We're cousins. You can't ask me that.

Brenda laughs.

> BRENDA
> I mean, do you think guys, in general, might find me attractive?

> BRIAN
> Guess so. If you want my unbiased opinion, I think you're gorgeous. This week, in a punked-out cool way. But you seriously need to melt that iceberg sitting on your shoulder and build a bridge to cross the ocean surrounding you.

Once you do, most guys
on this planet couldn't
resist you.

                    BRENDA
          Then I'm hopeless.

Brian smiles ruefully.

                    BRIAN
          As long as you're breathing,
          there's always hope.

Brenda examines the ends of her hair,
separates the strands by color.

                    BRIAN (CONT.)
                (skeptically)
          That was the crisis?

She scissor-kicks her legs.

                    BRENDA
          Angie asked me if I'm gay.

                    BRIAN
          Ahh.
                (beat)
          Are you?

                    BRENDA
          No, I don't think so.
          I'm not really attracted
          to anyone. Maybe...there's

something wrong with me?
Maybe I'll never be
attracted to anyone?

> BRIAN
> Hmmmm, how's the hand
> play? Or do you prefer
> electronic devices?

Brenda attempts to punch Brian, but
he dips out of the way. She frowns.

> BRENDA
> Don't joke.

> BRIAN
> Sorry. I didn't mean
> anything by it.

Brenda shoots him a look that's
forgiving, but also a warning not to
mess with her again.

> BRIAN (CONT.)
> There's nothing wrong with
> you. And who said you have
> to find anyone attractive?
> I dunno much about it, but
> maybe you haven't found
> the right person to be
> attracted to? Or maybe you
> need to find the right guy
> or girl to explore your
> feelings? You've lived in
> small-town Wisconsin all

your life. Maybe things will be different in New York?

> BRENDA
> (sullen)
> Maybe.

> BRIAN
> (beat)
> Remember when you told Tricia you'd go Norman Bates on her if she ever two-timed me?

Brenda's face lights with surprise. She laughs.

> BRENDA
> She told you? I was only half-serious.

> BRIAN
> Yeah well, Tricia hates Alfred Hitchcock movies, especially *Psycho*, so bad choice. She made me take down her shower curtain and put up a glass door.

> BRENDA
> Really?

Brian smirks.

BRIAN
No. Anyway, I explained to Tricia what happened with your mom and my dad and how your mom cheated and how my parents got together after. Maybe that traumatized you more than you think? Maybe that's why you aren't interested in any relationship? Maybe, subconsciously, you think someone will cheat on you?

Brenda stares off toward the trail, visibly shaken. She swipes a tear away.

BRIAN (CONT.)
Geez, Bren. This is serious. You never cry. What's going on? It's not just the attraction issue, is it? Did something happen at home that you needed to get away?

She continues to cry and wipes the tears away. For each of Brian's next six guesses, she shakes her head.

BRIAN (CONT.)
Does it have anything to do with your mom or dad? My parents? School? Someone

being mean to you? Because I'll beat 'em up for you. Moving to New York? Are you worried about attending Tisch?

Brenda covers her face, then looks mournfully at Brian.

> BRENDA
> I-I—
> (pleading)
> Can we give it a rest? Just for a little while so we can have one perfect afternoon kayaking?
> (beat)
> We'll talk about it later, okay? I promise.

Brian scrutinizes Brenda, sighs deeply.

> BRIAN
> Fine. But Bren, I really hate seeing you so upset and I'm done begging. You wanna tell me, I'll listen. I'll support you. I'll help you if you need help. But I won't ask again.

EXT. BRIAN'S HOUSE - LATE AFTERNOON

Brenda's SUV is parked next to Brian's truck. Brian is untying one of two kayaks from the bed. Brenda watches him, duffle in hand.

                    BRENDA
          If you're sure you don't
          need my help, would you
          mind if I went inside and
          took a shower?

Brian picks up the kayak and carries it toward the storage shed.

                    BRIAN
          I'm good. Go ahead.

INT. BRIAN'S HOUSE - CONTINUOUS - LATE AFTERNOON

Limping slightly, Brenda enters the house through the side door. She walks through the clean, 1970s-style kitchen and into a hallway. The walls are cluttered with family photos and PAPIER-MACHE and CLAY MASKS made by Brian, showing a progression of his artist skills.

Brenda enters a small bathroom, drops her duffle, locks the door, checks it, unlocks, locks, and checks the door again. She sinks to the floor, breathes deeply, looks toward the toilet.

BEGIN FLASHBACK:

INT. LARGE BATHROOM - NIGHT

Brenda (12) sits on a toilet, underpants around her ankles, T-shirt gathered in her hands. A small nightlight dimly illuminates the space. ANTIQUE DOLLHOUSE PIECES fill several shadow boxes. The door creaks open. A muscular tattooed MAN, mid-thirties, slowly creeps into the bathroom, locks the door, moves toward Brenda.

Young Brenda attempts to scream.

A scarred hand covers her mouth. He presses his mouth against young Brenda's ear.

                    MAN
          Shhhh. Not a sound.

Pee DRIBBLES into the toilet. The man kneels, removes young Brenda's underwear, runs a hand up her inner thighs, spreads them, then tears off toilet paper and hands it to her.

END FLASHBACK.

INT. BATHROOM, BRIAN'S HOUSE - LATE AFTERNOON

Brenda blinks at the toilet, slowly becomes acclimated to her surroundings. She stands up, checks to make sure the door is locked again, then undresses and showers.

INT. HALLWAY BRIAN'S HOUSE - LATE AFTERNOON

Brenda walks past a section of wall filled with family photographs, then backs up and removes one of Brian and Tricia taken at Schoolhouse Beach.

INSERT - PHOTO

With smooth, round stones FOREVER is spelled out between Tricia and Brian's towels. Tricia is gazing at the lake. Brian is smiling at Tricia, a look of adoration on his face.

Brenda wipes some dust off the glass, then returns the photo to its spot.

FADE OUT.

TWELVE

"The ray of light passes invisible through space, and only when it falls on an object is it seen."
Ralph Waldo Emerson

TRICIA
WASHINGTON ISLAND   TUESDAY, 4:02 P.M.

FROM THE LANTERN room high above Boyer's Bluff, I spot Mr. Welsby's Chevy Tahoe bounce along the driveway ruts. I duck and huddle against one of the wooden panels supporting the octagonal glass dome.

I'm confused. The last time he came over I'm sure I was crystal clear when I said that I'm not selling Boyer's Bluff and that I'd call if I changed my mind. After he left, I threw out his proposal to parcel off ten out of Boyer's Bluff's thirty-five acres. His plan was to build luxury green condos to, as he put it, "cover the costs of maintaining the lighthouse." What I refused to tell him is that my father and grandmother's deaths left me with a small fortune in stocks, bonds, and life insurance.

Welsby hefts himself out of the truck. Guilt sinks down to my curling toes. He's a thoughtful man, and I'm hiding out from his goodwill and concern. I hold my breath as the doorbell's faint *tink, tink* is followed by loud raps against the front door. After what seems like an hour, the racket stops. Crouching, I brace myself against the beveled lens casing and crane my neck to see if he left. No such luck. He's bent over his hood, and I get an unpleasant view of his plumber's crack. He straightens, slips a pen into his shirt pocket, and picks up a large manila envelope with my name printed in gigantic, bold letters across the front.

A light flashes behind him, and just my luck, the island's police force Ford Expedition crests the hill and parks behind Welsby. Jeremiah steps out and shakes Mr. Welsby's beefy hand. Welsby gives Jeremiah the envelope and bobs his balding head toward my house. I don't have to have lip-reading skills to figure out he's telling Jeremiah that he knows I'm inside. Just because my truck's in the driveway doesn't mean I'm home, right? Brian could have driven me…

Brian. Of course I would think of Brian.

When Welsby's vehicle descends out of view, I make my way down the galley stairs and through the house. Experience has taught me that if I don't see Jeremiah now, he'll be back in an hour or two. When it comes to me, our police chief is like those old-fashioned doctors who make house calls, regularly checking up on a sick patient. I'm getting better. Maybe he'll notice?

I step onto the porch. *Where is he?*

"Heard you ventured into Mann's Mercantile today," he calls out. I track his voice to the side of the garage.

I smile. No need to respond since I'm certain Jeremiah got a full report. When Finn greeted me from behind the counter, Mrs. Sanderson, Mother Cornell, and Mrs. Neilsen practically materialized out of thin air like fairy godmothers. Nearly an hour later, after the ladies shared a barrelful of home decorating tips, I was out the door with painting supplies.

Buying paint supplies was the result of a restless night thinking about Brian and running through the minute details of my conversation with Emerson. Emerson was right about so many things, and I realized that saying I wanted a fresh start and doing something about it were two different things. As dawn crept through my window, I flipped and flopped until I couldn't stand the rotisserie routine. Looking around my room, I had a flash of clarity. I was surrounded by memories and mementos that shackled me to the past. I boxed up my father's dog tags and footlocker, threw out my funeral dress, and relegated Brian's pillow to the closet. I couldn't bring myself to box up his things or remove the photo montage of the two of us.

After dusting, vacuuming, and rearranging the furniture, I carried five boxes of memories to the basement, then started in on the parlor. The 1940s curtains were weeds in the pristine room filled with antiques. I took them down; faded patches on the dull green walls made the space look colder, vulnerable, naked. That's when I decided to paint.

Jeremiah rounds the lighthouse porch. He waves Welsby's envelope toward me. An understanding smile softens his rugged face, and I can't help but smile back. No need to explain why I hid from Welsby.

Jeremiah points to a tree with a splintered limb dangling halfway up. "I'll have Alec Mann cut that down. Next storm could topple it and damage the roof. And I'll talk to Brian. There are some deep ruts in your driveway that need filling. You can save some money if he helps Kevin spread gravel."

"No," I say.

"No?"

"I can take care of it."

"It's not a problem." He walks toward me. At six-foot-five, Jeremiah can be intimidating, especially when he uses his swagger to say *I'm in charge.* This feels like one of those moments. "I'll see Kevin and Ray tonight for poker."

"No," I repeat, doing my best not to shrink into myself.

"Tricia." God, I hate it when he says my name like that. Packed with disappointment, disapproval. A plea to be reasonable. He climbs onto the porch. "May I come in?"

I step aside, follow. He stops in the parlor entryway, touches the painter's tape I used to protect the woodwork. "The blue will look great. Brian did a nice job with the primer. The shutters outside could use—"

"Not Brian. Me. I'm painting. I realize it's hard for you to believe, but I *am* capable of doing a few things myself."

His voice turns sympathetic, a match to his expression. "I know that, Tricia. Everyone on this island knows it." Frustration rattles his exhale. "Honestly, I wish you'd be a little more willing to accept people's generosity and help without resenting their kindness."

I quiver with a restrained boatload of annoyance, anger, and disappointment, some directed at myself. "Look, I'm not ungrateful. I get that people care. But sometimes people can care too much, and it's not helpful. There are enough venison steaks and sausages and fish filets and casseroles in my two freezers to feed me for the next three years. Just the other day, Mrs. Andersen stopped in to reorganize my pantry, and when I told her I didn't want the pantry reorganized, she ordered me to drink a glass of milk and eat the chocolate chip cookies she'd brought. Then, she pushed up her sleeves and alphabetized my canned goods. Two weeks ago, Mr. Swenson stopped me in the snack aisle at Mann's and asked if *Brian* had changed the batteries in the smoke detectors and flashlights."

I promise myself, I won't crumble. But I'm so close. Any reproof from Jeremiah and I'll leak like a punctured garden hose.

He fiddles with his badge. The tick of the grandfather clock punctuates the silence. Finally, he breaks it. "Okay Tricia. I hear you, and I get it. I'll back off and I'll do my best to tactfully spread the word."

"Forget tact. Be blunt."

He laughs. "Okay."

The tension between us completely disappears. I want to reach out and hug him, but then his face loses its humor and color. "Would you really sell Boyer's Bluff?"

His question chills the air, squeezes my heart, crushing me with loss. "I...don't know. I never seriously considered it."

He nods ever so slightly, purses his lips into a thin line. He slips the envelope out of his pants pocket—folded into a mangled mess—and places it on the carved console table in the hall. His attempt to smooth out the creases is futile. "Welsby asked me to give this to you." I don't touch it. Jeremiah shifts uncomfortably. "So, since I'm here, anything you need me to do?"

"Matter-of-fact, yes." I smile and his face lights in a way I haven't seen in a long time. Like I gave him a gift. After leading the way to the den, I hand him the key to my dad's gun cabinet. I ignore his flash of surprise. "I don't plan to hunt. You'll take them?"

"Done and gone," he says. In five minutes, he has the cabinet and Dad's rifles loaded in the Expedition.

He shuts the liftgate. Turning around, his eyes shift from me to the lighthouse, and I can't help but cringe as I follow his gaze to a broken shutter, the flaking trim. I hadn't even noticed. But now I look at the house through Jeremiah's eyes. At least the limestone is solid and strong.

"Day or night, you'll call if you need anything else?"

I focus on a streak of white paint on my holey jeans, then lift my eyes to his. "You don't have to feel obligated," I say, immediately wishing the words hadn't slipped out.

His shoulders drop and his stance reminds me of Brian and the dejection I've put on his face. Jeremiah's tone is a perfect blend of sorrow and conviction. "Tricia, you know I loved your father like a brother. I'm not trying to replace him. I care about you. You're not an obligation. I—" A call interrupts his speech, and I'm relieved. I've heard this all before. Jeremiah rattles off a code, then returns the phone to its holster. "A boater in distress," he says. "I need to go." As he moves toward the Expedition, he says, "Tricia, I'll do my best to give you more space and not drop by so often, okay?"

I hesitate, then say, "Jeremiah?"

"Yeah?"

"I don't mind too much that you stop by. I, uh—My dad would approve."

He nods, and there's a soft smile on his face that reassures me that I said the right thing. I said it because I know it's true.

As he drives away, I want so much to run after him, to get swept up in a fatherly embrace. But what I really want, I can't have, and that's my own dad.

THAT ENVELOPE. I'M tempted to tear it into a hundred pieces or burn it in the fireplace, but it won't make the message inside disappear, and certainly not its deliverer, who probably has copies in triplicate. I rip open the envelope and slide out a piece of paper.

Charles Willmington, III *<Willmington@WillmingtonEnterprises. com>*

To: **Zachariah Welsby** *<info@Welsbyrealestate.com>*

Dear Mr. Welsby,

As I explained over the phone, last summer my family and I spent a week in a rented home on Washington Island. During our stay, we were particularly attracted to the lighthouse and the secluded area of Boyer's Bluff, which would be the perfect location to construct a summer retreat for family and guests. After doing some research, I discovered the home and land are in probate. That's why I am retaining your services.

Please accept this email as a formal request for you to contact the owner and offer 1.6 million dollars for Boyer's Bluff. It's well within the high range of fair market value.

If you have any questions, do not hesitate to reach me at 312-555-9897 and my secretary will assist you.

Once I receive an affirmative response, my lawyers will draw up the paperwork.

Sincerely,
Mr. Charles Willmington, III
Chicago, IL

One million, six hundred thousand dollars. I grab my phone and tap my Favorites list.

Brian's hesitant hello snaps me back to reality. How easy it was to forget about our breakup. To call him is as instinctual as blinking. All I wanted to do was tell him about this crazy offer.

After I say hi back, I can't form a coherent thought.

"What's up?"

"Umm, I was, uh..."

"Yeah?"

"Cleaning."

"Cleaning." He sighs. "Well good for you."

"Welsby stopped by. Then Jeremiah—"

"Look, Tricia, this is really hard for me right now, and I'm busy. So if this isn't important—"

"I'm sorry."

Brian sucks in a breath. His voice loses its hard edge. "Sorry for what, Tricia?"

So many things run through my mind. Sorry for calling? Sorry for disappointing you? Sorry for not being the girl you once loved? Sorry you walked out?

"What is it that you want from me?" he asks. Frost crystalizes in my veins and spreads through my body like a layer of ice over the lake.

"I—There was this letter, an offer to buy Boyer's Bluff. I-I wanted to know what you think."

"You wanna know if you should sell Boyer's Bluff?" His voice cracks like he's going through puberty again.

"Um, we could talk about it? You could come over? There are probably other things we should talk about too, right?" I sound desperate, needy.

"I'm busy," he repeats. He's never used such a sharp tone with me, not even when he's been angry.

"After?" I really need to put duct tape over my mouth.

"I have plans after."

"Oh."

There has to be a way for us to salvage...something.

"I gotta go. Brenda's here."

Brenda? The ceiling greets me. My hope to rescue my friendship with Brian has a better chance with Brenda on my side. He's close to her, respects her, will listen to her. I don't care if I'm being unreasonable or if he's having a hard time. Friends don't bail on friends, and our friendship is worth a lot to me. Brenda just may be our salvation.

Desperate, I begin to ramble. "Brenda? You didn't tell me she was coming up. I mean, not that you had to or anything..." Blah, blah, blah. I prattle on and ask him about her plans for New York. He says something about auditions as I wander through the house. Brian's size-twelve hiking boots sit on a carpet square next to my size-sevens by the back door. His tackle box and fishing pole are tucked away in the closet near the kitchen.

He interrupts me as I say something about laundry. "Tricia, are you okay?" It's not warm or kind. It's clinical, like he's diagnosed me with lunacy.

I want to shout, *"What happened to you? Where is my friend? I miss my best friend!"* But I don't. I claw at the tender skin on my wrist to channel the pain and answer, "Yeah. I'm okay."

"Good." I don't think he means it. I don't think he believes it. I know his tones, and there's no faith in it.

I turn pathetic. "You could bring Brenda? I'd love to see her. It's been a long time."

"Call her if you want to."

"Really? I don't have her number." He gives it to me.

The room sways. A two-story bonfire wouldn't melt the glacier between us. The tension grows unbearable. And then I add to it. "You must need your things. D-do you want me to pack them up? Bring them over? Or..." *Are you coming back?* But I can't say it.

I hear a loud bang, like he slammed a book onto a table. Except Brian's not a reader, at least not of novels. Comic books and graphic novels. He loves the drawings. Then I know. He's working out air bubbles in a slab of clay. "Are you in your studio?"

"I gotta go," he mutters, and hangs up.

THE DAY OF my grandma's funeral, people stuffed the house with food and stories and so many memories and "I'm sorry" (*I know, please stop saying it*) and "She's in a better place" (*Then why am I still here?*) and "You're not alone; we're your family now" (*Yes I am; no you're not*), that by 6 P.M., I couldn't take anymore. I excused myself and escaped to my bedroom, leaving Brian to say good-bye to the last mourners.

About a half-hour later, he walked into my room and crawled into bed with me. I turned to him, buried my face in his shoulder, and cried. At first, he just held me. Exactly what I needed. Exactly what I *asked* for. I wanted to talk about my grandma. I did—for a while.

Enough time passed for some of the heaviness to lift, for me to breathe more steady. That was when Brian whispered, "Let me make you feel good." He reached behind me, unzipped my dress, unhooked my bra.

I shook my head, but in the pitch dark there was no way for him to see. I choked out "Brian." Tears overflowed in a torrent I couldn't stop. Trying to soothe me, he stroked my back, slid the dress and bra off my shoulders, off my arms. He stroked my breasts and kissed my neck. He stroked my thighs and between. Still sobbing, I reached down, stilled his fingers. Held his hand in a way that I hoped he would understand that this wasn't what I wanted. Not then. Like always, he was attentive to my body. He wasn't demanding or forceful. But he also wasn't paying attention.

"Shhh, beautiful. It'll be okay. Let me take care of you. Let me show you how much I love you. I love you so much, Tricia." Drained, I loosened my grip, and he lifted my palm, pressed it against his beating heart as if to prove he was alive. He set his hand over my heart, then traced my breast with his fingertip. It felt good. Too good. *Wrong.*

The more Brian touched me, the more my body responded, then shuttered and tumbled, and in a way betrayed me. I felt betrayed by *him.*

I'd made love with this beautiful guy so many times I couldn't count.

But...

For someone who knew me so well, for so long, *forever,* how could he have been so clueless? For someone who loved me, how could he fail to understand how shattered I was from burying my grandma only a few hours before? Thousands of fractured pieces of me blown away like dust, left behind in my grandma's kitchen, office, bedroom, *grave.* The rest of me separate. Empty. How did he not see it? Hear it? Understand it?

When Brian left the bed to take a shower, I dressed and drove to the cemetery. He found me huddled against my father's gravestone, shivering and feverish.

Days later, I pushed Brian away and worried whether he had used a condom the night of the funeral. I'm pretty sure I had told him I hadn't taken birth control pills for a couple days. Who thinks of those things when their grandmother's dying, then dead? I counted the number of unused foil squares in the box I kept in my nightstand. We hadn't used them since

I started taking the pill ages ago. No clue if he did or didn't, and there was already enough tension between us that I decided not to ask. I immediately made sure to get back on schedule, and hoped for the best.

Three weeks later I got my period, a spotty one, but blood just the same. I've never been more relieved.

~

5:13 P.M.

I'VE LEARNED MEMORIES don't contain magical glue to hold a relationship together. I've learned the greatest gift a friend can give is to listen and understand. Brian and I had that brand of friendship, and lost it. Now I want to see if there's a chance to reclaim it. I look up and utter a quick prayer.

I don't know Brenda well. We haven't spent much time together. But she respects me. The one time she came over, her tongue was like a knife. "I'd kiss a cobra before wearing that sackcloth." And "Who cut your hair, a blind man?" I called her a bitch and she laughed. Said, "You'll do."

Once, I caught her watching Brian and me in a PDA. She deemed us "the cutest couple ever." Said her best friend was going out with some guy who didn't love her. That he was some super-smart, overachieving, straight-laced jock who was too nice to—Brian cut in. "I thought I was your best friend?"

She jumped on his back and said, "For a guy."

I walk outside, lean against the porch rail, and dial Brenda's number.

THIRTEEN

"Don't trust children with edge tools."
Ralph Waldo Emerson

BRENDA
WASHINGTON ISLAND   TUESDAY, 5:36 P.M.

FADE IN:

EXT/INT. BRIAN'S HOUSE AND ART STUDIO
- NIGHT

Brenda walks from Brian's house to
his art studio. LED ZEPPELIN blares
from inside. Brenda slides the barn
doors open.

Brian sits behind a POTTER'S WHEEL,
taking out his frustrations on a huge
hunk of clay.

                    BRENDA
              (yelling)
          Hi.

Brian stops the wheel, turns down
the music.

                    BRIAN
          What?

Brenda waves her hands, indicating
the mess Brian's made.

                    BRENDA
          Welcome to the movie set
          of *Ghost*. Except from
          the likes of you, Ms.
          Moore, I'd say you've been
          possessed by a real ghost.
          You look like death warmed
          over. What's the matter,
          Demi?

                    BRIAN
          Tricia called.

                    BRENDA
          Oh.

                    BRIAN
          She wanted my advice on
          whether or not she should
          sell Boyer's Bluff, like
          I would have any say in
          that.

                    BRENDA
          Wow.

Miserable, Brian looks at Brenda.
She takes a clump of hair and sorts
the strands by color again.

Brian attacks the clay, destroying
the pot he made.

> BRIAN
> She asked if she should
> box up my stuff.

> BRENDA
> Ouch. I'm sorry.

Brenda sits on a high stool next to
a table, uses her fingernail to pick
at dried clay.

> BRIAN
> She wanted me to stop over.
> I told her you're here and
> that we're busy. But um,
> she wants to see you, so
> I told her she should give
> you a call.

Using various tools, Brian gouges
the clay, then dips his fingertips
in water and smoothes away the holes.

> BRENDA
> What? Why would you tell
> her that?

> BRIAN
> Because she sounded
> genuinely happy that
> you're here, and I wasn't
> going to decide for you.

Brenda raises an eyebrow. She sweeps the crumbs she's made from scraping at the clay into a small pile. She pinches the flecks between her fingers and sprinkles them like salt onto the mound.

                    BRENDA
          Uh huh. Do you want me to
          pick up your stuff?

                    BRIAN
               (sounding hurt)
          You'd actually go see her?

                    BRENDA
          Sure. I'll grab your stuff
          and run. But if you want,
          I'll take your tools and
          carve "Bitch" into her
          front door.

Brian smiles a little.

                    BRIAN
          You would, wouldn't you.

Brenda laughs.

                    BRENDA
          If it would make you happy.
          But I doubt it. In the end,
          the only one who'll be
          thrilled for some action
          is Johannson, and I'll

                    have to call my father for
                    bail money.

                         BRIAN
                    Just tell me, how the hell
                    does Tricia think we can
                    be friends?

Brenda starts drawing circles in the
dried clay flakes with her finger.

                         BRENDA
                    Don't know. Why don't you
                    ask her? Maybe you need to
                    go over there and talk this
                    out. You're like Joseph
                    Gordon-Levitt's character
                    in *(500) Days of Summer*.
                    Wrecked. Stuck in the same
                    stupid cycle. And if you
                    don't want this to ruin
                    your life—

Brenda's finger freezes on the
circle. She looks intently at it,
then stares off into the distance.
Brian notices and frowns.

                         BRIAN
                    What's the matter?

                         BRENDA
                    I just realized something.

She hops off the chair, holds up her phone, and motions toward the door.

> BRENDA (CONT.)
> I'm going to call my dad.
> He can help.

Brian looks at Brenda, utterly confused.

> BRIAN
> You think I need a lawyer?
> We only lived together for
> five months.

> BRENDA
> No. Not for you. Me.

Brian's confusion deepens. He gets up from his potter's wheel and moves toward Brenda.

> BRIAN
> You? Wait. What's going
> on? Are you in some kind
> of trouble?

> BRENDA
> No. I'm not in trouble.

Brian reaches out to her, but Brenda backs away.

> BRIAN

Then how did we go from my nightmare to you calling your dad?

BRENDA
Talking to you about Tricia. You made me realize... something. I need my dad's advice. He's the only one who might be able to help.

BRIAN
So—

Brenda reaches for the handle, anxious to leave. Brian braces his hand on the door, not ready to let her go.

BRENDA
So, I appreciate you helping me figure that out. And I appreciate you not asking any more questions. At least not until after I speak with him.

Brian hesitates.

BRIAN
Just tell me, are you okay?

BRENDA
No, not really. Are you okay?

                    BRIAN
          No.

                    BRENDA
          So I think we understand each
          other.

Brian's expression changes, like he's
pieced together a puzzle. He rubs his
hand on his jeans. Concern fills his
face.

                    BRIAN
          The reason why you're here.
               (beat)
          It was something so horrible
          you need a lawyer?

She looks at him, silently pleading
for him not to push her. Brian backs
off, removes his hand from the door so
Brenda's free to go.

BRENDA's PHONE RINGS. Caller ID shows
TRICIA. Brenda holds up the phone to
Brian.

                    BRENDA
          What do you want me to say?

                    BRIAN
          Whatever you want. Just
          leave me the hell outta
          your plans. I'm not ready
          to face her.

                              FADE OUT.

FOURTEEN

"We must be as courteous to man as we are to a picture, which
we are willing to give the advantage of a good light."
Ralph Waldo Emerson

TRICIA

WASHINGTON ISLAND   TUESDAY, 5:45 P.M.

BRENDA'S PHONE RINGS and rings and rings. I'm
about to hang up when... "Hey Tricia, what's up?"
Underneath her greeting is a ripple of annoyance, like
I'm an invasion. I cringe, seesawing between hanging
up or saying hello.

I fumble through, "Hey, how are you? Brian said
you're on the island?" My stomach flutters from the
hummingbird wings beating frantic within it.

Brenda doesn't respond. Sweat trickles between
my breasts.

"Um, I'd really like to see you. Any chance we could
get together? I could meet you somewhere, or you
could come over?" My voice becomes a whisper. "You
both could come over."

I'm hit with another wall of silence.

"Weird day." I half-choke, half-laugh. It sounds more
like a sob. "Yeah, someone wants to buy Boyer's Bluff
for one point six mill. M-maybe we could celebrate?

Order pizza? I found some champagne my grandma was saving. We could open it." I dig my nails into the porch railing. I'm a freakin' idiot.

Brenda confirms it. "Champagne? Screw that. Your Dr. Jekyll and Mr. Hyde routine's messing Brian up. You know that, right? What do you want from him?"

I meet the rolling ground with a jaw-jolting *thunk*. Browns and greens and whites blur to gray. I close my eyes, edit the screw-you words in my head, and manage to say, "Nothing. Forget I called. I'll see you." *Like never.* I fumble with the phone, listen to the various beeps caused by pushing numbers instead of the END button. I rub my eyes, and even then my vision remains a thunderstorm.

Through the speaker, I hear, "Tricia, don't hang up. Please? I put my bitch away." She groans, and it tosses me out of the storm and back onto dry ground. "Dammit girl, are you crying?"

"No." I sniffle.

"Talk to me. Brian loves you. He thinks you don't love him or need him anymore or some other ridiculous nonsense."

"I called," I say, lamely. "He's the one who—"

"Look, I'm certain he doesn't want you to sell Boyer's Bluff. But that's not what this is about, is it?"

"I-I—"

"No one but me knows Brian walked out. He made some excuse to his parents and Savanna about coming home to get a few things, and then falling asleep. Now I'm his cover for being away from you. Say the word, and I'm certain I can convince him to move back in before the sun sets."

"I-I'm not ready for that," I choke out. "I just—Never mind. Really. It doesn't matter anymore. If I don't see you again, good luck in the Big Apple." I swallow the sandpit in my throat. "Wait, sorry, I should have said break a leg, right?" I bite my thumb hard enough to leave marks.

"Tricia, you and Brian need to talk."

"I know. But I've tried a hundred times already. He doesn't want to listen to what I have to say." It comes out as a plea. I feel like I ripped my chest open, exposed my heart and soul and everything in between.

"Of course he'll listen. He loves you. I'll see what I can do about stopping by tonight. Just so you know, you're both killing me."

"Sorry," I say, again. I can almost feel the coffin lid closing over me. I'm not sure I have the strength to lift it.

"Yeah, well good thing I've survived worse. Much worse. Hanging up now."

And she does.

FIFTEEN

"Life invests itself with inevitable conditions, which the unwise seek to dodge... If he escapes them in one part, they attack him in another more vital part."
Ralph Waldo Emerson

BRIAN

WHEN BRENDA RETURNS to the studio after talking to Tricia, she looks weary, uneasy. An expression I've become all too familiar with since I've worn it myself numerous times during the past five months. It pings my heart, notching it with more guilt.

I walk over to my shelf of glazes and begin to check inventory as much to avoid Brenda as to make sure I have the colors I'll need for my *Island Beauty* series. It's hard to concentrate. My mind wavers between wanting and not wanting details of their conversation. I settle on *not*, pick up the almost-empty container of purple moon and set it aside to reorder.

Brenda slides her petite frame between the wire shelves and me. Her challenge is almost amusing, even though her face is anything but. I reach above her head and shake the seaweed green container. It's half-full, so I set it down and pick up the next one. Brenda elbows me hard enough to make my ribs ache. Trying to ignore her, I step to the side, but she shuffles like a goalie. She's utterly impossible and annoying. Time to put the spotlight on her.

"Did you call your dad?" I ask, nonchalantly.

Her back bangs into the middle shelf, causing the whole unit to shake. I grab the side bar and steady it before anything topples over. Angry red lines streak from her nail beds to her knuckles. Okay, so I won't do inventory.

As I walk away, she follows like a shadow.

"I texted him," she says. "He's in the middle of reviewing documents for a criminal trial that starts next week. We'll talk later."

"Uh huh."

"Aren't you at all curious?"

She's not referring to her dad's trial, but to Tricia. A door inside my mind slams shut. I lower my gaze, meet Brenda's eyes. "No. I'm really not."

I hit the play button on my iPod and blast Led Zeppelin through the speakers.

Brenda shouts, "I'm going over to Tricia's."

I glare at her, at first not sure if she's trying to get a rise out of me or if she's completely serious. It doesn't take long for me to recognize her defiance. Before her betrayal worms its way deeper into my gut, I turn into stone.

She shuts off the music just as Zeppelin finishes belting out the chorus to "Communication Breakdown." It's ironic how perfect these lyrics fit my life.

"Don't do that," she says softly.

"What?"

"Make me feel guilty."

I laugh, dark and ugly.

"She sounded desperate."

"Not my problem." Bitterness burns my throat like a shot of whiskey.

"She loves you. I know she does. Just listen to what she has to say."

"Now who's buttering guilt on the bread?"

"I'm going, Brian. With or without you." An obstinate, challenging line creases her brow, daring me to cross her. If I weren't so frustrated, *hurt,* I'd laugh.

"Without me."

10:22 P.M.

IRRITATION AND RESENTMENT become fuel for creativity. Using photos of places on the island, I sketch and sketch.

My mind races through Tricia's phone call and Brenda's disapproval and betrayal. Why the hell should I have gone with her? Tricia doesn't want me. Not really. Did she say she misses me? That she loves me? No. She asked if she should box up my stuff.

Major gut punch. But I heard a tremble in her voice. Oddly, that gave me a speck of hope. Maybe she doesn't want me to leave? The thing is, I've learned my lesson. Since her grandma's death, I've been a dog—come, fetch, roll over, play dead. I'm done with that. If there's any hope to salvage this relationship, I need Tricia to say she wants me to stay. Then we'll talk. It *all* comes down to respect. Is that too much to ask?

It hits me then, a truth that's been hovering around me like the early morning mist rolling off the lake. I'm not sure getting back together is the right thing for us.

Admitting it, *knowing* it terrifies me. I stare at my last two sketches as I let this revelation settle. Amazing what the subconscious does. I drew two of the most important places on the island for Tricia and me.

The first was where we planned to marry—the Stavkirke. But the second is the one that holds the best memories. Jackson Harbor at sunrise. The place Tricia and I first kissed. It's the moment she finally decided our relationship could evolve from friendship to being a couple. The happiest day of my life.

No, the happiest day of my life was on a Sunday last summer. But I most definitely can't sketch that one. Tricia's grandma had left for an unexpected trip off-island for shopping and dinner with friends in Green Bay. Tricia called with news. "I'm ready," she said. "How fast can you get here?" Sparks crackled over the phone.

"You mean...*ready*, ready?" I asked making sure my sizzling brain cells hadn't misunderstood the signals.

"Hurry," she said. Only wings would have gotten me over to her faster.

She met me at the door in a Hello Kitty extra-short bathrobe, flashed her lavender bra and panties and a smile more seductive than any other she'd ever given me. I almost exploded from anticipation. She held up a condom. My mouth met hers, consuming, receiving, confirming the want, need, *love*. A half-second later, clothes were strewn in every direction. Even though this was our first time, we had plenty of practice with everything else. I already knew exactly how to make her body shudder into the palm of my hand. But this... This was fast, furious, fire. After that, she slowed me down, set the pace. Let's just say we never made it past the foyer.

An incoming text from Brenda brings me outta the memory. *"Get yr ass here NOW. Need u!"*

My head buzzes with all sorts of horrors and I'm overwhelmed with fear. I text back, *"911?"*

I decide not to wait for a response. By the time I reach the Bethel Evangelical Free Church at the intersection of Main and Jackson Harbor Road, the speedometer hits seventy—double the speed limit. Johannson would have my ass, but I don't care. The truck flies over a bump, catches air, and clunks down onto the road. It's a hilly straight shot until the dirt turnoff to Boyer's Bluff.

Less than five minutes from the time I started the truck, I'm barreling through Tricia's front door, ready to face disaster. Instead, I'm struck with laughter and strains of the Red-Eyed Loons emanating from the kitchen. Breathing hard, I storm in.

My brain struggles to register the scene. Brenda is spraying champagne into the mouth of a brown-haired girl—Tricia. Back to her natural hair color. Her shirt is drenched and clinging. She's halfway to drunk. I'm pissed, relieved, and wondering what the hell is going on.

I grab the champagne from Brenda just as she's about to shake it up again. "What the hell are you doing? This Dom Pérignon costs over two hundred dollars."

I've seen this bottle before. It was supposed to be for Tricia's father's homecoming. Last year, Tricia's grandma said we should save it for our wedding.

"We're celebrating life." Tricia snatches it from my hands and guzzles a good quarter of what's left. A loud belch blasts from her gaping mouth, which sends her into a giggling fit. As she staggers around the kitchen, she waves the bottle in wild arcs. She slips on a patch of wet floor, flailing her arms. Somehow, I catch her, catch the bottle, and land on my ass in what might be the only dry spot in a five-foot area. Tricia's on my lap, alternating between laughing and gasping for air. She twists around to face me, wiggles forward until we're hip to hip. Before I blink, I'm pulling her toward me. I can't say who kisses who first. My mind only registers that her sticky, sweet lips are on mine, and I want more. She tastes so damn good.

Without rational thought, my hands trail under her shirt, over taut skin, narrow ribs, to her barely-there breasts. It feels absolutely amazing—a gift—to touch her, kiss her, and to have her respond. This is what I've waited for. Like God Himself breathed new life into a lump of clay. I deepen the kiss and gently stroke the sensitive skin at the base of her hairline in slow, slow circles while I silently chant *I've missed you. I've missed this. Thank you God for bringing her back to me.*

Tricia pushes me away and jumps up, sobering us both. She's across the kitchen and yanking down her top before I catch my breath. Through glassy eyes, she looks at Brenda, looks back at me like she doesn't have a clue what happened.

"Brian." My name comes out as both a surprise and a question and I'm so floored by the switch I can't think. It passes. Guess she still finds my touch revolting. Who could blame me for being confused? Angry? Crushed?

Brenda glares at me. "Time for you two to talk."

She takes Tricia by the arm and guides her to the kitchen sink, wipes her face and neck with a damp washcloth as if Tricia has a fever. Then she straight-arms Tricia against the counter, eyes her fiercely, more like a prison guard than the tender mother role she played a moment before.

Tricia nods, stares down at herself. "I'll just...um... go shower and change." She glances at me through her lashes. Hoarsely, she says, "I did the laundry." She points to a chair next to the kitchen table and then walks out, not quite steady.

My clothes are neatly folded and piled in a basket.

I pluck a school T-shirt from the basket and replace the one she soaked with champagne.

Brenda starts to wipe up the floor with the same rag she used to cool Tricia's face. Seething, I wrench open the closet and thrust the mop at her. When I hear the rumble of the upstairs pipes, I speak through clenched teeth. "What the hell is going on?"

She looks at me, all innocent, like I'm the one who's lost his mind. "Just as Tricia said. We're celebrating life. She's going to have a bash here Friday night. Actually, a slumber party, since Mainlanders won't have any way to get back until morning."

"What?" My vision wavers and an ocean crashes in my ears.

"The champagne was her idea. The party was mine. She's at a crossroad, Brian, and for the first time ever she's wondering whether or not she should sell Boyer's Bluff and leave the island. She lost her family and she thinks she's lost her best friend too. So, what's left for her here?" Brenda's eyes narrow, daring me to contradict her. Her words feel like a slap and I'm too stunned to argue. "But maybe, just maybe bringing a little fun, *life* to this place might change her mind. This is her home. She should stay."

I swallow, but it doesn't help me breathe.

"And get this, the Red-Eyed Loons are going to play."

"The Red-Eyed Loons?"

"I know, amazing. I called Michaels right after I texted you, and he said yes."

It's very possible Brenda and Tricia have flipped their lids, gone complete loony. "Is this some joke? Because it's seriously not funny. I thought she was dying. I thought—" The kiss and Tricia's rejection hit me a second time.

"I'm sorry. I didn't know how else to get you here. We want your help planning the party."

I shake my head, but it's not the only part shaking. My hands, my legs, my heart. The last time we had a party here was for the Super Bowl. I had invited all the upperclassmen from school, arranged the food, *everything*. A half-hour before the game, people started showing up. As usual, Tricia was holed up in her grandma's office. Okay, so maybe I shoulda told her. But I figured since I was living here I had every right to have our friends over. I had hoped that if she were surrounded by people who love her, she'd get outta her head, her misery, and relax and have fun. BIG mistake. She put on a decent show, talking and even smiling. But afterward, Tricia was livid. "How dare you," she said. "You had no right to invite people without talking to me, asking me if I wanted company."

The conversation disintegrated from there. No matter what explanation I gave her, it wasn't good enough. I finally said, "Well, if I had asked, you woulda said no." And she said, "We'll never know, will we?"

Two days later, I tested it out, asked if some guys could come over to play XBox and maybe watch a movie. The answer was, "Can't you do something at their house or at your parents'?" When I said no, that I wanted to be here with her too, she relented, but spent the night in our room. I only wanted to help her. To show her how much she means to me, to others.

And now Tricia's having a party?

"I'm leaving."

Brenda follows me to the front door. "Don't, please? You two need to talk. You can't leave things this way."

I spin around. "What did you think you'd accomplish by forcing me to come here wh-when you knew, *knew* I couldn't handle one more slap in the face? Sh-she can't even stand me touching her."

A change in light draws my attention upward. I release Brenda. Tricia's standing at the top of the stairs dressed in black yoga pants and her dad's oversized Army sweatshirt. Her wet hair is plastered against her cheeks and shoulders. My first impulse is to tell her to go dry it, that she'll catch a cold if she doesn't. I keep my mouth shut. Her ashen complexion and sullen eyes are reminders that not much has changed. What's really going on here?

The spell of our suspended motion breaks when Brenda's phone plays Jay Z and Alicia Keys's "Empire State of Mind." Instantly, Brenda's attention and tension divert from Tricia and me, to herself. She answers, "Hi Dad, hold on a sec," as she hurries away toward the den.

But then, she halts. Turns around as if she forgot something. Her eyes meet mine with the same fierce determination she had lobbed at Tricia earlier. She points to me, the stairs, her heart, presses her palms together like a plea. She points to the phone, herself, then coordinates one swift, defiant hand chop and foot stomp. When it comes to charades, you want Brenda on your team. I get the message, and prove it by releasing the doorknob. Guess I'm staying. Her whole face shines with triumph. Sometimes, she's really annoying.

The den door clicks shut. I hope she'll finally deal with whatever problem sent her running to this island. Now it's my turn.

Except I can't move.

What am I supposed to say? Sorry I'm not enough for you? Sorry my touch disgusts you?

Yeah, I'm angry. I'm slathered in it. Who's to blame for that, huh?

Tricia makes her way over; her small, fragile frame stops inches from me. I feel her heat, wanna reach out. But I'm no fool. I won't touch her again. With my peripheral vision, I see her hand move toward my face. "What are you doing?" I ask.

She places her palm on my cheek. *Arrrrrrrrrrrrrg.* I can't bear it, so I close my eyes as she presses into my body. She inhales the smell of my shirt, a habit of hers I've always loved—like she can't get enough of what she once described as a combo of clay, BBQ, and my soap. Her arms work their way to my back and I cave, pull her in. I don't know if I should be holding her. Is this the girl Tricia once was, or a stranger? It feels... wrong.

It's almost as if she reads my mind, because she steps back and gives me an apologetic smile. "Can we talk?" she asks.

Talk? I'll be lucky if I can squeak out a syllable, but I nod and follow her. That's when I notice the parlor. It's light blue. The color a cloudless sky just after sunrise.

How I missed it earlier, I dunno. Stunned, I say, "You-you painted?"

Tricia nods. She weaves a bit, extends her hand toward the wall for balance, but keeps moving. As I trail her, I notice she's made other changes to the house. The rooms are spotless, free of clutter. But she didn't touch my things. Good sign? On a few walls, there are rectangular outlines where paintings once hung. Taped-up boxes sit in corners. Only when she passes her grandma's office do her feet slow. The door's open. It hasn't been unlocked for months.

The collage of Boyer family photos remains the same. The furniture's in the same place, but overall the space is cheerier, neater. I'm so fixated on the space that I stumble on an open box. I right myself and am at once mesmerized and freaked by the contents.

Tricia turns. "You okay?"

"Wh-why'd you box up your dad's comic book collection?"

"Don't need them," she says, like it's no big deal. Like they've never been a big deal. But that's a lie. To Tricia, that collection is—was—worth *everything*. As an artist, I've always appreciated the drawings. If I wanted to look at them, I needed permission. They were kept in a cabinet in her grandma's office, stored in binders, organized by title and issue. Each one has its own clear, heavy-duty polypropylene folder. Tricia guarded them like a dragon protects its lair, along with everything else in that room. *Don't touch my grandma's things,* she had said when I had gone in search of scissors. And now the comic books are in a box? "They're yours if you want them," she says. "I want you to have them."

I swallow. "Okay."

When we get close to the tower stairs, Tricia removes two large knit afghans from an old trunk and hands them to me. The lantern room had always been our space, the place we spent hours together talking and later on, kissing and so much more. But I won't think about that.

When we enter the small space, Tricia slides to the floor. Her head clunks against the wood panel. I hand her an afghan and sit next to her. Not touching, not looking at her. I focus on the shadows of trees and cliffs, the ghostly glow cast around us by the moonlight. For a few silent minutes, we take it in. Under the blankets, her hand reaches for mine. I slip my fingers between hers.

Why wasn't I enough? The words repeat, louder and louder until I'm screaming them in my head. "Why wasn't I enough?" I ask.

Tricia releases my hand, tucks her afghan under her, trapping the arm closest to me. We might as well be talking on the phone. "You don't understand."

"Explain it to me then."

"I never wanted or needed you to be enough, as if you could fill the void left by my grandma or my father or my mother." She presses her free fist into the spot above her heart. "You can't replace them. No one can. I'll always have something missing. Here." The thump against her chest is solid. No echo to that emptied chamber.

"Geez, Tricia. You really thought I believed I could replace them? Never. I was trying to *show* you that you're still alive, that you have a life, I had hoped with me. That you mattered. To me. That you had family. Me. I know now that I wasn't enough."

Shaking her head, she says, "That's not true. You have always been enough for me. You never had to prove it. I needed to grieve. I'm still grieving."

"I wasn't trying to prove anything. I just wanted you to acknowledge my presence. Appreciate me being here for you. For you to attempt to be happy once in a while."

She frees her arm, twists off and on her mother's promise ring. "I did appreciate you, but I couldn't change how I was feeling just to please you. What I wanted was for you to listen. To understand I have something missing that can never be replaced. Not by you. Not by anyone. What I needed was for you to be my friend."

I stare at her in disbelief. "I am your friend! I've *always* been your friend. But you and I, we're supposed to be so much more and you shut me out and shut me down. You blocked me every time I tried to get close to you. You froze me outta your bed and outta your life."

She faces me. Her anger and misery match mine. "The night we buried my grandmother I asked you to hold me. I needed you."

I look at her, even more confused, startled. "I *did* hold you."

"For a little while. And while I tried to talk to you about how I was feeling, you shut me down, like listening to my pain was a burden. I was distraught and you wanted to have sex? You undressed me and I was crying."

My mouth hangs open. I can barely believe what I am hearing or—my God. Does she think...? "Are you saying...I raped you?" Tears well in my eyes.

Her eyes grow wide. "No! Of course not. What I'm saying is that you didn't pay attention. I didn't want to be touched that way. Not when I had buried my grandmother only hours before. Not when I was exhausted and worn out, wrecked. The more you touched me, the more it made my heart hurt because you know exactly how to make my body respond. And I love it. Love how incredibly good it feels. But at that moment, I didn't want to feel good. My body was yours, but my heart and soul were shattered from losing my grandma. I had been *crying.* Shaking, sobbing harder than I have ever cried in my life. How could you not notice?"

My mouth drops open again as Tricia's words sink into my gut and twist it into a knotted mess.

"For some reason you stopped listening to me, respecting my space, respecting my needs, respecting *me.* You stopped being my friend when what I needed more than anything was for you to be one."

Sick to my stomach, I brace myself against the glass and choke out, "Wait a minute. That's not fair!"

"Not fair?" She laughs mournfully.

I hold up my hands, a peace offering. "Okay, so I-I—Just hear me out. It-it was never my intention to—" The memory of making love to her that horrible, heartbreaking night flashes like an exploding tank truck—blinding, burning outta control.

I had walked into her darkened room. The light from the hallway only illuminated a few inches past the threshold. I didn't see her. I said her name. No answer. After a minute, my eyes adjusted. She was on the bed curled into herself, so small, so quiet I thought she was sleeping. But then, I saw her eyes. Empty, dead eyes. So near lifelessness that the fear of losing her gripped me by the throat. And every day since.

I shut the door, crawled into bed with her, and held her until she soaked my shirt. Believe me, I wasn't aroused. Then she talked about having no one left in her family, how she didn't know if she could live without her grandma, how much she would miss her. It was too much, too painful. I thought making love would help distract her, help her feel better, ease her pain. Our pain. Hell, was *I* wrong.

Tricia needs to know—no matter what happens from this moment on—I'm not a heartless bastard.

"You're right. I shoulda listened. The whole situation was screwed up, Tricia, and I couldn't cope. I swear when I held you in my arms, the last thing I was thinking about was making love to you." She looks at me absolutely defeated. "I thought if I could make you feel, if I could feel you it would help both of us. The only thought in my mind was taking care of you. I thought..." Realizing how much I failed her, failed *us*, I squeeze my eyes shut. "I thought I was doing what was best for you."

A tear rolls down my cheek. "You have no idea how absolutely terrified I was when I got outta the shower and you were nowhere in the house. Your truck was gone." My skin goes cold from the memory.

"When I found you on your family's graves, I was more convinced I'd lost you forever. I was outta my mind with worry. You were shaking so badly. I put my arms around you to warm you up and you pushed me away. Do you know how hard it was for me not to break down? To stay strong for you? And when I said, 'Let me take you home,' you said, 'I am home.' Do you realize how that scared the crap outta me? How that nearly killed me?"

Great, I'm the one sobbing. Tricia runs a hand over my thigh. Back, forth. Back, forth. Small comfort.

I pull myself together.

She says, "I couldn't talk to you. You were there, and I felt utterly alone."

"So were you, and I felt the same." Any lingering anger is gone. Only deep, aching sadness is left.

"I know." She shrinks into her afghan. "I wish I could have been more for you. Better for you. I knew pulling away hurt you. I let you down. I ruined us too." Tears dampen her cheeks. "Maybe I *should* leave Boyer's Bluff. One point six million dollars and I can be free of all of this. The memories." Now it's her turn for the waterworks.

I can't believe how messed up we are. A few drops escape from my eyes. "Tricia, we both deserve some happiness. Whatever will make you happy, that's what I want for you. But...I don't think that's me. I don't think you're—" I cut myself off, take a moment to think, redirect. "About selling Boyer's Bluff, as your friend, as your *best* friend, I can't tell you what to do. It's your decision alone because you're the one who has to live with it. But I will say that this is your home. Despite everything that's happened, I know you love this lighthouse, this land. A year from now, two years, whenever, I know you, and you'll miss it. Don't make any quick decisions, okay?"

Sniffling, she nods.

"I'm sorry." It's for a hundred different reasons. I hope Tricia knows it covers all of them, including the biggest loss of all. Us.

Her gaze glides from the stairs to the topside view of Boyer's Bluff, then settles on me. "I'm sorry too." Her shoulder presses into my arm, anchoring us together. "We both did the best we could, under the circumstances."

I wipe my face with a sleeve. "That night we buried your grandma? A part of me broke too." She nods. "I love you, Tricia. I wish there were a way to fix this. Us. But I just don't know how, or even if we should."

"I love you, too. Always." She slides in front of me, crosses her legs, and takes my hands in hers. "We'll be okay. We'll figure out how to be friends again."

Her touch burns. I withdraw my hands, flex them at my sides. "I'll move my stuff out tonight."

She nods. "I can't imagine a life without you in it."

"I can't imagine life without you, either. I'm here for you. I'll be a better friend."

"Me too." She cloaks herself tightly within the afghan.

I kiss her cheek and scoot away, feeling lousy, a failure, and also relieved. I admit that deep down I wanted us to be over. It was the how and Tricia's reaction that I feared the most.

I allow the sight of her to sink in. Her chestnut brown hair, her delicate cheekbones, her beautiful, soulful green eyes. Will I look back at this moment and have no regrets? I hope so, but I'm not sure.

"I'm gonna get my clothes and pack up the rest of my stuff," I say with a voice that doesn't sound like my own.

"Do you want my help?" she asks, sounding just as strange. "Or Brenda's?"

"No thanks. Tell her I'll meet her at my parents'."

SIXTEEN

"Our strength grows out of weakness."
Ralph Waldo Emerson

BRENDA

WASHINGTON ISLAND   WEDNESDAY, 2:34 A.M.

FADE IN:

NEXT. TRICIA BOYER'S LIGHTHOUSE -
NIGHT

A disheveled, sleepy Brenda opens
the lighthouse front door, stumbles
onto the porch in her bare feet,
a T-shirt, and her underwear. She
stares after Brian, who's driving
away.

Tricia is upset, but not crying. She
stands in the middle of the circle
drive also watching the truck. When
Brian's gone, she turns and climbs
onto the porch.

> BRENDA
> Where's he going?

> TRICIA
> Home.

> BRENDA
> You mean—-

Tricia turns back toward the driveway, lost, stunned. After a minute, she faces Brenda.

> BRENDA (CONT.)
> But, the two of you were supposed to work things out.
>> (beat, slightly irritated)
> Why didn't you wake me?

Tricia ignores Brenda's question, sits on the bottom step. She looks as if she's suffering from a hangover. Upset about Brian, she moans. Covers her face with her hands.

> TRICIA
> It's over. We're really over.

> BRENDA
> Maybe a little time away from each other will be good for you two?

Brenda shivers from the cold, blows on her hands to warm them. Tricia spots Brian's BASEBALL on the porch. She jumps up, grabs it, and whips it at the trees.

                    TRICIA
          I hate this island. I hate
          Boyer's Bluff. I can't
          stay here. I won't be able
          to deal with seeing Brian
          every day and pretending
          everything is normal. I
          could backpack through
          Europe, explore the world
          and forget all this.

                    BRENDA
               (with a touch of amusement)
          Not before Friday. We're
          having a party, remember?

Tricia moans again, but this time it's in protest.

                    TRICIA
          I never should have agreed
          to it. Not when everything
          in my life is falling
          apart.

                    BRENDA
               (frustrated)
          Stop! You think you're the
          only one who's had to deal

with shit in her life?
You think you should be
exempt? Stop being self-
absorbed and wake up.
Other people are suffering
too. Get over yourself and
deal with it.

Tricia steps back, almost like Brenda
slapped her. Brenda puts a hand over
her mouth, chokes, then reaches out,
hugs and releases Tricia quickly.

                    BRENDA (CONT.)
          I'm sorry. God, I am so
          sorry. I shouldn't have
          spoken to you like that.
          I can't imagine what it's
          like to be you. I'm sorry
          about your family. I'm
          sorry about Brian. But
          trust me, you can't run
          away from your problems.
          No matter what, they'll
          find you.

Tricia looks at Brenda and sees
she's visibly shaken. Tricia's
expression morphs with understanding
and sympathy.

                    TRICIA
          You want to tell me about
          it?

                    BRENDA
          There's nothing to tell.
          I'm just sayin'. Now let's
          go inside, I'm freezing my
          ass off.

INT. TRICIA BOYER'S LIGHTHOUSE/
FOYER/HALLWAY - CONTINUOUS - NIGHT

Tricia notices Brenda hasn't followed
her to the kitchen. She retraces her
steps and sees Brenda lock the front
door and then check to make sure
it's secure.

Brenda unlocks and relocks it three
more times. Tricia is curious about
Brenda's behavior.

Brenda looks up and glares at Tricia.

                    BRENDA (CONT.)
          What?

Tricia shrugs. Brenda walks toward
the den. Tricia follows.

INT. TRICIA BOYER'S LIGHTHOUSE/DEN -
CONTINUOUS - NIGHT

Brenda grabs her jeans from the
floor, sits on the couch, and slips
them on. She removes her phone from
her pocket.

INSERT - BRENDA'S PHONE

Brenda texts Brian: B @ yr house asap. Wait up 4 me.

                    TRICIA
          Was that a text from Brian?
          Is he okay?

                    BRENDA
          He's fine.

Tricia attempts to get a glimpse of Brenda's phone by peering over her shoulder. Brenda moves away, scrolls through her emails. Her face lights up.

                    BRENDA (CONT.)
          Awesome news. Colin Michaels
          confirmed that the band'll
          play from eight 'til
          midnight. They need a
          thousand up front in cash,
          two breaks, and as much
          beer and food as the guys
          can stuff in their faces.

                    TRICIA
               (shocked)
          A thousand dollars? But—

                    BRENDA
          That's dirt cheap for
          the Red-Eyed Loons. They

usually get five for a
rave. You can send it to him
through PayPal. I posted
the party on Facebook and
sent out a group text to
most of my contact list.

Brenda holds out her phone to Tricia.

INSERT - BRENDA'S PHONE: FACEBOOK
EVENT PAGE: WASHINGTON ISLAND BASH,
THIS FRIDAY NIGHT

                    BRENDA (CONT.)
Look. I told you people
would want to come. Sixty-
eight RSVPs so far. I
wouldn't be surprised if
we hit two hundred by
tomorrow.

                    TRICIA
You're kidding?

                    BRENDA
Nope. I invited all
upperclassmen from the
island, Sturgeon Bay,
Gibraltar, Sevastopol, and
Southern Door High.
    (beat)
Hey, unfreeze the frown
face. I'm seeing some
lines, and they look
permanent. Get excited,

girl. Focus on how amazing
this will be.

                TRICIA
            (glumly)
        How am I going to feed all
        those people? I don't even
        know what to buy.

Brenda slips on her shoes, acts
completely unperturbed.

                TRICIA (CONT.)
        What if it rains? Where
        will I put everyone? What
        if the band doesn't show?

                BRENDA
        You worry too much. I
        checked the forecast. It's
        supposed to be amazing.
        As for the rest, stay
        organized and you'll be
        fine. Keep a list.

Tricia removes a notebook and pen
from a built-in cabinet drawer. She
flips to a blank page and looks at
Brenda for guidance.

                BRENDA (CONT.)
        The food should be simple.
        Do roast-your-own hot
        dogs, brats, veggie dogs
        over the bonfire. And

za Wiemer

chips. Or… I have a better
idea. Let's do the roast-
your-own and a fish boil!

                TRICIA
        But—

                BRENDA
        C'mon. Door County tradition.
        Everyone will love it.
        We'll borrow the equipment
        from Charlie's Pub and
        Grill. Aunt Elana and
        Uncle Charlie won't mind.

Tricia frowns, adds ASK BRIAN FOR
FISH BOIL EQUIPMENT, CUPS, NAPKINS,
PLASTICWARE, PLATES to the list.

                TRICIA
        What else?

                BRENDA
        I sent an email to a port-a-
        potty company in Green Bay,
        in case you don't want the
        guys using the woods and
        the girls tramping through
        the house. Everyone's
        supposed to bring camping
        equipment, except my
        friend Angie. I promised
        her a bed. Don't worry
        about drinks. I put BYOB
        on the Facebook event.

Brenda stands, swings her purse onto her shoulder.

                    BRENDA (CONT.)
          I better head out.

                    TRICIA
          What? Why? We barely have
          a to-do list. Who's going
          to   shuttle   people   from
          the ferry? And what about
          breakfast for everyone?

                    BRENDA
          Make muffins.

                    TRICIA
          And...decorations?

Brenda laughs.

                    BRENDA
          This   isn't   a   birthday
          party.

She grabs Tricia's notebook and pen
from her hands, flips to a blank
page. In bold letters she...

INSERT - NOTEBOOK

...writes WORRY PRODUCES WARTS. STOP
WORRYING!

RETURN TO SCENE

Brenda rips out the message from the notebook.

INT. TRICIA BOYER'S LIGHTHOUSE/ KITCHEN - CONTINUOUS - NIGHT

Brenda marches into the kitchen with Tricia scurrying behind and sticks the note up on the fridge. Brenda sets her hands on Tricia's shoulders and gives her an affectionate shake.

> BRENDA (CONT.)
> This party's going be kickass fantastic. The best ever. I'll come help you set up Thursday morning. We have Senior Skip Day on Friday, so I'll recruit help if you think we need it.

She steps back, takes a good hard look at Tricia.

INT. TRICIA BOYER'S LIGHTHOUSE/FOYER - CONTINUOUS - NIGHT

Brenda drags Tricia to the mirror in the foyer, spinning her around so she can see herself.

> BRENDA (CONT.)
> Listen up. I did a perfecto job on the hair color. You

almost look like yourself.
No ponytail for the
party. And if I see that
sweatshirt, I swear I'll
toss it, and maybe you,
into the bonfire.

Brenda lifts Tricia's chin.

> BRENDA (CONT.)
> Forget the natural look.
> The whole emo scene is so
> last year. You need makeup.
> I'll bring my bag.

Brenda gives Tricia a playful shove.

> BRENDA (CONT.)
> Later.

She leaves.

Tricia continues to stand in front
of the mirror. She takes her hair
out of the ponytail and combs her
fingers through it. She sighs, reties
the pony.

EXT. BRIAN'S HOME - NIGHT

Brenda's SUV pulls into Brian's
driveway. The house is dark and so is
the studio. Brenda carefully slips
her keys in between her fingers and
steps outside. She checks both the

front and side door. They're locked. After trying to reach Brian on his phone, she moves to his bedroom window and knocks. No answer. As she attempts to slide the window open, a shadow reflects on the outside of the glass. Brenda spins around, ready to strike until she recognizes Brian.

> BRENDA (CONT.)
> What the hell are you doing sneaking up on me like that?

She puts a hand on her heart, then flops onto the ground. Brian joins her.

> BRIAN
> Shh, I didn't know it was you until I turned the corner. You're shaking like a scared puppy.

> BRENDA
> No shit, Sherlock. Where were you? Didn't you get my text?

> BRIAN
> In my studio. And obviously not. I shut off my phone.

Brenda slaps Brian on his shoulder.

                    BRIAN (CONT.)
                    (in a louder whisper)
          Ow! What'dya do that for?

                    BRENDA
          For   breaking   up   with
          Tricia. For not waking me.
          For   not   looking   at   your
          phone. And this…

She jabs him in the stomach.

                    BRENDA (CONT.)
          …is for scaring me half to
          death.

Brenda gets to her feet. Brian stands
too, blocks Brenda's path of escape.
She puts her hands on her hips,
scowls at him.

                    BRIAN
          Cut me some slack, Bren.
          You might think you can
          barge in and figure out
          what's going on, but you
          can't. This is what's best.
          I saw it with my own eyes.
          Tricia's making changes,
          doing things around the
          house. Having a party. She
          wouldn't be doing any of
          that if I were still there.
          And if you don't think that
          doesn't hurt, then—

                    BRENDA
            Then I'm an idiot.

Dejected, Brian slips a hand into
his pocket and pulls out a chunk of
dried clay. He rubs it between his
fingers, squeezes it in his fist,
and lets it crumble over the grass.

Brenda sighs, tilts her head up to
take in the night sky. She glances
at Brian, who's stargazing, too.

                    BRENDA (CONT.)
            Maybe you two were too
            close? Like scrambled
            eggs. Too mixed up in
            each other's lives.
            Maybe breaking up was the
            only way to unscramble
            yourselves for a while?
            You know what I think? I
            think that after a break,
            maybe the two of you will
            decide that you can't live
            without the other.

                    BRIAN
            Don't count on it.

                    BRENDA
              (beat)
            Listen to me. At least
            work on being friends.
            This island is too small

to avoid each other day in and day out. Help her with the party. That will go a long way to smooth things over.

Brian turns to her, eyes narrow.

> BRIAN
> (sharply)
> Is the party for her, or for you?

Brenda pauses, then laughs, absolutely delighted by his question.

> BRENDA
> Thank you. That was truly insightful.

Brenda smiles at a confused Brian, then her expression changes. She becomes dead serious and determined.

> BRENDA (CONT.)
> I told you earlier that it's time for me to face my issues. I'm taking the first ferry today and heading back. My father's flying in and I'm meeting him in Sturg. Together, we're going to face my nightmare. I don't want to. But I have to. Then I'm

coming back and helping
Tricia with this party. So,
to answer your question,
yes. The party is for both
of us. She just doesn't
know it.

                  BRIAN
            (concerned)
      Are you gonna be okay?

Brenda shrugs.

                  BRENDA
      I believe so. I'm tired of
      living in the past. I've
      replayed the same scenario
      hundreds of times and it
      never changes. It always
      has the same ending. You
      know what I realized?
      No one else lives in my
      memories but me. The past
      is a lonely, depressing
      place to live, and I'm
      done.

She looks at Brian as if she suddenly
had another revelation.

                  BRENDA (CONT.)
      I'm writing a new
      screenplay for my life.
      That's what I'm doing.
      And this time, I'm the one

who's in control of how it ends.

INT. BRIAN'S HOUSE/SAVANNA'S BEDROOM - EARLY MORNING

Brenda's cell phone alarm beeps on a NIGHTSTAND next to her bed. The time flashes 6:30 A.M. In a second bed, SAVANNA (17) stirs, then opens her eyes.

> SAVANNA
> Hey, cuz. What's going on?

> BRENDA
> Going home. I'm taking the seven.

Brenda climbs out of bed, collects the things she scattered near her backpack, and pulls out clean clothes. She changes out of her nightshirt.

> SAVANNA
> (disappointedly)
> But…we didn't get a chance to hang out. I have so much to tell you.

> BRENDA
> I'll be back tomorrow to help Tricia with the party. Can we talk then? You're coming, right?

                    SAVANNA
          'Course.
             (beat)
          Should I be worried about
          my brother?

                    BRENDA
          What has he told you?

                    SAVANNA
          Nothing. He never confides
          in me. But everyone knows
          they broke up.

                    BRENDA
          They do?

                    SAVANNA
          I don't know how, but yeah.

Impatient to leave, Brenda stuffs
her nightshirt into her backpack and
hoists it onto her shoulder.

                    SAVANNA (CONT.)
          Mom put out a gag order on
          the island. She said she'd
          strangle anyone who talks
          to Tricia or Brian about
          the breakup before they
          make it public.

                    BRENDA
          Whoa, way to go Aunt Elana.

                    SAVANNA
We   figured   it   out
immediately. Brian hasn't
slept at home for months,
so it was obvious something
was up. Then Dad saw him
crying in his truck before
school.
    (beat)
They said if he doesn't
come talk to them by
tonight,   they're   gonna
make an excuse to take him
off-island. They've only
waited because you're here
and they thought that's
why you came. Because
Brian needed you.

Savanna pulls her knees up and hugs
them.

                SAVANNA (CONT.)
I love Tricia. I always
thought she'd become my
real sister. But after
the last few months, I'm
relieved it's over. Brian's
whole   world   revolved
around her. Everything was
Tricia, Tricia, Tricia. It
was unhealthy, and I told
him so. But did he listen
to me? No.

Brenda checks her cell phone for the time. Holds it up for Savannah to see. 6:42 A.M.

                    BRENDA
I need to go. See you tomorrow?

Savanna hops out of bed, surprises Brenda with an embrace. Not sure what to do with her hands, Brenda pats Savanna's back. Savanna steps away.

                    SAVANNA
          Promise me we can talk
          more when you come back?
          I want your advice about
          Oliver.

                    BRENDA
          Oliver? Umm, I'm not sure
          I'm the right one to talk to
          about that. Maybe...someone
          with dating experience?

                    SAVANNA
          (dejected)
          Yeah, well, I would have
          talked to Tricia, but
          whatever.

Brenda hesitates at Savanna's door, feeling guilty. Savanna hops back into bed, pulls her blankets over her head. Brenda turns and exits.

EXT. FERRY - DAY

Brenda stands on the top deck looking toward the mainland. She pulls out her phone.

INSERT - BRENDA'S PHONE

Text from Angie: When r u coming home? Need 2 talk 2 u. So much going on w Emerson. Need advice on Jordan. Call me.

Brenda sends a text message to Angie: Bad reception on the ferry. Can't c u later. My dad's coming 2 town 4 business.

FADE OUT.

SEVENTEEN

"Life is a succession of lessons which must be lived to be understood."
Ralph Waldo Emerson

ANGIE

STURGEON BAY   WEDNESDAY, 5:38 A.M.

Skipped school
yesterday.
Unexpected
holiday.
One hundred
twenty-eight
"Likes" on a
gif of me
soaking wet,
revealing way
too much.

Emerson, the gentleman,
addressed nasty accusations,
with a simple statement:

> "Don't believe
> what
> your eyes see.

                    I
        never touched
            Angie."

He ~~deleted his social~~
~~media accounts~~. Changed
his cell phone number.
Doesn't matter when the
  gif   is   E   V   E   R   Y   W   H   E   R   E.

School's different
cause he can't avoid
silent shunning, staring, shame, shame, **SHAME.**
Social suicide complete
for our
F
A
L
L
E
N
hero.

Golden boy no more.

What have I done?
Hide. I'm so ashamed.

⤴

Two hours
until school.
Two long   s t r e t c h e d   o u t   h o u r S

Liza Wiemer

before I face
the mob
and lies, lies, lies, lies, lies, lies, lies.

Jordan thinks
I should
tell the truth.
I told
him (most of) the truth
and
survived.

For
some strange
reason
he still likes
me. Why
when I don't
like
myself?

Confess?
 How can I
  lose my reputation,
    face public humiliation
      when so many friends rallied
      behind me? Won't I be the one who'll be
      getting the glares and silent shunning?
  Who'd still respect an eighteen-year-old toddler
throwing a temper tantrum? Jordan said he would.

Will Brenda be there for me?

Concern pricks the back
of my mind, questions

unanswered from our talk.
She's obviously keeping
a secret. If she's not gay,
then what is it?

I imagine losing my best friend
forever. Heart breaking each time
her image graces the movie screen,
gossip shows, *EW, People* Magazine.
Acting, screenwriting in Hollywood.
Tony, Academy, Emmy Awards.
Our dreams for her success.

Will she forget me
once she's in NYC?
Small, simple, boring
life in Sturgeon Bay
against lights, glamour,
excitement in the city
with Times Square,
Broadway, Fifth Avenue,
Chinatown, Little Italy.
The sweet, juicy apple
to our tart and tiny
Door County cherries.

Kind of feel forgotten already.

BECAUSE...

She's planning a party
on Washington Island,
a massive celebration
not to be missed. Emerson's
favorite band the Red-Eyed
Loons. Why did she hire
them to play?
Camping, dancing, BBQ. BYOB.
Posted on Facebook: juniors,
seniors, friends invited from
ALL Door County high schools.

My LIFE
is
F
A
L
 L
 I
N
G
A—-P—-A—-R—-T.

7:24 A.M.

I text Brenda:
When r u coming home?
So much going on w
Emerson. Need advice
on Jordan. Call me.

Hello?

Brenda texts me:
Bad reception on the ferry.
Can't c u later. My dad's
coming 2 town 4 business.

Dial, ring. She answers.
Brenda's mysterious
about her dad. Business?
Dropped call. Sigh.

7:43 A.M.

Ican'tgotoschool.Ican'tgotoschool.
Ican'tgotoschool.Ican'tgotoschool.

Text from Jordan:
I'll drive u to school.

I text Jordan:
Not going.

Jordan texts me:
Oh yes u are.
Even if I have to drag u
and tie u on top of JJ.
Be outside in 15.
PS I'll be there for u. :)

I text Jordan:
Ok.

Sigh.

Liza Wiemer

Last night, under
a **dark sky,**
I climbed
through Jordan's
window, crawled
into his bed,
cuddled next
to him. We talked
about the past
when I'd been
a frightened
little girl.

Jordan had kept me safe from the Demon lurking
across the street.

No Demon now.
Mom, Dad, baby Emily. Me.
A happy home sweet home.

EXCEPT...

ghosts linger.
Fingerprints,
footsteps, history.
Can't erase memories.
Secrets.

BUT...

Jordan knows
about burns, bruises,
blows, broken bones,
scrrrrr-eeeea-mmmms.
Pain, pain, pain

Mommy endured
from the Demon
I'd called Daddy.

AND...

Brenda knows

BECAUSE...

I told her how I hid
under Jordan's bed.
The night the Demon
was arrested.

Four-year sentence
for reckless injury.

AND...

once, in seventh grade,
while Brenda and I
were asleep
he came back. We
didn't know
it was him 'til later.
He stole Mom's
Tiffany lamp
and the antique
silver candlesticks
belonging to her
mother, the grandma
I've never met. Secretly,
I've watched Mom
polish, clutch them

Liza Wiemer

to her, sometimes

                    C
               R   R
          Y   Y
          I   I
          N   N
          G   G

We
don't talk about it.
No
never.

The Demon
was caught,
locked up
again when he attempted
to pawn the lamp and
candlesticks for a gun.

Brenda and I have never
talked about it for more
than a minute. Later,
years later, I tried. She
changed the subject.

So, I didn't tell her
about the letter
the Demon sent
me eight weeks ago.

                    Dear Angie:
              Happy 18th Birthday!
         That's how old your mother
           was when I met her. You've

Hello?

grown up so fast. I can't
wait to see how much
when I'm released.
Love, Daddy

Mom called the attorney.
Nothing he could do.
No threat from the Demon.

EXCEPT...

it feels like one.

CONFESSION:

Last night,
I told Jordan.
I'm terrified
the Demon will
come for me
in 342 days,
his scheduled
release. Must
get away
from Sturgeon
Bay before then.
Jordan said he'd
help. Don't know
how he'll help
from college.

**Mom's
motto:**

The past

stays in
the past.

Don't
talk
about
it.
Don't
tell
anyone
family
secrets.

I never
told
Emerson
about
the
Demon.

Dating Emerson,
I knew he'd
never, never, never ————————————————
—— ⟩
(physically)
hurt me.
I knew he'd
always
be kind,
loyal, keep
me safe.
Protective
when a drunk
guy hit on me,
danced

suggestively.
When Jordan
rejected me,
I chose
Emerson.
Did I
use him?
~~Never.~~
I was
(sometimes) a (giving, loving, considerate,
thoughtful,) needy, jealous
girlfriend.

I don't want
to be
needy, jealous
with Jordan.

Can I change?

EIGHTEEN

"Undoubtedly we have no questions to ask
which are unanswerable."
Ralph Waldo Emerson

EMERSON

STURGEON BAY   WEDNESDAY, II:3I A.M.

I'VE LIVED THROUGH nearly two days of hell.

And did nothing to avoid it.

I'm actually proud of that.

Angie's back in school and I've watched her walk from class to class with a posse of overprotective, sympathetic girls who've made me into an enemy of the entire female race. The lies. Whisper talk pitched perfectly so I couldn't miss the disgust and indignation.

I thought I had cleared things up when I had gone over to Angie's house Monday after school and apologized. I talked to Angie about Brenda and told her I was worried about Brenda's comments and reaction. We talked about Travis and that stupid gif. She was mortified, upset. I thought she'd set everyone straight. But there she is, walking around like a victimized princess.

It just reaffirms I could never trust her.

Under the veil of her bangs, Angie follows an array of shoes clopping along the linoleum floor and lets others do the talking, glaring. Earlier, between first and second block, I deliberately stepped into her path, forcing her to raise her head and meet the truth and silent anger I crafted onto my face. I couldn't hold it.

Fear flickered in her eyes with a plea that stunned and shut me down. Marina Martinez grabbed Angie's arm, pulled her aside, and shoved me in the chest. "Get out of her way, douchebag."

I did. Not because of Marina, but because Angie reminded me of someone dying, trapped in an undertow she didn't have the strength to swim out of, so she'd given up, given in. In that one second, my anger washed away a fraction, replaced with... sympathy? Did I really feel sorry for her?

Sucker.

I called after her. "Angie." The tone, I hoped, was a question and my answer: *What are you doing? You're better than this. Fix it!* She froze, shoulders stiffened. I have no idea if she turned around because I walked away, radiating confidence and calm.

I spent the next hour and a half hating myself for caring, still wanting to protect her, even at my own expense. *Sucker. Idiot. Wimp.* Yeah, I do self-loathing well.

A text from my sister Mia chirps onto my phone. "So sick of this. Tell everyone Angie's a liar." Mia's been questioned like a trial witness by half the school, and she made it her personal mission to defend my honor. Waste of time, I told her.

Now I'm repeating myself. *Calling her names won't help.* I hit SEND. I've already made it clear I hadn't touched Angie, hadn't done anything wrong other than make fools out of both of us by breaking up over a picnic lunch. People either believe me, or they don't. Most don't. After thinking about it, I came to the conclusion that people relish in seeing someone fall from grace. It makes their lives less pathetic.

Mia texts back, but I don't bother to look at it. I tuck my phone away, open my locker, and kneel down to organize my books.

A hand clasps onto my shoulder and I flinch. Matt grins down at me, amused. Okay, so maybe I'm a little on edge. "You want to go off campus for lunch? Wouldn't mind tossing this for Culver's." He holds up a brown paper bag.

Tempting.

I'm about to say that I'll drive, but Jordan's words drift from across the hall and stop me. Despite looking directly at me, he's talking to Angie. "I'm not taking you home. Deal with it. Deal with this." His tone is firm, unshakeable and without malice. From his "this," I can only conclude that he's referring to me. Marina bounces over to Angie, hooks her arm in hers, and says, "Let's go. French fries are on the menu."

"I like fries," I say loud enough for everyone to hear. I'm not backing down.

Matt shrugs, and we head to the cafeteria.

❧

FOUR STEPS INTO the caf and Marina shoves a ketchup-filled paper plate into my face. "Oops. I'm so sorry," she says with mock horror.

I stumble back. My eyes snap shut at the burning, stinging sensation. Matt hurries away and returns with a stack of napkins. I swipe the ketchup off to clear my vision, but the best I can do is squint.

Mia sprints over, a wiry tiger ready to pounce on anyone else who might attack me. It might be comical if I weren't seeing red literally and figuratively. She says, "Leave my brother alone," and takes my arm to guide me out of the cafeteria.

Travis shouts, "Look who's got the balls in the family."

In a second, I'm on Travis, grabbing him by the shirt and laying him flat on the floor with my knee pressed into his throat. Ketchup drips from my bangs and chin onto his face and collar. My boot is an inch from inflicting permanent damage to his manhood. I expect whichever teacher's on lunchroom duty to come over and intervene. The idea of a suspension or expulsion turns my stomach. But I'm sick of Travis and now he's going to pay.

"Stop!" A shrill voice cuts through the frenzy and freezes everyone. Fueled by adrenaline, my breath comes out in pants as I search the crowd, knowing the source but not seeing her. Travis takes advantage of the distraction and attempts to buck me off, but I readjust my grip. He's not going anywhere until I want him to. Mia plants herself at my side. I'd tell her to stay clear of this trouble, but telling Mia to do anything she doesn't want to do only makes her more stubborn. I don't need to battle her too.

From a tabletop only ten feet away, Angie's eyes sweep the room, then settle on my slit lids. Her foot slides forward, almost like she's going to jump and flee. Curtly, I nod, hoping she gets the message: *End this.*

Her spine straightens, her chin juts out. Jordan stands below, slightly off to her right like a sentinel guarding royalty.

She opens her mouth, then closes it. Everyone's mesmerized. The spotlight shines on her like so many times before. Normally she loves it. But by the way she's tugging on her ponytail, she's not loving this.

Neither am I, but in my head I urge her on, willing her not to bolt, and to admit the truth.

Her voice comes out loud and clear. "Emerson didn't do anything. I'm the one who smashed the picnic basket. I'm the one who dragged the blanket to the water, and I'm the one who slipped and fell on her ass. Emerson tried to help me. That's all. Now leave him alone. Leave us both alone. And please, if you shared the gif, delete it."

Jordan grins up at her, like her confession was the first step to rehab. He raises his hand, offers it to her. She takes it, hops down, and powerwalks to me.

I yank Travis up by his red-stained collar and shove him onto the bench seat. Jordan hands me another napkin. It doesn't do much other than smear more ketchup around. My eyes sting and burn even more.

"I'm so sorry," Angie whispers. But it's not just directed at me. Something passes between her and Travis, and I can't tell if he's more pissed at her or me. I don't care. Not for a millisecond do I regret bringing him down. I step real close and get into his face with my narrowed, swelling eyes. "Delete the gif. Contact whomever you have to and remove it from every site, or I'll be calling an attorney." I shift toward Angie. Jordan moves slightly in front of her. I ignore him. "Angie, you backing me up on this?"

She squeaks out a yes.

Mr. Bordon, our basketball coach and my math teacher, comes over. He looks at Travis, then Angie and Jordan, then Mia and me. "Everything all right ladies and gentlemen?"

"Yes, sir," I say.

Travis nods and walks away. Smartest thing that asshole's done in years.

"The bell's about to ring. Wash up, son, and if you need to go home for a change of clothes, come see me and I'll give you a pass." He leaves to make his rounds. If it had been any other teacher, most likely we would all be hauling ourselves to the principal's office. But Mr. Bordon knows us well. He knows my record, knows Travis's, and probably decided to give us time to work it out before stepping in. As our coach, that's always been his modus operandi, MO. I wonder, did he see the gif?

Mia grabs my arm. Her voice is laced with concern. "You okay?"

"Eyes," I answer. They're doing a watershed I can't stop, no matter how much I squeeze them shut. I'm not crying, but I'm sure someone would grab onto that conclusion and run with it. It's the damn vinegar from the ketchup.

I hiss in a breath, yank my shirt over my head, and use it as a rag to clean my face. My lids barely open, but it's just enough to guide myself out of the cafeteria without smashing into walls and tables.

Jordan follows me into the men's bathroom. Must say, the dude has balls. I turn the faucet on full blast, duck my head under the stream, and splash handful after handful of cool water while trying to force my eyelids to remain open.

"You can go, Jordan," I mumble.

He grabs paper towels and holds them out for me. I shake my head as I continue to flush my eyes. The sting dissipates and my vision clears enough that I can assess the temporary damage. Red, bulging eyes like the massive orbs of a fly. If anyone brings out a phone to snap my picture, I swear I'll smash it into a million pieces.

I look over at Jordan. He's staring at the ugly scar slashed across my chest.

"Open heart surgery, heart defect," I say, answering his unasked question. "When I was five."

The bathroom door opens. A puny freshman steps in, apologizes for the intrusion, and backs out. It's kind of comical after everything, but with my mood still black, I scowl. I turn my shirt inside out, toss it over my shoulder, covering most of the scar. The warning bell rings. My stomach grumbles. I really could have used those fries. I sigh out a river of frustration and move toward the door. Jordan offers the paper towels again, but I don't want anything from him. Why is he here?

Grasping the door handle, I turn. "You know what, Jordan? You should ask Angie to prom. She really wants to go. Stargaze lilies are her favorite, but roses will work too." And then I walk out. It's Jordan's shocked expression that finally makes me smile. My frustration, agitation, and the guilt I've felt since I messed up the breakup dissipate a bit as well.

3:26 P.M.

THANKS TO ANGIE, by the time school ended a few minutes ago, life was back to normal. At least on the outside.

Inside, I'd been having one-sided conversations with Frankie. I can't stop thinking about her and I'm beginning to wonder if I'm on the verge of crazy. Maybe all the stress, the roller-coaster of emotions, and the lack of sleep from the nightmares are finally catching up?

I wish I could talk to her again. She's the one person I know would listen. I'd tell her everything that's happened since we hung up. Of course, it's impossible. I made sure of it Monday after school. *Frankie's a phantom,* I remind myself for the hundredth time.

The morning we spoke I had this flash of what she looked like, and I was able to describe her. But now, that image is as elusive as trying to capture a cloud in a net. Discontent rumbles inside me like an earthquake. This is not who I am, and I don't know what to do with myself. I need to let her go. She can't be important or real to me. I'd have a better chance of catching a shark in Lake Michigan than finding her. I'm plagued with unanswerable questions. *Why was I the one to get her grandmother's old phone number? Was it random? Or was there a greater purpose I'll never understand? Is she okay? How is it possible to miss someone you've never met?*

I intended to go straight home to work on an AP English paper due on Monday. Instead, here I am driving around Sturgeon Bay looking at strangers to see if by happenstance I'll spot a girl who is more beautiful than Ava Gardner, the actress Frankie's grandma compared her to. I had googled Ava on my phone, but it's hard to take the image of a 1960s bombshell and translate it to the modern-day girl I had pictured in my head. After twenty minutes of this asinine activity, I give up and drive home.

$$\sim$$

4:48 P.M.

I PARK IN the driveway next to Isabelle's Camry. It's not unusual for her to come home and hang out with

Mia on her day off. All my sisters are close and as the one and only brother, I'm often the outsider or the special one, depending on the day. Now that it's just Mia and me at home, being the only boy isn't as big of a deal.

When I enter the kitchen in search of last night's leftover Cacio e Pepe, bean soup, and a baked treat from Nonna, I'm greeted by both Mia and Isabelle. Well, "greeted" isn't exactly the right word. They stand in front of the island like defensive ends on a powderpuff football team. Mia's face twists into something menacing and tough, the same one she flashed earlier today in the cafeteria, very intimidating if she weren't my little sister. I'm actually proud of that look—it's kept a lot of hormonal adolescent jackasses at bay. With her unyielding stance and perfected death stare Isabelle mastered from Mom, she's as scary as hellfire.

Now I'm not scared of anyone or anything other than death, but when these two gang up on me, they're a formidable sisterhood of high-octane estrogen. Anyone who has sisters knows that's highly combustible and whether I like it or not, I'm about to enter the burning building.

Isabelle: "A picnic in the park, Emerson? What were you thinking?"

Me: "I wasn't thinking, okay?" I bite my tongue, realizing they won't let me off he hook so easily. "So I messed up. Next time I'll use the stupid phone and break it off that way."

Mia: "That would be an improvement."

Isabelle: "Well, I'm glad you broke up with her. I didn't like her."

Me: "Since when?"

Isabelle: "Since day one. I told you she didn't appreciate you. I told you that you could do better. Mia, did you like her?"

Mia: "She had her redeeming qualities, and she was always nice to me whenever I saw her at school. But—"

Me: "Just stop. Angie and I were good together. Until we weren't. Leave it alone."

Done with this, I turn away, but Mia pushes me onto a stool.

Isabelle signals Mia through their secret sisterly language, which Mia answers with a knowing nod and walks out of the room. I moan in pure agony. I protest again, but Isabelle's Sith stare holds me in place. "Emerson, I need to talk to you. This is important."

"I don't need a lecture, Iz."

"I don't want to lecture you. I want to talk this out. I get it. I get you."

"Don't." My tone holds a threat, but Isabelle ignores it. Of course, that's why Isabelle delivers the lectures. She's the Great Wall of China. Mia's a hall monitor with no authority.

"Don't what? Care about you? Worry about you?"

I lower my voice so that Mia can't hear, because she's probably right around the corner listening in. I know exactly what Isabelle's going to say and I don't want to hear it for the thousandth time. "Don't bring up the past with me. I broke up with Angie. I'd say that's making progress."

"When was the last time you saw Dr. Shale?"

I knew it. Whenever she thinks I'm stressed out she starts worrying about my mental health. "What does Dr. Shale have to do with me breaking up with Angie?"

She doesn't answer my question. Instead she says, "Mia told me you barely defended yourself over any of the outrageous things people were saying about you."

"You don't know bullcrap from chocolate pudding. I made it clear that I didn't touch Angie, but I wasn't going to become a broken record. People will believe whatever they want to believe. And I wasn't going to throw Angie under the bus to save my butt. Most people would say that's admirable."

"Letting people smear your reputation?"

"Who cares about my reputation when I knew the truth? And what about Angie? I embarrassed her, humiliated her by breaking up with her in public. I screwed up. I took responsibility for it."

"Really, so her behavior, her childish actions were *your* fault?"

"No. I—" I shut my mouth, because yeah, I feel partially responsible, but also relieved that Angie set the record straight. "She spoke up. She did the right thing. Sometimes having a little faith in people—"

"At what price? Did you think about how this would affect Mia? How it could have affected your future?"

"Mia's as tough as all the Carusos, and I didn't need her to defend me."

"She defended you because she loves you."

"I know that." I take a deep breath. "It worked out. That's what matters."

Isabelle's expression drips with what I interpret as pity, and I can't bear it. I focus on the collage of family photos on the refrigerator. "You need help, Emerson." She slugs me on my arm, not hard, but to get my attention. "You can't save everyone from being hurt and you can't punish yourself every time you do something stupid, but that's exactly what you did over this breakup."

"You don't know what you're talking about."

"You bought Angie a dozen roses and apologized *after* you broke up with her."

"How did you know about that?"

"Everyone knew. It was like an admission of guilt."

"I was being—"

"—nice. We know."

"I messed up. I needed to apologize."

"Why is everyone else allowed to mess up but you?"

"Because—" I cut myself off and huff out frustration. Maybe I do hold myself to a high standard, but I hardly consider that a character flaw. "There's nothing wrong with apologizing when you're wrong."

"That's not what this is ultimately about, and you know it. You have an excessive need to take care of people, to protect them, to make sure they're okay or safe."

We stare in a face-off, neither one of us budging. "Fine," she says. "You want another example, I'll give you an example. The last time we went to Nonna's you grabbed my shoulder and stopped me from crossing the street until you were certain no cars were coming. Really Emerson, I know how to look both ways and cross the street safely."

"Jaywalk all you want. I don't care."

"Oh yeah? Do you realize you do that all the time? If you don't believe me, go ask Mia."

I stand, poised to storm away, but she seizes my arm.

"I don't want to discuss this!" I'm desperate to wrench out of her grip. But I won't, and she knows it.

She pushes. "Just say it, Emerson."

I protest with another guttural groan.

She'll continue to push until I give in. I refuse to give in.

"That lady who died—"

I shove her away, not enough to hurt her, but to give me space. And then I bolt up and move for the door. "I don't want to talk about it! Why do you always have to bring it up?"

She shouts after me. "It all comes down to her. What happened wasn't your fault. If you're not going to talk it out with me, you need to see Dr. Shale."

I spin around. "I know I'm not responsible, okay? I got over that years ago. So stop. There's nothing wrong with me. *Nothing!* And I'm tired of everything I do being analyzed by everyone in this family, especially *you!* I'm a nice guy. There's nothing wrong with being a nice guy."

"You can't spend the rest of your life trying to be a superhero or superhuman to make up for what happened. You were a boy, Emerson. Let that boy off the giant fishhook stuck in the back of your neck."

"Shut. UP!" I grab my jacket and sprint out the door to my car. Isabelle and Mia run after me. If they get anywhere near this vehicle, I'm stuck, so I ram the gearshift into reverse and hit the gas, only slowing down when I reach the road to check for traffic.

I decide to head toward Egg Harbor, get away from my annoying, know-it-all sisters. When people say they see red when they're angry, it's no lie. I've seen more red today than my fair share. And then, oh happy days, I see more. Red and blue lights flash through my rearview mirror when I turn north on Michigan Street toward Highway 42. Dammit!

I pull over. As the officer walks my way, I take out my wallet, remove my driver's license, and stick my hands on the steering wheel where he can see them.

The officer is Matt Busby's dad and I'm not sure if I should be relieved or mortified.

He nods. "Emerson."

"Yes, sir."

"You were driving twelve over the speed limit."

"Sorry, sir."

"License and registration." I reach into my glove box for the registration and hand over the documents. His eyes sweep over the car's interior. "Sit tight."

I watch his unhurried gait as he returns to the squad car. He takes out a clipboard and begins to write. I can't believe I got pulled over in front of the police station. *Idiot.* I slouch in my seat, not that it'll do me any good. The whole town knows my Camaro—an ultra-cool classic my nonno bought new in 1968 and sold to me for two grand on my sixteenth birthday.

Minutes tick slowly off the clock. With trepidation, I glance out the window and search for a familiar face.

That's when I spot Brenda sitting on a bench outside the police building. Her fingers weave behind her head and her forearms sandwich her face as she rocks slowly forward, the way we do stomach crunches in PE. This goes on for a short time until she slides her palms forward to cover her eyes. Her ragdoll stance is so unlike her usual take-on-the-world posture, I actually question if it's really her and not a lookalike. But yeah, it's her. The pink-streaked hair and combat boots are dead giveaways. All at once I'm curious to know why she's outside the police station and also praying she doesn't notice the flashing lights, which are a beacon right to my humiliation.

A tall, solemn-faced man, perhaps late thirties or early forties, dressed in a fancy suit walks out the door and sits next to her. She reaches out to him and he cradles her to his chest. Her body begins to tremble like she's crying. He runs a hand over her hair, brushes it aside, and says something to her. She nods. He reaches into his breast pocket, pulls out a white fabric square, and wipes her eyes. She curls her fingers, drops them on her thighs. He kisses the top of her head. The similar round shape to their faces and eyes are enough to justify my guess that he's not a cradle robber, but her father.

I relax a bit, still transfixed by the scene.

Busby taps my window, pulling my attention abruptly away from Brenda. I roll it down. "Since your record's clean, I'll let you off with a warning. Watch your speed." He hands back my paperwork. I slip my license into my wallet and set it aside. Busby leans over, lowers his mirrored glasses until I see the rims of his dark eyes. "I heard you've had a couple rough days."

Oh, great. Bet the whole freakin' town knows. "Yes, sir."

He chews on the edge of his mouth, perhaps to hide the whisper of a smile. He pats my arm. "Take my advice, son. Don't let it get to you."

"I won't, sir. Thank you." He walks away, and I accept both the warning and his well-intentioned advice with a solid head bang onto the steering wheel.

I look at Brenda, hoping she hasn't noticed my car. Don't think so. I continue to watch her. When a female police officer comes over, Brenda raises her tear-streaked face and nods. The woman removes a business card from her shirt pocket and shakes both Brenda and her supposed father's hands.

As Brenda and the man step closer to the parking lot, he wraps his arm protectively around her. And that's when she looks my way. Our eyes meet for under a second before I slide and huddle as close to the floor as my body allows. I begin to count, figuring she'll be gone by the time I reach one hundred.

Wrong. Brenda raps on the window, presses her nose against it, and glares at me. I produce a pen from the floor and hold it up, as if it was my purpose all along. From the police parking lot, the man watches us. She opens the passenger side door, and leans in until half her torso's inside. "What are you doing here?" she asks. Her hand snakes out and clasps my arm. Through the layers of my jacket and shirt, her nails mark my flesh as her thumb presses into bone.

"Speeding." I wave the warning in front of her.

"I'm not here."

"Who are you?" My attempt at humor fails to relax her crushing grip.

"Exactly."

I'm released. Without another word, she slams the door and runs back to the parking lot, says something to the man who narrows his eyes at me in warning.

Brenda's always had a hard shell, but we got along, hung out. Not friends exactly, but better than the cactus she's turned into the last two days, jabbing me with her needles every chance she gets. My arm throbs, confirming it.

I slide my jacket and shirt to my elbow. Small, crescent-shaped marks already begin to bruise. I rub the area, but it does nothing to ease the pain. This is turning into the second-worst day of my life.

∼

5:06 P.M.

TEN INCOMING TEXT messages—all from Isabelle and Mia.

Mia's latest one: *"R u all right?"*

In my family, there's a fine line between worry and panic. I'm close to sending Isabelle into a panic, and I know it. We have history.

I text Mia: *"Fine. Need my space."*

She texts back: *"Don't do anything stupid. <3 u."*

Right. I'd love to take a look at their list of stupid things they think I would do. I doubt I'd contemplate any of them. Also, I've had my fill over the past few days. I'm done with stupid.

I text: *"I'm fine. I promise. Don't worry."*

And then one more text comes through.

It's from Angie. *"I need to see u. It's important. I'm at Otumba Park w Jordan. Can u come by?"*

My thumbs hover over the keypad. I'm not sure how I'm going to answer or if I'm going to answer at all.

NINETEEN

"Don't waste yourself in rejection, nor bark against the bad, but chant the beauty of the good."

Ralph Waldo Emerson

ANGIE

STURGEON BAY   WEDNESDAY, 3:16 P.M.

Note found in my locker:

Dear Angie,

Please join me at our climbing tree.
Four o'clock today.

Don't be late.
Don't try to guess why.

Yours,
Jordan

RSVP: Text me

4:02 P.M.

Our climbing
tree. Jordan's,
mine. Snarly,
gnarly, tucked
behind a grove
of pines in the
southwest corner
of Otumba Park.

Discovered summer
of sixth grade,
our special space
up, Up, UP, UP
we climbed.
SunriseS, suNsets
over Sturgeon Bay.
Secrets, dreams,
tears, laughs,
poetry. Years
of camaraderie.

UNTIL...

that good-bye.

I shhhiver from
the memory.
Jordan's lips
brushing mine,
salt from munched
potato chips never
more delicious.
Our first and only

kiss in our old
oak tree, before
he left for Haiti.

I spot Jordan
before he
spots me,
legs dangling,
in our tree.
Closer, closer
until he waves.
I tremble with
anticipation.

"Hello!"
Rose petals
                s
            s
        s
pink,
   red,
   yellow,
white,
 cream
d
 r
o
 p
d
   o
w
   n
     on
my
    head.

Jordan holds up cardboard
signs:
1. Would you
2. please go
3. to prom
4. with me?

Mouth open,
eyes tear,
heart bump, bump, bumping.

G R i n n i n N G
W i d E!

"Absolutely!"
Bark, rrrOUgh
against my palms
imprint ~~lines~~
on my knees
as I scoot, crawl,
shimmy up, uP, UP.

Jordan takes
my hand
as we hug
the thick branch
between our thighs.

"Prom, huh?" I say.

"Yup," he says, smiling.
One beat. Two.

"But you hate dances."

Sophomore and junior year,
he's refused several
Sadie Hawkins
invitations.
Professed he hates dances.
So why prom? Why now? Cause
Emerson dumped me? Probably.

I hate pity.

　　　Smile
upside　　down.

Jordan sees.

　　　　　　"I don't hate dances. I never
　　　　　　　　　wanted to go
　　　　　　　if I couldn't go with you."

The world $^{t}il_{t}s,$
　　　　　sh i f t s when his mouth meets mine.

I ~~never~~ loved Emerson,
not
like　　　THIS.

LATER...

much later,

after we climb
d
o
w

n...
rose petals f ^{l} u $_{t}$ t ^{e} r
across the ground
littered with pine needles,
last year's leaves,
smelling like a mixture
of summer and winter
potpourri.

I scoop
a handful,
inhale,
and accidently
snort bits
of decay.
Sneeze,
one,
two,
three.

Can't believe Jordan went
to this much trouble for me.
Climbing tree.
Rose petals.
Promposal. *Poetry.*

I need
to tell
Jordan. Let
him decide, if
I'm worth
his time. But
first I need
to confess
to Emerson.

~

Emerson parks
the Camaro next
to JJ. Walks over
to our picnic bench.

Confusion crosses
Jordan's face. I didn't
mention texting
Emerson. Should
I confess or pretend
it's coincidence?

Lift-chin-nod from Emerson.
Jordan does the same. Glances
at me. "?????????????????????"

I spit out
my confession.

"IwastheonewhotoldTravisyoupushedmeinto
thelake."

Emerson: Blink. Blink.
Blink. Blink.

Jordan: Mouth

249

H
A
N
G
S
open.

With a shake,
thick, unruly
hair covers
Emerson's deep
disappointment.

"Oh Ang."
A looooooooooong
raspy sigh.

I've never, never, ever
been so ashamed.
I can't look at Jordan.

Emerson says,
"Well, it's good to know,
good you told me. But...
WOW."

One beat. Two.

"Th-that's nnnot all."

My voice drops
to a whisper.
"Remember the girl
from Sevastopol High School?
The one who came on to you?
I was jealous, unsure, insecure.

She was your test. You passed."

"*What*?"

"I'm sorry."

"You set that UP?
You set ME up?"

"I'm sorry.
So, so sorry!"

Wish it were
~~enough.~~

Emerson rubs
his brow.

"Okay. WOW.
This—You—
Give me a
minute.
Or two. I need
to digest
this."

Thirty beats. Times two.

"Here's the bottom
line. What you did?
It really sucks.
But it's over,
and we're done."

He glances at Jordan

tracks a seagull
F L Y I N G by.

"So, whatever it's worth,
I forgive you."

One beat. Two.

```
TEARS SILENTLY
     SS
    T   T
    R     R
    E     E
    A     A
     M  M
        d
        o
        w
        n
    MY FACE
```

Emerson continues. "Ang, do
us both a favor. Can we
figure out a way not
to hate each other? At school,
parties, with our friends?
We shouldn't have to avoid
each other or choose, right?"

One beat. Two.

I nod. "So...friends?"

Jordan sighs,
shakes

his head hard
looks away.

Won't fall into a pit
of self-pity.
I put myself here.

"Yeah. Friends."

Emerson. *Always the gentleman.*

"Thank you."

One beat. Two.

"I need to..." He points
to his car. "...go. See you
Jordan."

Emerson walks away
one, two, three
steps. Turns back.

"I saw Brenda in town
with an older guy.
Her father?"

I nod.

"She was upset."

"Upset? What did she say?"

"Nothing.
But...maybe you can text her? See

253

what's up? Whatever you do, don't
tell her I told you. Act normal.
Routine. She'll be angry
that I mentioned
it to you."

"I'll check up on her."

"Good. Thanks."

He's thanking *me*?
I never deserved
Emerson. I hope
to deserve Jordan.

"Hey, Emerson!" He opens his car
door, turns to me. "Friday there's
a party on the island. Red-Eyed Loons
are playing. I'm going, so are a lot
our friends. You should go. Brenda
helped plan it with a girl she knows."

"Brenda? Don't think so.
I'm on her
'Wish You Weren't Born' list."

"Don't worry
about Brenda.
Just come.
It'll be fun.
I'll text you
the info."

A small smile slips
onto the lips I liked to kiss.

Hello?

No more.

"Red-Eyed Loons.
Maybe. I'll see."

⁓

5:42 P.M.

Later, a looooog time
later.
Jordan finally speaks.

"Ang,
those lies
took my
breath away."

"I'm sorry."

"Why? How
could you do that
to Emerson?"

"I...don't know."

He shakes his head
s l o w l y.
"Not good enough."

"I-I was afraid."

Jordan waits
patiently.

Liza Wiemer

"Emerson was texting
pics of girls coming
on to him. Made me
jealous, insecure."

"You trusted Travis?"

"I-I'm not
good.
Not nearly
good
enough."

"Bullshit."

"You know
my DNA.
You know
my history,
what I hide
every day. It's
a part of me."

"You're your
mother's daughter,
not his."

"That's better? Who is she?
Why did she marry
the Demon? Who are her
parents? My grandparents?"

"Does it matter?
Be whoever
you want to be."

"What if I
can't choose?
What if I'm
stuck? No
money for college.
Mediocre grades.
My future's
working at Mom's
Turn Back
the Clock
Antique Shop
until I'm old, gray."

"Only if you see
your life that way."

Otumba Park
glows. Pink,
purple, orange,
yellow sunset.
Sigh. So pretty.
Nature's
sanctuary.
Sparrows
squabble.
Gusts of wind
rattle maple
branches,
carry rose
petals away
to the beach.
Runnnnnnnnnnnnnnnnnnnnnnnnnnnnnnnnnnnnnnnn
Reach down, scoop,
hold on, one, two
three petals

dropped from
the old oak tree,
a perfect place
for fantasies.
Jordan watches.
Waits. Waits.
Welcome back
to reality.

I return, sit
next to him.

"I have dreams:
to know my
maternal
grandparents,
to go to college,
to move to a
city like NYC,
Chicago, or
Milwaukee."

I look at him
through lashes
and see his hazel
eyes focused on me.

"I'm tired of
being afraid
all the time."

"Then don't be.
Trust me that you're dreams
can come true."

His face is
so sincere.

"You're
my BIGGEST
dream."

"You were mine
too."

PAST TENSE.

Briefly, he
covers his
sad eyes.

Did I
RUIN my
chance with
him?

~~Hope~~

Worry.

Doubt.

Fear.

EMOTIONS
s
c a t
t   e
r

everywhere.

259

Liza Wiemer

"Do you
still want
to go to
prom
with me?"

Jordan
shakes
his head
like he's
trying
to decide.

"Depends. Can I trust
you? I need to know
what
you did to Emerson
you won't do to me."

I stand, move
in front of him,
take his hand.

"I won't.
Promise. Why
I confessed
was so I could
be a person
worthy of
your trust.
I wanted you
to see the worst
of me. No secrets.
Only honesty."

One beat. Two.

THEN...

~~lines on Jordan's face~~
disappear.

He draws
me into his arms,
whispers
into my hair.

"That's a start."

6:11 P.M.

Alone,
emotions
bubble, burst.
How did my life
become
out of control?
I need my best
friend.

Text to Brenda:
Can u come over now?
I need to c u.

Brenda's text to me:
Your mom told u?

Text to Brenda:
Told me what?

AND THEN...

Oh.
Emerson was worried
about Brenda,
and I'm a horrible friend.

Vow:
I will
be a better,
less insecure,
more selfless
PERSON.
For Brenda.
For Jordan.
For me.

TWENTY

"It was a high counsel that I once heard given to a young person,
—'Always do what you are afraid to do.'"

Ralph Waldo Emerson

BRENDA

STURGEON BAY   WEDNESDAY, 6:02 P.M.

FADE IN:

INT. MAGNOLIA INN - NIGHT

Brenda and her father, JOEL HANNES
(42), descend from the grand stairway
and enter the lobby. MARYBETH (41),
dressed in sixties vintage clothes,
straightens the VISITOR INFORMATION
PAMPHLETS. She turns, sees Brenda
and Joel, and offers a standard
hospitable smile. Her expression
changes to a full-out grin when she
recognizes Joel.

                    MARYBETH
          Well if it isn't Joel
          Hannes. My gosh, I haven't

seen you since Laura's
party.

She skips over and throws her arms
around him. He hugs her back awkwardly.
Recognition spreads across his face.
He smiles down at her.

> JOEL
> Marybeth Jameson. It's
> been a long time. Twenty
> years?
> > (beat)
> You haven't changed. Still
> lighting up a room.

> MARYBETH
> > (slightly embarrassed)
> Don't look too closely.
> A lot has changed. I'm
> Marybeth Gotting, now.

> JOEL
> So you married Rex?

> MARYBETH
> Divorced, two years.
> > (beat)
> I work the nightshift here,
> so let me know if you need
> anything.

Marybeth runs her hand down her hair.

                    JOEL
        Thanks.

                    MARYBETH
        So, where have you been
        all these years?

As Joel talks to Marybeth, Brenda
wanders over to the brochures, picks
several up, puts them back in the
wrong places. She then walks to an
antique BREAKFRONT with TEA, COFFEE,
and a GLASS-COVERED PLATE WITH OATMEAL
RAISIN COOKIES. Brenda removes one,
plucks out the raisins, and takes a
bite of the cookie.

                    MARYBETH (CONT.)
        This pretty thing must be
        your…daughter?

Marybeth looks at his ringless left
hand. Brenda notices and flicks a
raisin toward Marybeth. It hits her
on the shoulder. She spins around
like she was stung.

                    BRENDA
        Oops.

She opens her palm, exposing the
small pile of raisins.

                    BRENDA (CONT.)
            One of these little buggers
            got away from me.

Joel lifts an eyebrow, then moves to
Brenda's side and gives her shoulder
a quick squeeze.

                    JOEL
            Yes, this raisin slinger is
            mine. Brenda's graduating
            in June.

Brenda smiles sweetly. Marybeth
extends her hand to Brenda, who brushes
the raisins into a wastebasket and
completes the handshake.

Marybeth wipes her hand on her skirt
and walks behind the check-in desk.
Joel follows her, stands on the other
side. Marybeth winks at him.

                    MARYBETH
            Remember when Corbin flashed
            his boxers at our graduation?
            Principal Lorman—

Brenda's phone CHIMES with an incoming
text, interrupting the conversation.
Brenda walks toward the stairs to
read the text and get away from
Marybeth.

Marybeth rests her elbows on the countertop, leans forward toward Joel, who also leans toward her. She plays flirtatiously with the beads on her blouse and talks quietly to Joel, who is clearly taken in. He laughs at something she says.

INSERT - BRENDA'S PHONE

Text from Angie: Can u come over now? I need to c u.

Brenda texts back: Your mom told u?

Text from Angie: Told me what?

BACK TO SCENE

Distressed, Brenda looks at Joel.

> BRENDA
> (loudly)
> Dad!

He turns away from Marybeth and hurries to Brenda's side. Brenda shows him the text from Angie.

Marybeth makes herself busy with the computer.

Joel takes Brenda's arm, guides her up the stairs.

INT. UPSTAIRS SITTING ROOM - MOMENTS
LATER

Joel sits on a couch near the
fireplace. Brenda sits in a chair
opposite him. She irons her palms
against her jeans, then jumps up and
starts looking through books on a
bookshelf. She slides one out and
absently flips through it.

                    JOEL
          Mrs. Beckwell told me
          she'd talk to Angie as
          soon as she closed the
          antique store. Maybe she
          got delayed?

                    BRENDA
          Maybe. What do you think I
          should do?

Brenda receives another text.

INSERT - PHONE

Text from Angie: Mom couldn't talk,
last-minute customer. What's going
on?

Brenda texts back: One sec.

BACK TO SCENE

                    BRENDA (CONT.)
                 (anguished)
          Maybe I should be the one
          to tell her?

                    JOEL
          No matter what, she'll
          want to talk to you.
          You're in charge. It's
          been a difficult day. It
          can wait.

                    BRENDA
          I think I'd rather be done
          with it.

                    JOEL
          Do you want me to go over
          there with you?

Brenda frowns, sets the book on an
end table, picks up a magazine, rolls
it into a tube, wrings and releases
it.

                    BRENDA
          I'm not sure. I'm kind of
          scared, ya know? What if
          she despises me?

                    JOEL
          There's no way she could
          despise you. She loves you.
          If anything, she's going
          to be terribly upset. Just

like Mrs. Beckwell, but
she's coping with it, and
so will Angie.

Brenda shrugs, non-committedly,
releases the magazine. Joel fidgets
with the tassels on a throw pillow.
His eyes follow Brenda, trying to
read her cues.

                    JOEL (CONT.)
          I could drive you over,
          wait for you in the car
          until you're done, if you
          want to talk to her in
          private?

Brenda's eyes flicker toward Joel.
She moves to the couch, sits by his
side, and rests her head against his
shoulder. He drapes his arms around
her, closes his eyes briefly, fights
back his obvious distress. When
Brenda abruptly sits up and looks at
him, his face relaxes.

                    BRENDA
          I couldn't have dealt with
          this without you. Thanks
          for handling Mom.

                    JOEL
             (quietly)
          It would have been a little
          easier if you had told her
          I was coming.

                    BRENDA
          But then I would've had to
          explain why, or lie, and I
          didn't want to do either.

Joel frowns slightly, nods. Brenda
becomes more animated, upset. She
moves away from Joel.

                    BRENDA (CONT.)
          You see how she carried on,
          made it about her? Like
          what happened to me was a
          judgment on her parenting
          skills? Sometimes I get sick
          of being the responsible,
          rational one.

Joel stands, walks to the fireplace,
turns to Brenda. He loosens his tie,
rolls up his shirt sleeves exposing
a small knotted CELTIC TATTOO with
Brenda's name.

                    JOEL
          You know, you two have a
          lot of positive traits in
          common.

                    BRENDA
            (skeptically)
          You're kidding?

                    JOEL
          No, not at all. You have her
          courage,   determination,
          loyalty.

Brenda snorts loudly.

                    BRENDA
          Dad, this is Mom. The woman
          you barely speak to?

                    JOEL
          Yes. One and the same. Do
          you know what she went
          through to have you?

Brenda's eyes grow wide.

                    JOEL (CONT.)
          Normally I wouldn't speak
          ill of the dead, but your
          grandparents   were   the
          worst   kind   of   parents
          imaginable. Has she ever
          talked to you about them?

                    BRENDA
          No. Never.

Joel sits in a chair, leans toward
Brenda. His face is pensive.

                    JOEL
          When   your   mother   found
          out she was pregnant and

we decided we weren't going to marry, your grandparents insisted she have an abortion.

            BRENDA
    An abortion? Why? Because I was…a mistake?

            JOEL
Oh God, Sweet B. Your mother never saw you as a mistake. She may have regretted the fight with Charlie, then sleeping with me. But not once did she regret you. She wanted you. Her parents turned their backs on her. There's no explanation for their behavior, other than to hurt your mom. She moved out of their house and made a life for the two of you. That took incredible courage. She's done her best. I hope you know that.

Brenda fidgets with her hair.

            BRENDA
I do, it's just hard sometimes. She's constantly fighting with Aunt Elana.

                    JOEL
          Elana was always the perfect
          one. Even when Elana and
          Charlie got together,
          your grandparents sided
          with Elana. Rubbed it in
          your mother's face. It
          wasn't right. Elana knew
          your mother still loved
          Charlie.
               (beat)
          I don't think Elana
          intentionally set out
          to hurt your mother, but
          she did, and she used me
          to justify her actions.
          Despite everything, your
          mom has stayed loyal to
          her. Your mom's a good
          person, and I admire her
          for her strength.

                    BRENDA
          Then why didn't you marry
          her?

Joel hesitates. Brenda looks at him
with eyes filled with pain, then
drops her gaze to her lap. She uses
a finger to trace the pattern on the
sofa.

                    JOEL
          You knew we never loved
          each other, right? And

even though I asked her to marry me, she didn't want us to end up resenting each other. She knew I wanted NYU law school, and she knew I'd give it up. She didn't want me to.
(beat)
That's loyalty and courage and determination and a hell of a lot more. She made the choice. In the end, it was best for all of us.

Joel moves over to Brenda's side, and even though Brenda won't look at him, he stays focused on her.

JOEL (CONT.)
Just so you know, if it weren't for her, I wouldn't have the most important person in my life—you. I will always be grateful to her for being brave enough to stand up to her parents, for choosing to have you.

He tucks a piece of hair behind Brenda's ear. A tear rolls down her cheek. He brushes it away.

JOEL (CONT.)
(whispering)
I love you, Sweet B. And as
much as what you've gone
through kills me, I'm also
proud of you for being
courageous and strong, and
for being a loyal friend
to Angie.

Brenda turns her head, rests her
cheek against her knee.

BRENDA
I'm not sure about that.
Most of the time, I've
been scared and confused
about how I feel about her.
Sometimes I can't stand
being near her, sometimes
she frustrates me, but
she's also my best friend.

JOEL
Well…that's understandable.
And yes, you were scared,
are scared, but you could
have isolated yourself
from her. You could have
stopped being her friend.
You didn't. This was a
huge secret to hold for
all those years. But even
now, you're thinking about
how it will affect her.

You even protected your
mother, knowing I'd cope
better than she could.
   (beat)
It took courage to pick up
the phone and tell me what
you went through. It took
courage to tell the police.
You own that courage, okay?
Know you did the right
thing. Because of it, that
animal will remain locked
up for a long time.

Brenda becomes more distressed,
surprising Joel. She stands, picks
up the curled magazine, rolls it
tightly again.

            JOEL (CONT.)
   What's the matter?

She faces him.

            BRENDA
   What if they can't extract
   the DNA evidence? Could
   the case get dismissed?

Relief spreads across Joel's face.

            JOEL
   This is textbook. By not
   washing your clothes you
   preserved the sample

impeccably. To put them in the shoebox took tremendous foresight. I'm confident there'll be no issues.

                    BRENDA
               (mumbling)
          I think we can credit "Law
          and Order: SVU."

                    JOEL
          No. You.

Brenda's phone CHIMES with an incoming text.

INSERT – BRENDA'S PHONE

Text from Angie: Freaking out here. What's going on????? Call me!!!! Fyi. Jordan asked me 2 prom!

BACK TO SCENE

                    BRENDA
          I don't feel very brave
          right now. The whole world
          feels like it's crashing
          down on me.

Brenda waves her phone.

                    BRENDA (CONT.)
          I'm not sure I can get
          through this.

He walks over to her, lifts her chin.

> JOEL
> (with conviction)
> One day at a time. One
> step at a time. Whatever
> it takes, understand? I'm
> here for you, and we'll
> get through it together.
> You believe me?

She nods.

> JOEL (CONT.)
> What do you want to do
> about Angie?

INT. BRENDA'S CAR/EXT. ANGIE'S HOUSE
- NIGHT

Joel parks Brenda's SUV in front of
Angie's silhouetted house. Brenda
picks at the soles of her sneakers.

> JOEL (CONT.)
> I won't go anywhere. Text
> me if you need me.

The moment Brenda opens her car door,
Angie comes running out of the house
and hugs Brenda. Angie holds the door
open, sees Joel looking at her.

ANGIE
(enthusiastically)
Hi Mr. Hannes. Thanks for
dropping off Brenda. Are
you sure I'm not taking
her away from you?

Brenda's eyes focus on the house. She
takes a step toward it. Joel huddles
down to look at Brenda. Angie tracks
his gaze, turns around, eyes Brenda
inquisitively.

BRENDA
(to Angie)
I need to use your bathroom.

Angie smiles at her, but it dies
when Brenda doesn't smile back.

ANGIE
Okay.

Joel steps out of the car, watches
Brenda with concern. Angie turns to
Joel, unsure of what's going on. Her
eyes bounce between Joel and Brenda.
Brenda walks into the house.

ANGIE (CONT.)
Is everything okay with
Brenda? She's…been distant
lately.

> JOEL
>
> No, not entirely. But
> she'll explain. She's
> working through it.

> ANGIE
>
> So...you know why she was so
> upset the other day?

> JOEL
>
> That's why I'm here.

> ANGIE
>
> Just so you know, my
> feelings for her haven't
> changed. No matter what I
> love her as a friend.

Angie smiles at him. Joel is baffled
by Angie's comments.

> JOEL
>
> Well, that's good. I'll be
> right here in case Brenda
> needs me.

Angie's eyes dart between Joel and
the front door. She opens her mouth
to ask Joel a question, but decides
against it. She turns, walks to the
house. When she reaches the door and
steps inside, MRS. BECKWELL (44)
pulls up and parks in the driveway.
Joel waits for her.

INT. ANGIE'S HOUSE/HALLWAY OUTSIDE
BATHROOM - NIGHT

Brenda pushes the bathroom door wide
open. She takes a step forward,
places her toes at the edge of the
threshold, but can't step in. She
extends her hands, braces herself.
Her eyes sweep across the bathroom,
focus on the ANTIQUE DOLLHOUSE PIECES
displayed in shadow boxes.

BEGIN FLASHBACK:

INT. ANGIE'S HOUSE/BATHROOM - NIGHT

Brenda (12) sits on the toilet; a
scarred hand covers her mouth, another
one pushes against the interior of
her thigh. Her underwear's against
the wall. A large, tattooed MAN yanks
her off the toilet, shoves her onto
the floor. He climbs on top of her.
She tries to fight him off and he
laughs a soft, menacing laugh in her
ear.

> MAN
> (throaty whisper)
> You struggle, you attempt
> to scream, you flinch, and
> I'll kill you and then
> I'll do the same to Angie.
> Stay still and I'll leave

her alone for now. Nod if
you understand.

He blocks her nose, presses his hand
harder against her mouth. Her eyes
grow wild with terror. She nods, and
the second he frees her nostrils she
sucks in an audible breath.

A ZIPPER OPENS.

INT. ANGIE'S HOUSE/BATHROOM - MOMENTS
LATER (FLASHBACK)

The man drags Brenda (12) to her feet.
His hand still covers her mouth. He
shoves her against the vanity so she
can see the dim image of herself
in the mirror. He leans over her,
shoves her head forward, pushes her
hair aside, and marks her with his
teeth at the back of her neck.

> MAN
> (raspy whisper)
> You're going to sit in
> that bathtub, count to a
> thousand, and then you're
> going to get up, go back
> to bed. If you ever say a
> word, I promise you I'll
> find you and kill you and
> Angie and her whore mother
> too. Not a word. Nod if
> you understand.

Brenda nods.

END FLASHBACK.

INT. ANGIE'S HOUSE/HALLWAY OUTSIDE
BATHROOM - MOMENTS LATER

Brenda crumples to the floor and
begins to rock. Angie sees Brenda,
sprints to her side.

                    ANGIE
          Brenda? What's wrong?

Brenda moans. Angie drops down next
to Brenda. Brenda stares into the
bathroom. Angie notices, shoves the
door open farther with her foot,
trying to understand what Brenda's
looking at. Angie becomes agitated.

                    ANGIE (CONT.)
          Brenda? Are you okay?
             (beat)
          You want me to call your
          dad?

Brenda takes a deep breath, exhales.
Her eyes refocus on Angie.

                    BRENDA
          N-no.
             (mumbling to herself)
          Safe. I'm safe.

ANGIE
(softly, with concern)
Of course you're safe. I'm
right here.
(beat)
Did you see something in
the bathroom?

Brenda's hand twitches at her side.

BRENDA
(whispering)
The night the Demon broke
in. The last time I slept
over. The reason why I
don't want to spend any
amount of time here?
(voice drops lower)
I was raped. In there by—-

Brenda's voice chokes. Angie's face
morphs into shock. Then she starts
to freak out. Brenda watches her
reaction, then diverts her eyes.

ANGIE
Oh my God. Oh my God! Th-
the Demon did that to you?

Brenda nods. A tear spills from her
eye.

                    BRENDA
              (choking up)
          I woke up during the middle
          of the night and had to
          go to the bathroom. I-I
          didn't lock the door. He-
          he said he'd kill me, kill
          you, your mother.

Tears stream down Brenda's face.
Angie also starts to shake, cry.
She clutches Brenda. They hold each
other.

                    ANGIE
          Oh my God. Oh my God. I'm
          so sorry. I'm so sorry.

Brenda looks into Angie's eyes,
unsure how to feel. Brenda pushes
Angie away suddenly, needing to
escape. She stands.

                    BRENDA
              (mumbling   mostly   to
              herself)
          Not your fault. I told. I
          finally told my dad, the
          police. I'm okay. It was
          a long time ago. Memories
          I had to face. I'm okay.
          Safe.

Brenda clutches at her shirt, yanks
down the hem.

> BRENDA (CONT.)
> I need air.

Angie stares at her in shock. Panic starts to overwhelm Brenda. She weaves her way through the house to the front door. Angie follows her, scared.

> ANGIE
> Don't go. Please talk to me. Tell me what I can do.

> BRENDA
> Just leave me alone!

EXT. ANGIE'S HOUSE, STREET — CONTINUOUS - NIGHT

Brenda runs out of the house, down the porch steps. Angie follows, calls out to her. Brenda ignores her, picks up speed. Joel is standing outside Brenda's car comforting Mrs. Beckwell. He breaks away.

> JOEL
> Brenda! Angie, what's going on?

> ANGIE
> I'll go after her.

Angie kicks off her FLIP-FLOPS and tries to catch up. In flight mode, Brenda doesn't hear her father. She runs faster, wanting to be away from the house, the memories, and Angie.

EXT. OTUMBA PARK – CONTINUOUS – NIGHT

Brenda doesn't slow down until she's partially hidden in moonlit Otumba Park. She stops by a clump of birch trees near the beach, rests her hands on her knees, and catches her breath. As she straightens up, someone reaches out and grabs her shoulder. Brenda instinctively goes into self-defense mode, attacks her attacker, kneeing him in the groin. He goes down. She runs, never seeing who attacked her.

> ANGIE
> (out of breath)
> Brenda, stop! That was Emerson!

Emerson curls into a fetal position, moaning. He turns his head and gets sick. Angie hovers above him, unsure what to do.

Brenda stops. Her chest is heaving as she tries to catch her breath. She turns around and faces Angie and Emerson. Still breathing hard, she walks slowly and cautiously over to them.

Remorseful and distressed, Brenda crouches down.

> BRENDA
> What were you doing scaring the crap out of me like that?

> EMERSON
> (through intense pain)
> I...saw you running. I... called your name. A few times. I...just wanted to make sure...you were okay.

Emerson rolls onto his knees. Grunts. Angie helps him to his feet.

> EMERSON (CONT.)
> (embarrassed)
> I'm fine.

Emerson tries to laugh it off, but it comes out as a grimace.

> ANGIE
> I thought you left the park hours ago?

> EMERSON
> Yeah, well. I had. But I couldn't find my wallet.

Emerson pauses. Fortifies himself before he continues.

> EMERSON (CONT.)
> I came back to search for it. I thought that maybe it fell out of my pocket.

> ANGIE
> Did you find it?

> EMERSON
> No.

Emerson takes a few bowlegged steps. Bends over.

> ANGIE
> C'mon. We can go to my house and get some ice. Then Brenda and I can come back and look for your wallet.

> EMERSON
> No. That's all right. Really. The pain's not so bad anymore. My car is over there.

He points to the parking lot.

> EMERSON (CONT.)
> I'll just rest for a few minutes.

Angie drapes his arm over her shoulder, wraps her other one around his waist. Brenda walks next to them, head down, as Emerson hobbles toward his car.

Angie releases Emerson. He unlocks his door. Brenda holds it open while he gingerly climbs in.

> BRENDA
> I'm so sorry, Emerson.

> EMERSON
> My fault too. I probably shouldn't have come up behind you like that. I didn't mean to scare you.

> ANGIE
> Isn't that your wallet?

Angie points to the floor between Emerson's seat and the driver's door. Disgusted, Emerson reaches for it, tosses it onto the passenger seat.

> BRENDA
> I hope you'll be okay.

> Emerson nods, turns the ignition.Brenda shuts his car door.

> FADE OUT.

TWENTY-ONE

"To go into solitude, a man needs to retire as much from his chamber as from society. I am not solitary whilst I read and write, though nobody is with me. But if a man would be alone, let him look at the stars."

Ralph Waldo Emerson

EMERSON

STURGEON BAY   WEDNESDAY, 10:12 P.M.

I DRIVE AWAY from Otumba Park, from Angie and Brenda, and am tempted to go home, pull the covers over my head, and not emerge until graduation. Those two have managed to make my life a living hell, and I'm beginning to wonder if Frankie's call detonated a cosmic explosion that's now spinning my life out of control.

Unfortunately, right now, home is not an option. For the thousandth time, my phone chirps with another text message from Isabelle. I ignore it like I've ignored most of her other texts and calls along with the rest of my family's. I already said I'm fine, that they have nothing to worry about. How many times and how many ways am I supposed to say it? Even though it's getting late, my balls are killing me, and I'm tired, the statistical probability of someone still being awake and waiting for me to come home is one hundred percent. The last thing I need is another lecture.

Craving caffeine and something cold, I turn into the McDonald's drive-thru and order a cup of coffee, a cup of ice, large fries, and a Big Mac. I set the cup of ice between my thighs, sip the coffee, and devour the rest of my food. I've had enough of driving around. I need a place that's quiet and deserted. I head toward Whitefish Dunes State Park.

As I hoped, I'm alone. Walking along the beach is like having my own private Caribbean island minus sunshine, seventy-five degrees, and a cabana. So it's not paradise.

But a close second.

Barefoot, I twist my feet until they're buried in the cool sand. I stare at the water and am lulled by Lake Michigan's waves peaking and crashing and retreating. The beauty of the blue-black sky, the hazy reflection of the three-quarter moon on the water, the smell of damp beach, and the gritty sand between my toes all bring a calm I haven't experienced since before Frankie's phone call. This is exactly what I need—solitude.

A call from Isabelle shatters it. I let the call go to voice mail and plan to delete it, but some unknown force stops me. Collapsing onto the beach, I hit PLAY and SPEAKER and listen to her message.

"Hey bro. I know you're angry with me, and I wish you wouldn't be. Do me a favor. No, do yourself a favor because you deserve it. Stop living your life like you can change the past. You can't. Stop trying to be everyone's hero. I love you. We all love you. You know that, right? Oh, and don't be pissed with me. Or Mom. Especially Mom. We're *all* looking out for your best interests. Go with it. I know you're okay, but text Mom anyway. You know how she worries. Bye."

It takes me a few minutes to regain my composure.

I text Mom: *"I'm fine, Mom. Bought McDs. <3 u."*

As I power down, she texts back. *"Love u. School night. Don't be out too late."* Yeah, thanks for the reminder. I have a tendency to mix up my weekends with weekdays. That's why I'm a beer-bellied high-school dropout.

Snark aside, I think about what Isabelle said and decide she scored a few points, but missed some too. I'm not trying to punish myself for the past. Or relive it. What I'm trying to do is make sure the past doesn't repeat itself. We're obligated to do that.

When we studied the Holocaust in European History, we had a survivor come to our school. He showed us the number tattooed on his arm. He talked about the horrors he endured in Auschwitz and Dachau. He said, "Never forget."

If you forget the past, you're doomed to repeat it.

I can't and won't forget my past.

I get that I was too young, too oblivious, too late to help the woman who sacrificed her life for mine. But that doesn't mean I shouldn't be prepared to help someone else, right? If we see someone we can assist, don't we have a moral obligation to do so?

Yeah, I definitely can see this as a main topic of conversation at our next party, especially since I most likely would be the only one sober. I need...more.

I wish I could talk to Frankie.

Or knock my head against a wall. Why am I thinking about her? I'm letting her infiltrate my brain, giving her way too much importance. I scan the lake, searching for the horizon, but water and sky blend seamlessly into one. A seagull squawks and rides the air currents over the lake, and I realize I'm as close to reaching that bird as I am to finding Frankie. She's already turned my life upside down, inside out, and wreaked havoc on my perfectly organized, not-so-normal life. Never again will I make a promise to a stranger.

It's time to get her out of my system and get my mind focused on what's real. I glance around, relish in the peace, then strip down. Instead of wading into Lake Michigan's frigid spring water, I dive in. The shock of it sends thunderbolt daggers into my bones, a pain that wakes me up. I flip onto my back, stretch out my arms.

The cold disappears, the past disappears, the future disappears. For one perfect minute *I* disappear. I'm mesmerized by the universe, by endless possibilities, and then I'm struck by the idea that somewhere Frankie could be looking at the same constellations, the same moon, the same vast sky at this very minute. It frustrates me and makes me hopeful.

Along with many other confusing emotions, I've been angry with her, too. For shaking me up, for rattling my world, for using a nom de plume. *Enough already.* I stand, dip my cupped hands into the lake. As the water drips between my fingers, I resolve to stop obsessing over Frankie, and I let her go.

I drag myself onto the beach. Compared to the water, the air's warm. I use my T-shirt for a towel and brush the grit from my numb skin. Putting on my boxers and jeans is like trying to grab a flopping fish with my hands. I'm shivering so much that my limbs don't cooperate the way my brain wants them to. My jaw aches from my chattering teeth.

I trudge back to the car and collapse onto my seat. I crank the heat to high, then flip through radio channels. Frank Sinatra croons "New York, New York," bringing Frankie to mind—again—endangering my vow to forget about her. I change the station, opting for hard rock, and drive the twenty minutes home.

To my huge relief, no one's awake. I fork out leftover lasagna onto a paper plate, forgo heating it up in the microwave, pour a glass of milk, and bring the food to my room.

TEXT FROM ANGIE: *"R u ok? Pain?"*

Without a doubt there are stranger things in this world than having your ex check to see whether your balls still bounce. I could ignore her, but I'd prefer that we don't add this to our list of public discussions.

I text back: *"Fine. How's Brenda?"*

Text from Angie: *"I'll call u."*

She does. That guy, whoever he was and whatever horrible things he did to Brenda, must be one Evil Bastard.

I'M PROFOUNDLY GRATEFUL these swimmers will be able to dive in and score a ten in the gene pool. Yeah, I was worried whether or not the head-banging Brenda gave me would impact my solid platform, especially since I haven't jumped off the high dive yet. Thankfully, before I collapsed from exhaustion, life was looking up.

TWENTY-TWO

"Every sweet has its sour; every evil its good."
Ralph Waldo Emerson

ANGIE
STURGEON BAY   THURSDAY, 12:14 A.M.

Shivvvering,
I squint,
press my nose
against shadowed
glass. Jordan sleeps
propped up in bed.
His window's unlocked,
sash sssssssssslides up,
creeeeeaks. I climb
in. Jordan's eyes
open.

He taps
a spot next
to him. I snuggle
in against his chest,
bare but for a sheet,
I peek. Boxers
underneath.

He whispers,

"If your sperm donor ever sees
the light of day and gets near you,
I'll take these hands
and strangle him for what
he's done to Brenda, to you."

Jordan shifts, holds
me tightly, strokes
my hair, strokes
my back, calms
the gripping
fear. Wipes
away my

```
     t   t
   e   e
  a       a
   r   r
     s
```

"Talk to me."

"I didn't know.
Ididn't know. Ididn'tknow!"

"How could you?"

"The morning of
the burglary Brenda
was sick, throwing
up, shaking. Mom
said it was the flu.
The missing Tiffany
lamp? Precious silver
candlesticks? Collection
of first-edition books?

I didn't care. My worry?
Catching Brenda's bug
and missing our summer
family trip to Six Flags
Great America. That's
what I cared about.
Even then I was a
lousy friend."

"You were twelve."

Images carve
into my mind,
evil, terrible,
horrifying.
Brenda bruised,
branded, raped
while I slept
sound and safe.

Silence. Years of secrets
kept to protect
against the Demon's threat
to kill us. It makes
me wonder about Brenda's
OCD. Her odd quirk
she always brushed off.

Doors. Windows.
Lock/check. Lock/check. Lock/check. Lock/check.
Lock.
Pause.
Lock/check. Lock/check. Lock/check. Lock/check.
Lock.
She hated when I

questioned her.

> "There's nothing
> wrong with wanting
> to make sure a door is secure,"
> she had argued.

What could I say?

When I wasn't with
Emerson, Brenda
would pick me up,
drop me off, but never
step inside.
I teased. I cajoled.
I begged. I laughed.
The worst friend. I am
a certified evil bitch.

I snuggle closer
to Jordan. His
eyes pop
open. I say,
"It should have
been ME.
NOT Brenda.
He wanted ME.
It should
have been me."

> "It shouldn't have been anyone."

But it was.
Guilt
cloaks my skin.

Regret
coats my tongue.
Sour.
Spit
it out
and forget.

I
lean in
to Jordan for
a kiss, run my hands
over his thighs, higher, higher,
higher until...

"Stop."

"But...why?"

One beat. Two.

"Angie, I'm here
to be your friend."
He holds me closer.
"It's late. Relax. Let's
get some sleep."

"But I don't—"

My cell vibrates.
Incoming call from
Brenda. I answer.

"Hi, how are you?
Are you
okay?

I'm sooo
sorry, Bren.
What can I do?"

Did you speak to Emerson?
Is he okay?

"No permanent
damage.
He's fine.
He wasn't upset. Only
worried
about you. When
I explained—"

What? You didn't tell him, did you?

"No! 'Course
not. He saw you
at the station. You
went ninja on him.
He's smart.
He knew something
happened. So
to explain, I said
that a guy—"

A guy? That's brilliant, Ang. Real smart.

"Emerson doesn't
know. I swear I didn't
give any details. I
promise I—"

       Tears

     r   d

   r   o

  r   w

  i   n

   c   d

  k   o

   l   w

    e   n

      my

     cheeks.

You shouldn't have said ANYTHING!

NOT ONE

WORD!

My life, my story,

and it's

NOT

yours to tell.

I'm going to text Emerson.

Tell him to mind his own damn business.

You should too.

If this gets out, I'm blaming YOU.

Click.

TWENTY-THREE

"Why should I hasten to solve every riddle which life offers me?
I am well assured that the Questioner, who brings me so many
problems, will bring the answers also in due time."
Ralph Waldo Emerson

EMERSON
STURGEON BAY   THURSDAY, 7:18 A.M.

MY DOOR CREAKS open, startling me awake. "Mia, don't you know how to knock?"

"It's Mom, and I did knock. You must not have heard me. If you don't get up, you're going to be late for school." She's dressed for whatever fitness class is in fashion this month: yoga, Zumba, Pilates—I can't keep track.

"I'm getting up." I say, hoping she'll take the hint and leave. No way am I giving her a full view of my boxers. But just like the rest of the torrential rain of luck pouring down on me this week, she comes in, sits at the foot of my bed.

"How's my boy today?" Her voice is filled with love and concern, reminding me of when I was a fearful little kid hovering by her side. A part of me wouldn't mind being small again, to crawl into her lap and let her hold me tightly.

"In need of a shower."

She nods, but it's clear from the way she avoids my eyes, she was expecting more than an answer on hygiene. Just as I'm formulating something to reassure her, she says, "I made an eleven o'clock appointment for you to see Dr. Shale."

"What? No! I'm not going."

"Yes. You are."

"I'm eighteen," I say through my teeth.

"And living at home and our responsibility. I already left a message on the school's attendance line."

So this is what Isabelle meant when she said don't be pissed at Mom. "Screw that," I say.

"That'll cost you the bathrooms," she says, calmly. "You can scrub them after school." Of course. The one job she knows I despise.

"It's your money," I call after her.

∽

10:53 A.M.

I PARK, CLIMB out of the car, and glare at the medical office building. What am I doing here? Am I that much of a conformist that I refuse to defy my mother? I could pay the last-minute eighty-dollar cancellation fee and be done with it. I've always hated this parking lot, hated this building, and standing here is as close to traveling back in time as I'll ever get. Yet, here I am, seriously considering going in. Why can't psychologists make house calls? Why do people have to risk public humiliation?

Welcome to my life, a perfect storm to sink the little dignity I have left. Brenda stomps toward me like a prizefighter aiming for a knockout, and clearly I'm the unwilling sparring partner. "Why are you here?" she shouts.

I hold my ground, but watch her clenched fists swinging at her sides. "None of your business. Why are *you* here?"

"Same."

I should head inside, but I'm not sure it's safe to move. I study Brenda and I'd rather be in the Minnesota Vikings stadium wearing my Green Bay Packers sweatshirt than standing here with her. "Are you going to come after me?" I ask, cautiously taking a step toward the hood. "I have an eleven o'clock appointment."

In that instant, everything about Brenda changes. Her body shifts from ass-whipping warrior to... well, not quite friendly, but approachable, and her expression becomes a mask of composure. "Sorry I didn't expect to see you here."

"Same." I slide my feet forward and keep watch.

"What did Angie tell you?"

"Absolutely nothing. I haven't seen or talked to Angie since we broke up. Days ago," I add for emphasis.

Catching on, her eyes narrow with a heavy dose of skepticism. "What about the police station?"

"Again, I have no idea what you're talking about."

She nods and almost, but not quite, smiles. Her gaze drops to my crotch. "Sorry about...you know." She looks away, shamefaced.

"There's a club," I say.

She turns to me and I swear she has more expressions than a mime. "What?"

"The 'My Life Sucks Club.' I'm a full-fledged member. It's free to join if you're interested."

Apparently, I've rendered Brenda speechless. Then she bursts out laughing. "You? Perfect Emerson? Breaking up with Angie and getting your balls bashed qualifies, huh? Poor baby. I am *not* sympathetic."

No, I wouldn't expect her to be. I let a slow smile spread across my face and lock my eyes on her. Let her see my true colors.

"I have something, highly effective for shitty days. In my glove box. That is, if you're interested. Normally, I keep an inventory of six different ones. You can take your pick of blue or yellow. I'm out of green. That was always Angie's first choice when I got a fresh supply." I pause. "Now that I think about it, no little brown ones either. Thanks to you, I took those last night. You know, to help ease the pain. There might be one or two orange or red ones left, but I'm not sure. They're pretty popular. And since it's your first time, no charge. We'll call it a peace offering."

The shock and confusion on her face exposes are deeply satisfying. More than satisfying—vindicating. I'm happy to have whatever picture-perfect image she had of my life break into fine crumbs. I lift my chin and keep my gaze steady, an unspoken challenge tossed right back at her.

"Um—"

"Guaranteed to improve your mood and help you relax." I take her in from her combat boots—grateful not to have met those—to her electric-blue eyes. I feign superiority, as much as I can muster. "Clearly you need it. Trust me, they did wonders for Angie. So, what'll be?" If I could snap a picture of her face right now without risking Brenda smashing my phone to bits, I would.

"Um, whatever you think is best?"

Inwardly, I smirk. "Good choice." I open my passenger door, poke my hand into the glove box.

"So, how long have you been…um—"

"Making deliveries?" I suggest, raising one eyebrow and lowering the other, a genetic gift I inherited from my father.

Brenda comes around to my side with her hands in her hoodie pockets, way too close for comfort. It's not easy to concentrate when she scrapes her boot against the asphalt like a bull ready to charge a matador. I don't need a reminder of how long the sting of her slap can last, or the damaging force of her knee. "Do you mind?" I say, sweeping my hand toward her.

She takes two baby-steps back. I chomp down on my molars, take a deep breath through my nose, and pull out several snack bags. I don't bother to check the contents. Cradling them close to my body, I say, "Hold out your hand."

I drop an entire bag into her palm and scramble behind the trunk, getting far enough away to defend myself, if need be.

"What the hell?"

I laugh.

"I thought—"

"I knew what you thought. Your expression was priceless. A MasterCard moment."

"You asshole!" But at least she says it with a smile. She opens the bag and dumps the entire contents into her mouth, chewing and talking at the same time. "So Anee got the een ones? No onder she's a orny itch." Brenda swallows. "You actually sorted them for her?"

I shrug. Yeah, I was an idiot.

"More?" I don't wait, just toss the bag of blue M&Ms over the Camaro's roof. She snatches it out of the air like an infielder catching a pop-up. I check the time on my cell. Five minutes late. And even though it's an appointment with Dr. Shale, I get antsy not being punctual. "I better go." I lock my doors. "See you."

"Come to the overnight party on the island tomorrow," she calls. "We're camping."

I stop, glance back. "Will I live?"

"Highly probable."

"I'll think about it."

⌒

THOUGH I'M LATE, Dr. Shale is even later. I sit in one of six cushy waiting room chairs, flip through an old *Sports Illustrated* magazine. I force my leg to stop bouncing, but a few seconds later, it starts up again. The invisible band around my heart gives a quick squeeze as if to remind me of why I started seeing Dr. Shale in the first place. I check my phone and decide he gets four more minutes before I walk out.

I've skimmed this article on Aaron Rodgers three times and have barely comprehended a word. Moving on, I begin one on the athleticism of cheerleaders when I hear Dr. Shale say, "I'll see you next week."

I drop my head lower, practically planting my nose between my knees. My view of his exiting patient consists of black heels and the bottom eighth of a floor-length red skirt. I recognize Dr. Shale's worn loafers. The outer door clicks closed.

"Emerson."

Not one thing has changed in Dr. Shale's office. Same family wedding photos on his desk, same books on his shelves, which makes me think he's either anal about where he puts them or he never reads them. Same leather couch, but with more worn spots, same dead plant in the corner, same landscape paintings on the wall.

"You should toss that," I say, pointing to the pot of dirt. He eyes the petrified stalk like he's never seen it before and leaves it right where it is. He sits in the same chair opposite the couch. Picking up the same egg timer, he sets it for an hour and places it in the usual spot on his desk, just over his left shoulder. I have the worst case of déjà vu.

"All right, Emerson. It's been..." He flips through my chart, "...over two years since I've seen you. Why are you here?"

"My mother set up the visit. I didn't have a choice."

"You're eighteen. I believe you can make choices."

"Tell her that."

He leans back, assessing me. Once again, I force myself to stop bouncing my leg. "There must be a reason why you decided to come today."

"I don't know."

He waits and I watch the damn minutes tick off the timer. We could sit here for the rest of the fifty-seven minutes. I've done it before. Or I could walk out. I've done that too.

He's annoyingly patient.

I do not want to talk about Angie or the gif fiasco. Or Brenda. But Frankie?

"There's this girl," I begin. Interest stirs in his blue-gray eyes. "I don't even know who she is. I've never met her, but I talked to her on the phone. Once. I had her grandmother's old phone number and—" I wipe my damp palms on my jeans. "I guess she wanted to find out who it belonged to, so she called."

Dr. Shale's gaze flickers to my chest and I become conscious that I've been rubbing my scar. I clasp my hands together. "I'm pretty sure the reason why she called was because it was a test."

"A test?"

"To see if maybe her grandma was watching over her. You know, from the other side. When she called, it was like three A.M. I just happened to be up—studying—and I answered. She said that it was a sign from her dead grandma."

"Uh-huh. And do you believe in those kind of things?"

"Do you?"

He hesitates, then with conviction says, "I do."

"Why?"

He picks up a small oval photograph tucked between two larger pictures on his desk and hands it to me. It's of an adorable little boy, maybe two years old.

"Since my grandson died, my daughter finds his toys in the most unusual places, even after she's locked them away in a closet. So has her husband. If my wife and I hadn't witnessed it ourselves, I'm not sure we'd believe it."

I had no idea he even had a grandson. "I'm sorry for your loss."

He takes the picture back, returns it to its place. "It's my unscientific opinion that our grandson was letting us know that he's all right. My daughter finds comfort each time she finds a misplaced toy. It's helped her go on. The loss was hard on us all, but for her..." For a moment, his voice trails off along with his gaze. "I've read too many stories, talked to too many patients to dismiss the possibility. But that's me. You need to decide for yourself."

I let his answer sink in. A shiver sweeps across my arms, producing goose bumps as I remember the smell of lavender, the eerie sense that I wasn't in my room alone while I talked to Frankie, and the numerous other unusual signs. I say, "I believe it too."

"You want to talk about it?"

"I've been thinking about the woman."

"The one who saved you?"

"Yeah. And I uh...guess I've been wondering if maybe I owed some kind of payback. Like she saved my life, so I had to save someone else's? What do you think?"

"Hmm, personally, I'm not sure that's how the Universe works."

"Then how does it work?"

"What do you believe?"

"That's what I believe."

"So, you owe a life?"

"I—Yeah, I do."

"I'm not sure that's for you to decide."

"How would you know?" I challenge. "Who's to say what my purpose is? I mean, it doesn't seem fair that she was put on this earth to save me. That doesn't make sense. A person shouldn't have to die, not when—" I swallow. "Not when there are people who are left behind."

"What was it about your conversation with that girl that made you think about this again?"

I stretch out my legs, cross my ankles. "She was going to kill herself, at least I think she would have gone through with it. But I picked up, and...well, we made some promises to each other."

"Which were?"

"I broke up with my girlfriend, changed my phone number, and she promised she'd go on, live."

He folds his hands in his lap, rubs his thumb back and forth against his pointer finger. "And you trusted each other to keep these promises?"

I nod.

"So." He drags it out, lets it hang in the air.

I can't speak. I force my eyelids open as far as they'll go.

His head bobs in a slow, gentle rhythm. "You're wondering if you can stop? If you're even? If you've paid back the Universe for the woman who died in your place." The last part is a statement, not a question. Because he's right. It's exactly what I've been wondering. I nod again.

"I don't think that's how it works, Emerson. I know that's not what you want to hear from me. I could say it, but I don't think it would make you feel any better. Not for the long run."

I drop my face into my knees. Concentrate on my breathing and count backward from one hundred. When the room stops spinning, I sit up. "Then when will it stop? I need to stop." My cheeks are wet, but no matter how much rubbing I do with my shirtsleeve, they stay wet. "I need it to stop. When will it be enough? I need it to be enough! I-I can't be—"

"You can't be what?"

"I can't be perfect anymore."

He smiles, but it doesn't crinkle his eyes. "And you were before?"

"I—No...but I tried to be." The tears finally dry up. "My life had order and I've done well in school. Four point-o, scholarship to Madison. Thirty-five on the ACT, which isn't too shabby. Varsity basketball team captain. I hold three State track records. And I had Angie." *Why did I mention Angie?*

"Angie was perfect?"

I half-laugh, half-snort. "Heck no. Far from it."

"So why'd you add her to the list?"

I pause, then grin at Dr. Shale. "For one, Angie's gorgeous." He doesn't look amused and I let the smile slide off my face. "Okay, that wasn't the primary reason for being with her. Or even the second or third," I add. I close my eyes for a moment, refocus. "Being with Angie had nothing to do with perfection. I only hold myself to that standard."

I wonder how to describe her, our relationship. "With Angie...there were times she drove me crazy. Doing dumb stuff, and I was pretty much always there for her. Ready to step in, pick her up literally and figuratively wherever she needed me." I hear Isabelle's voice in my head. *Stop trying to be everyone's hero.* Is that it? Was that who I wanted to be for Angie? "Shit! Sorry." I meet Dr. Shale's eyes. "I didn't mean to swear. I-I think...I needed to be her hero."

"Her hero, huh?"

"Yeah, stupid."

"Not stupid. Understandable. But you broke up with her, right?"

"Because I promised Frankie."

"And why was that?"

"I didn't love Angie and knew I never would."

He does that slow nod again. "Look, Emerson. At this point, I'm not sure I can help you any more than you can help yourself. I can give you my theories, but you're the one who needs to decide how to live your life. For what it's worth, I believe we're born imperfect, and perfection, whatever that may be, is unattainable by us mere human beings. Seems to me that you already figured that out yourself. So I'm not sure it was perfection you were aiming for, but control.

"I also believe we're here to learn and grow and make a difference in this world for as long as we're blessed to be here. I've worked with people long enough to see how we can take the gifts we've been given and self-destruct, or use those gifts for good. You're a smart kid. You have many fine qualities and talents. Stop wondering why your life was saved. Accept that it was, and do your best with what you have, knowing you'll make mistakes. You're not perfect and you never will be."

I mumble under my breath, "I'm not perfect."

"And you never will be."

"Right."

"And it wasn't your fault your life was spared and that woman died, and just because it worked that way doesn't mean you lived to save the entire world. Or even that girl."

"But it's possible, right?"

"I'm not saying it isn't. What I'm saying is that you're only responsible for doing the best you can with what you have. No more. No less. Even if you become the heart surgeon you once said you wanted to be, you're not the mythical Asclepius. You can't bring people back from the dead. You're not God. You're just you. Be the *best* imperfect you. Okay?"

As he scrawls some notes in my chart, I let his words wash over me.

"Here's your assignment. Do something just for you, without any obligation to another person. Do it because it makes you happy. No looking for danger that might be lurking around the corner. Have fun. Will you do that?"

I nod.

"One more thing. Next time, if there is a next time, make your own appointment to see me. Got it?"

"Yeah."

"We have a few more minutes. Anything else you want to discuss?"

I shake my head.

This time the lines deepen around his eyes with his smile. "It's good to see you," he says, rising to his feet. I stand. "Good luck at Madison. Though I highly doubt you'll need it."

The pain along my scar eases a bit. "Thank you."

12:26 P.M.

I GO THROUGH the Culver's drive-thru and head to Sunset Park. I'm missing study hall, so there's no guilt. *Do something just for you.* This is a start.

It's a little strange being back here so soon after the breakup, but I'd rather face it alone instead of when I'm with a bunch of people watching a baseball game or when I'm here to play pickup basketball with my SBHS teammates. It's a given that someone will remind me of my idiocy.

To avoid Little Lake, I head to a glider overlooking the bay. A brisk wind rolls an empty water bottle along the cement path and carries the blast of a tugboat horn passing under the three Sturgeon Bay bridges south of the park.

I swing back and forth and polish off my burger and fries, letting the idea of attending that party Brenda mentioned rock with me. I've never been to Washington Island and, after Dr. Shale's directive, the possibility of a fun overnight sounds enticing. A free Red-Eyed Loons concert is definitely incentive.

As if I need convincing, a loon lands on the rippling bay. It lets out a long, soulful wail and ruffles its black and white wings. The first I've seen since last summer. A coincidence? A sign? I'll take it as one.

I slip my phone from my pocket and text Brenda: *"Sure u'r okay w me attending the party tomorrow?"* I delete it and type: *"I'll see u tomorrow nite. Need me to bring anything?"* My finger hovers over the SEND button, then I change my mind. After deleting the second sentence, I read it over one more time. *"I'll see u tomorrow nite."* I tap SEND.

Watching the loon dip its head and preen, I think about Frankie. But this time, it's not with trepidation. This time, I'm filled with a warm, tingling sensation. And I just know she's okay.

TWENTY-FOUR

"We must be very suspicious of the deceptions of the element of time. It takes a good deal of time to eat or to sleep, or to earn a hundred dollars, and a very little time to entertain a hope and an insight which becomes the light of our life."

Ralph Waldo Emerson

TRICIA
WASHINGTON ISLAND   THURSDAY, 11:12 A.M.

BRENDA WAS SUPPOSED to be on the 8 A.M. ferry, but she wasn't. I sent her two text messages to find out what's happening and she hasn't responded. Other than the payment confirmation she forwarded from the Rent-a-Toilet and the text yesterday saying to stop worrying, along with some inane comment about stress and zits, I haven't heard from her.

Doesn't she know how frustrating it is to wait decades for a response? Last count, there were over two hundred RSVPs. Times that by five, and that's how nervous I am. I've never done anything like this, and since it was her idea, this party is more hers than mine. Now, I'm left with the bulk of the work.

Yesterday, I placed an order through Mann's for chips, a total of three hundred hot dogs, brats, and veggie dogs, fifteen bags of marshmallows, ten boxes of graham crackers, and fifty chocolate bars. I have no clue if that'll be enough. Tomorrow, the order should be available for pickup before 10 A.M. The buns from the Island Bread Company will be ready by noon and the two port-a-potties are being delivered and set up around one forty-five. The Red-Eyed Loons are supposed to arrive on the five o'clock ferry.

What am I missing?

I wish I could reach Brenda. Why won't she pick up? Too many scary scenarios. So many real nightmares. Car accident? Ruptured appendix? The flu? *Don't go there.* I know she's okay. Of course she's okay.

Should I call Brian?

After our talk in the lantern room, I stayed up and tried to reimagine my life without Brian. It was hard to go too far in the future, but truthfully, I got excited about the possibility of an adventure. Traveling, meeting new people, making improvements to Boyer's Bluff, redecorating the lighthouse, and I've been toying with the possibility of attending some type of college. But at this point, I have no idea what I would want to study. Obviously, something interesting. Something I'm passionate about. Those people who know what they want to do with their lives? Right now, I envy them.

I also have been thinking about Emerson—a lot. I've come up with some wild ways we could meet. *Sleepless in Seattle* minus a dead wife and a kid came to mind. Other movies like *August Rush* and *Return to Me.* Each has one common theme—two strangers meet under serendipitous circumstances. I know. I know I know I know—real life doesn't work that way. But I wish it did. Even more pathetic, I fantasized about meeting Emerson on the streets of Sister Bay with a pregnant wife—carrying twins no less—and the deep regret that it could have been me, if only he hadn't changed his phone number.

It was because of that scenario I found out he followed my request. I called. *We're sorry. The number you have reached has been disconnected or is no longer in service. Please check the number and dial again...* I did. Twice. Three times.

I confess, I signed onto Facebook and checked the two hundred twenty-eight RSVPs. No Emerson. And, I searched Brenda's friends list—all 1,027 people. Again, no Emerson. If she doesn't know him, then I doubt he lives anywhere near here. The 920 area code covers eighteen counties, about a fifth of Wisconsin. Hundreds of miles, dozens of high schools. I could ask around, see if anyone knows him at the party, but what would I say? It's probably best to forget him.

12:06 P.M.

STILL NO MESSAGE from Brenda.

Needing a break from baking banana chocolate-chip cherry muffins, I head into Grandma's office to take care of the bills I've neglected to pay over the past couple of months. We'll need electricity for the party, and the threat to shut it off because of lack of payment is huge incentive to get my butt in gear.

When I enter Grandma's office, her 1950s Zenith record player draws my attention. A Sinatra album is on the turntable. I plug it in. The record spins and the arm automatically pivots and drops onto the vinyl. Closing my eyes, I can almost hear Grandma sing along with her rich, sweet voice, never overpowering Sinatra but blending in to form beautiful harmony.

I pull out Grandma's desk chair and sit. By the time Frank's last song ends, I've sorted through paperwork, paid the bills online, and acknowledged fifteen condolence donations made in Grandma's memory.

God, my heart aches.

With loneliness weighing me down and threatening to pull me into darkness, I push away from the desk, lock the door behind me, and run upstairs. Exhausted, I manage an impressive face plant onto my bed. Within minutes, I'm out.

～

1:49 P.M.

THE MUSIC OF "New York, New York" nudges me from sleep. Grandma's ringtone. It's muted and I strain to listen. Nothing. Now I'm certain it's my imagination or just a dream. Until seconds later it starts up again. I frantically search my room for the phone. I open my door just as Frank croons out the chorus. It seems to be coming from downstairs. There has to be a logical explanation. Except I can't think of one.

I run to the office, turn the key I had left in the lock. The second I open the door, the music stops.

My phone is on the desk. I check caller ID, but there's no record of an incoming call. Impossible. I heard it. Not my imagination. I swear.

My hand shakes as I dial Grandma's old phone number. *We're sorry. The number you have reached has been disconnected or is no longer in service.*

I glance at the record player. Unplugged. The windows. Shut.

I'm losing my mind. I look up. "Grandma," I whisper, "was that you? Play it again, just one more time."

Nothing. I drop my forehead onto the desk and a blur of color meets my eyes.

I sit up, not quite registering what's before me. I scan the entire room for anything out of place.

Everything is exactly how I had left it, but *this*.

This is a snapshot. One I have never seen before, and one so different from the lifeless photos hanging on the wall.

Boyer's Bluff is a carpet and canopy of greens. In the background, the sun illuminates the lighthouse and the couple standing at the base of the porch steps. My parents. My mother's wedding gown is a simple, fitted floor-length white dress without a train. A white orchid accents her updo. My father wears his US Army officer uniform. And Dad has his I'm-the-luckiest-man-in-the-world smile aimed at Mom. I remember that smile—filled with pride, love, gratitude. Mom beams back, stunning. Her gold band glitters from their twined fingers.

I twist the thin band of my tiny ruby and diamond promise ring, the ring Dad had given Mom, the ring I haven't taken off since Dad passed it on to me before his final tour of duty. Tears stream down my face, but I'm not sad. I look up. I look around.

This picture is Grandma's answer. In awe, I whisper, "Thank you."

Boyer's Bluff is home.

Missed text from Brenda: 1:28 P.M.

"Sorry, had a few things come up. I'll b on the 3."

Life finally has some semblance of order.

TWENTY-FIVE

"The best lightning-rod for your protection is your own spine."
Ralph Waldo Emerson

BRENDA
STURGEON BAY   THURSDAY, 11:19 A.M.

FADE IN:

EXT/INT. MAGNOLIA INN/SUITE - DAY

Brenda knocks on the door of her
father's suite and steps back. Joel
opens the door with a huge smile.
Brenda enters the sitting room. A
packed suitcase rests near the door.

> BRENDA
> Wish I were going with
> you. When do we have to
> leave for the airport?

> JOEL
> Twenty minutes. How did
> your appointment go?

She frowns at him, tosses her keys and purse onto the table.

> BRENDA
> I guess okay. The therapist didn't say anything I didn't already know.

Brenda removes her hoodie, lays it on top of the couch. Joel goes over to the wet bar, opens a bottle of soda and brings it to Brenda.

Brenda kicks off her boots, flops down on the couch, and stares at the ceiling. Joel picks up her legs, sits down, and sets them onto his lap.

> JOEL
> You're a survivor. You'll be okay.

Brenda's breathing grows heavy. She drapes an arm over her eyes. Joel looks at her deeply worried.

> BRENDA
> (muffled)
> Do...you think there'll be someone who'll love me? Someone who won't see me as tainted, damaged?

He removes her arm from her face, swallows hard. Peers down into her mournful eyes with love and conviction.

>   JOEL
> Oh Sweet B, there is nothing tainted or damaged about your body or your mind or your heart or any other part of you unless you believe it. What I see is an incredible, talented young woman. A strong woman. Please don't see yourself as anything less than that.

She scoots away from Joel, stands, walks to the window, and looks out.

>   BRENDA
> I can't wait to get out of Sturgeon Bay. Life will be a thousand times better in New York. Tisch is going to be the beginning of my real life.

Joel pours himself a drink, opens the ice bucket, and closes the empty container. He stares at the caramel-colored liquid, sighs, and puts it down on the bar. He walks over to Brenda.

JOEL

Bren, I won't deny how much
I'll love having you in the
city with me year-round.
Our summers were never
enough. As incredible as
New York can be, living and
working and improving your
craft there may very well
be a brutal experience.
It's tough for a lot of
people. It's inevitable
that you'll run into some
crappy individuals who
will want to crush you.
That's what real life,
as you call it, might be.
You think you can survive
that, after everything
you've been through?

BRENDA

I know what the competition
is like. I can handle it.

Joel opens the window wide, breathes
in some fresh air, then turns to
Brenda.

JOEL

Your summer workshops were
pre-school in comparison
to what you're going to
be doing, and people
play dirty. I want you
to be prepared, at least

mentally. There are going to be moments when you may even want to give up. I want you to talk to me if that happens. And, I want you to continue seeing a therapist.

BRENDA
Dad, I really just want to move on. Fresh start. I'm tired of replaying the horror film in my head like *Groundhog Day*. I'm tired of suffering in that place. I want to create new scenes and memories in New York.

JOEL
You will. We both know that. I won't make you see a therapist. It's your choice, but I do think it's important. Especially if you find that you can't stop the flashbacks or the OCD gets worse. You come first. Always. I want you to get whatever help you need. At least promise to consider it.

BRENDA
I will.

EXT. GREEN BAY AIRPORT - DAY

Brenda hugs Joel at the curb. His bag is next to him.

Joel reaches into his coat pocket and presents her with a WRAPPED GIFT. He smiles, excited with anticipation.

>   JOEL
>   It's your high school
>   graduation present. Don't
>   worry, I'll be here for
>   it, but I think you'll
>   appreciate this now.

He hands her the box, and she carefully removes the wrapping paper. She lifts the lid of a white BOX. Inside she discovers a VELVET RING BOX, which she removes.

>   JOEL (CONT.)
>   Open it.

Brenda does.

INSERT - WHITE GOLD KNOTTED RING WITH A SMALL DIAMOND.

BACK TO SCENE

>   JOEL (CONT.)
>   For you. As a reminder of
>   your strength, courage,

and for how much I love
you. I hope, whenever you
need a boost, you can look
at it and know how much
I believe in you. It's
a symbol too, for your
dreams, that some day in
the not-so-distant future,
you'll achieve them.

She slips the ring onto her right
index finger, holds her hand out,
and admires it. Brenda chokes up,
but manages not to cry.

                    BRENDA
          It's beautiful, Dad. Thank
          you.

She presses the ring to her heart,
then looks at it again. Joel hugs her
good-bye and walks into the airport.

INT. BRENDA'S APARTMENT/BEDROOM -
CONTINUOUS - DAY

Brenda packs clothes into a small
open duffle sitting on her unmade
bed.

INT. BRENDA'S APARTMENT/BATHROOM -
CONTINUOUS - DAY

She grabs toiletries off the vanity,
puts them in the duffle.

INT. BRENDA'S APARTMENT/HALLWAY -
CONTINUOUS - DAY

LINDA (39) walks through the front
door. She hears the HAIRDRYER in
the bathroom and heads toward the
sound. She stops just outside the
door and looks in at Brenda, who
is now wrapping the cord around the
hairdryer.

> LINDA
> You're leaving again?

INT. BRENDA'S APARTMENT/BATHROOM -
CONTINUOUS - DAY

Linda steps into the bathroom, sits
down on the closed toilet seat.

> BRENDA
> Hey, Mom. I told you,
> remember? I'm going to the
> island for the weekend.

Brenda eyes her mother's clothes and
blows out a frustrated breath.

> BRENDA (CONT.)
> Mom, I was looking for
> that T-shirt. I wish you
> wouldn't borrow my clothes
> without asking.

LINDA
You weren't here. How is
your father?

BRENDA
Good. I put an envelope on
the kitchen table from him
for you.

Brenda drops her hairbrush into the
duffle. Picks up the bag.

INT. BRENDA'S APARTMENT/BEDROOM -
CONTINUOUS - DAY

Linda follows Brenda into the
bedroom, stands at the threshold.
Brenda grabs her keys off her desk
and is ready to leave, but her mom is
in her way, looking miserable.

LINDA
I'm sorry, Brenda. I'm
just having a terrible
time knowing that you
suffered for so long and
didn't feel like you could
tell me. It kills me that
you hurt in silence.

BRENDA
It wasn't you. It wasn't
because I didn't trust
you. I was scared. Okay?
(beat)

I need to go, Mom. I don't want to miss the ferry.

Linda fidgets with the hem of the T-shirt, then crosses her arms and hugs herself. Brenda notices and her expression softens. She moves toward Linda, drops the duffle next to her feet.

> LINDA
> You're important to me. I love you.

> BRENDA
> I love you, too.
>   (beat)
> Mom, I'm strong because of you. I'm able to survive because of you.

Linda eyes become teary.

> LINDA
> Really?

> BRENDA
> Really. You raised me.

Brenda smiles at Linda, who pulls her into a hug.

> BRENDA (CONT.)
> Three o'clock ferry.

Linda wipes her eyes, smears her makeup. She kisses Brenda on the cheek.

INT. BRENDA'S APARTMENT/HALLWAY - CONTINUOUS - DAY

Linda walks down the hallway to her bedroom. At the door, she turns toward Brenda's room. She sees Brenda's legs sticking out of the threshold. Brenda's kneeling down. Linda hears the ZIPPER of Brenda's duffle.

> LINDA
> Say hello to Uncle Charlie for me, and the rest of the family, okay?

Brenda peeks out her door at Linda.

> BRENDA
> Sure, Mom.

Linda goes into her bedroom and shuts the door.

INT. BRENDA'S APARTMENT/BEDROOM - CONTINUOUS - DAY

Brenda pats her pockets, riffles through her purse and duffle. She goes into her bedroom and frantically searches for her phone. She finds it on her bed under a discarded T-shirt.

INSERT: BRENDA'S PHONE

Brenda checks the time. 1:24 P.M.
A series of texts from Tricia:

  1:06 Do u think I should have
  bug spray 4 ppl?
  1:11 I was going to make banana
  nut muffins too. What if someone
  has a nut allergy?
  1:23 Not making anything w nuts.
  I called Mann's, ordered more
  stuff for s'mores. Do u think
  I should order coffee from the
  Red Cup for breakfast?

Brenda texts back:
  Running late for the ferry.
  TTYL.

BACK TO SCENE

As Brenda walks down the hallway to
leave, she stops in front of Linda's
bedroom door like she's about to
say something to her. But then she
hears MUFFLED CRYING. Brenda's face
darkens with sadness. Her fingers
stroke the door, then her expression
turns resolute and she walks out.

                        FADE OUT.

TWENTY-SIX

"We talk of choosing our friends, but friends are self-elected."
Ralph Waldo Emerson

TRICIA

THE RED CUP'S small lot is packed, forcing me to park down the street. Definitely unusual for this time of day. I couldn't stay home for one more second. It was too quiet. For so long that's what I needed, wanted, *craved*. I barely recognize that Tricia Boyer. I refuse to think about what I could have done if Emerson hadn't answered. But I *am* deeply grateful. That call helped make life better, brighter, *beautiful*. I'm done fantasizing about a movie-style reunion and resigned to the idea that I'm more likely to be struck by a meteor than meet Emerson, especially here.

For now, I am going to stay. I love Boyer's Bluff, this island, *life*. The special gift from Grandma has left me giddy with excitement. Almost immediately after finding the photograph, instinct once again had me reaching for my phone to call Brian. But I squashed it quickly as much for his sake as for mine. It's okay. I relied on Brian for too long. One person can't be another's sun, at least not all the time. That's why the sun rises and sets, rises and sets, right?

Smiling, I slip the snapshot of my parents and Grandma into my purse pocket and climb out of my pickup. The glorious smell of fresh baked bread and brewed coffee embraces me like a good friend. When I step onto the porch, the door of the Red Cup flies open, blasting me with cheer. It looks like our entire school is inside with a sprinkling of adults. "What's going on?" I ask.

"Early dismissal, teacher in-service," someone shouts.

Through the hellos and hugs and smiles and laughter, my eyes meet Brian's. He sends me a weak smile and turns back to place his order with Caroline. Everyone starts talking at once about the party tomorrow night. I catch phrases like: "Can't wait!" "I'll help you set up." "My cousin Lillie is coming from Bailey's Harbor." Their enthusiasm is contagious.

Two of the youngest Hansen kids, Aislinn and Josie, elbow and nose their way into the circle and wrap their arms around my knees. I used to babysit them, and for some reason their hugs make me misty-eyed.

Brian navigates his way to our group, watching me watching him. Not sure how to act, I turn away and focus on Hunter. Within a few seconds, Brian's arms lock around my stomach and draw me in. His chin rests on my shoulder; his clean-shaven cheek is next to mine, warm and familiar. My breath mingles with his. *How many times has he held me this way?* For a few seconds, it feels so good, so normal, and then so, so WRONG. What is he doing? He whispers in my ear, "No one knows we broke up. Let's just leave it for now."

Hunter's baby sister Lydia grabs the back of my jeans and yanks hard enough to hoist herself up, forcing me to snatch the edge of my waistband before they drop and expose my bikini underwear. I laugh to hide the churning emotions Brian stirred inside—some wonderful, some painful—and scoop Lydia into my arms. I plant a kiss on her pudgy nose.

Hunter takes Lydia from me, settles her into the crook of his arm, and says, "So, for the party, Leif and Steven are in charge of the fish boil and are collecting all the ingredients. Brian borrowed the equipment from his parents' pub. Matt, Joey, and Brian will shuttle people back and forth from the ferry. Stef and Robin are going to help put up tents. Oh, and we were able to disassemble the stage from the old Washington Hotel for the band. Let us know when we can come over and where you want us to set it up."

I try to speak, but not a sound comes out of my gaping mouth. Hunter bends down, kisses my check, and says, "We're glad you're back."

Sarah hooks her arm in Linnea's. They grin like bridesmaids, and I find myself smiling too. Linnea says to Sarah, "Show Tricia what we've organized for the party."

"It's all worked out," Sarah says. She reaches into her pocket and hands me a folded piece of lined notebook paper. I open it slowly to draw out the anticipation, like it's a birthday gift.

I look up at Sarah, look at Linnea, look down at the list, look around at my friends' excited, proud, joyous faces. "But...my order at Mann's?"

"Taken care of," Sarah says. She loops her arms around my waist and gives me one of her signature hugs.

I'm so overwhelmed and grateful, I start to cry—good tears. Brian hands me a napkin and beams at me, a high-wattage grin that hasn't graced his face for what seems like an eternity. My fault. And there it is again: *guilt.* How much of this did he arrange?

Mrs. Cornell and Mrs. Jorgenson stop over to say hello and tell me they'll drop off the food tomorrow morning. I can only nod and hug them back.

For five months, I've resented the invasion of my space. But today, I realize these wonderful people have been a part of my salvation, my family. If there is heaven on earth, then it's here on Washington Island.

With the influx of more and more people into the Red Cup, it's nearly impossible for me to make it over to a table. Every chair is taken, but I ask Josh to borrow his for a minute. He doesn't hesitate, and I step up.

"Sorry to interrupt," I shout over the noise. Josh sticks two fingers in his mouth and whistles. Even the little ones quiet down. "Hi everyone." I smile at the chorus of greetings and choke back the soup of emotions. "I want to thank you all for your support the last five months. To say it's been the worst time of my life is the understatement of the century. All the food, your phone calls, your concern has meant a lot to me. To be honest, I wasn't sure if...if I would stay on Boyer's Bluff. But this is my home. *You* make it home."

The Red Cup erupts in cheers. Scanning the room, I find Brian. His expression conveys so much, almost like I'm reading the history of us. There's understanding and bewilderment, love and heartbreak. Most of all, there's the hint of that kindred friendship forged a lifetime ago. It's like Brian's giving me permission, *us* permission to move on. Anticipation ripples throughout the room as a sea of eyes bounce from me to him.

I open my mouth and say, "Brian..." I pause. My gaze is locked with his. "And I—" In that second, standing in front of everyone, I realize I wouldn't be here if we hadn't split up. Most likely I'd be at home, under the covers, in a state of complete despair. I never would have made that phone call. I never would have talked to Emerson.

Near the front of the packed crowd someone shouts, "We know!" Followed by another on my left. "*Everyone* knows." And there are chuckles throughout the room. My eyes dart from person to person. No one looks surprised, which come to think about it, isn't a surprise. Someone else says, "We love you both," and I realize it's Sarah.

That love epitomizes the island. Brian offers a hand and I hop off the chair.

In two heartbeats, the Red Cup talk returns to organic farming and the upcoming tourist season and the party. There's also a lot of buzz about the stupid kayaker who didn't wear a wetsuit and nearly died of hypothermia in the frigid Lake Michigan waters near Rock Island. If Randall hadn't been out on patrol, the idiot would be dead. No sane person swims in Lake Michigan, intentionally or unintentionally, this time of year. Even the wacky people—Brian included— who do our island's traditional New Year's Polar Bear Plunge are out within a few splashes.

Sometime in the shuffle of things, someone handed me coffee because—surprise—I'm holding a cup. I take a sip and it's perfect. Just the way I like it. A cappuccino with two packs of raw sugar.

Brian steps in front of me, touches my sleeve. "Let's go outside to talk." He must see the hesitation in my eyes because he adds, "Please." And I don't know what I'm thinking or if I'm thinking at all because I allow

Richter	20 lbs. potato salad
Hanson	10 bags marshmallows
Cornell, J	10 pkg hot dog buns
Jessen	10 pkg chocolate bars
Flecter	20 lbs. whitefish
Cornell, R	20 lbs whitefish
Marm	10 cherry/10 apple pies
Neilson	100 hot dogs
Whitman	20 lbs. corn salad
Peterson	3 kegs soda
Hutchens	10 pkg hot dog buns
Ottosen	8 doz. cookies
Schultz	80 venison brats
Waldron	chips & dip
Johannson	10 boxes graham crackers
McGrave	5 pgkg hot dogs
Lockhart	15 lbs coleslaw
Jorgenson	fixings for the fish boil
Swenson	8 pkg brats
Raymond	plates & napkins
Kickbush	plasticware
Foss	cups
Cornell, L	8 doz cookies

him to lead me outside. Immediately, I miss the crowd. He opens the passenger door of his truck and I climb in. I cling to the coffee to keep my hands busy.

As soon as he gets behind the wheel, he says, "I've been really worried about you. So, you're really okay? You're really gonna stay?"

I take a few more sips for fortitude, watch him over the lid.

"How is it?" he asks.

"Perfect, as usual."

And he smiles—a warm, satisfied smile. He bought me the coffee.

"Thank you." I tip my cup toward him in a salute. "And yeah, I'm okay."

"Good, and you're welcome." His eyes narrow like he's waging an internal battle. He takes a breath, points to the Red Cup, and says, "Well, I'm glad we got that out of the way. How long do you think we'll be the talk of the island?" His foot taps a mile a minute against the floor mat.

"I suspect it'll take a while. People are still talking about Katy and that Mainlander she ran off with and married, remember? He was here for a two-week summer vacation. She packed up her car, got on the ferry with him. And that happened ten years ago." I attempt to smile but it isn't so easy.

Brian leans over, opens the glove box, and pulls out a pack of cigarettes. He's smoking again? I don't smell tobacco.

"I thought you quit two years ago?"

"I did." He tears the cellophane and taps one out, holds it between his lips. But he doesn't light it and there are no matches in sight.

"Brian." The tone of my voice rips my heart out, and I can tell it has the same effect on him. It's filled with judgment and disappointment. He doesn't deserve this from me. Yet, I can't watch him fall back into old habits. "Please, don't start smoking again."

He gives his head a small shake, chews on the tip of the cigarette. Gently, I remove it from between his lips, take the pack, and squeeze the whole thing in my fist. If we needed one last confirmation that breaking up was the right decision, then this moment is proof. I drain the rest of my now-lukewarm cappuccino into my parched throat.

"You were right," I say. My statement catches him off-guard. "To leave. It hasn't been that long, but I really believe being apart is best for both of us."

He nods. "Takes getting used to, though."

"We were like old, holey socks."

He laughs. "Yeah, not exactly what I'd call sexy."

"Neither are these." I open my hand.

"They were my dad's." He gives me a sideward glance. A hint of a smile forms on his lips. "So? What now?"

"Well, there's the party." I pause. "Thank you for helping."

"I did it for Brenda." There's mischief and teasing in his tone.

I laugh and give him a playful shove. "Yup. I knew it all along."

Brian's cell chirps with a text. He pulls it out of his pocket. "It's from Brenda. She's checking to make sure we have enough wood for the bonfire."

My eyes widen as I picture myself trudging through the forest to gather and drag fallen trees and kindling. "Do we?"

He smiles. "Don't worry. Robin and Christian have it covered."

"Thank goodness, because I have no idea where my gloves are."

"In the toolshed," he says.

I can't think of another thing to say. Brian looks out his window toward the post office. A few of our classmates exit the Red Cup and head to their cars and trucks. "I better go," I say. "There's still tons to do for the party."

Brian wraps me in a hug, holds me close, friend to friend. There's so much history between us, so much happiness and sadness and everything in between. I'm not sure where this moment falls in the spectrum. It's too close, too raw, too new. I draw myself away from him, open the door, and hop out. "So, I'll see you?"

"Small island."

"Cliché." We laugh, and Brian's just far enough away that he doesn't hear the small hitch in the back of my throat. We wave good-bye and I watch him drive out of the parking lot toward his home.

When I re-enter the Red Cup, I spot Linnea, Sarah, Hunter, and Josh, who claimed a corner by the fireplace. Linnea holds up my purse. "No Tic Tacs or gum." She's joking. Linnea's too straight-laced to riffle through someone else's things.

"Thanks." I slide down next to her.

"You doing all right?" she asks, nudging my arm. Underneath her gentle smile, there's genuine concern in her light brown eyes, so similar to her dad's.

"Much better. Great, actually. It's good to see you. I'm missed you."

"I've missed you more." She loops her arm in mine and gives it a gentle squeeze. "Everyone knew about you and Brian by Monday afternoon. I was going to stop by on Tuesday, but my dad—"

"It's okay. Really." The lines above the bridge of her nose smooth out. "It's been good for me to have time alone. I've had a lot to think about. A lot to do. I'm excited for this party, and even though my grandma's gone, I know she would approve."

I unhook our arms, unzip my purse pocket, and pull out the wedding day photograph. Thinking about it, my parents' wedding was probably the last time there was a huge celebration on Boyer's Bluff. Finding this picture, I realize, is a sign that my grandma would approve of this party.

I hand it to Linnea, and say, "I found this in my grandma's office earlier." Pointing at my family, I add, "Even though they're gone, they're still so much a part of Boyer's Bluff, the lighthouse, me. How could I ever sell?"

Her smile spreads into a wide grin. "I'm so glad. My dad thought you'd really appreciate it. You look so much like your mom. And I love the dress. Do you still have it?"

I stare at her. Sound ceases to exist. I'm completely mute. Linnea's face fractures like a Picasso painting.

"What? What's wrong?"

I choke out, "This-this photo was from your dad?"

Linnea squints her eyes at me. "Yeah?"

Grabbing my things, I stumble to my feet, get my balance, and weave my way through the crowd. People call my name, but I ignore them. Jeremiah brought over the picture? He left it for me in Grandma's office? When? Why would he do that?

Linnea reaches the door before me and blocks my way.

"Where's your dad? Is he at the station?" My voice is frantic. It quivers with betrayal and angry tears.

"He should be. Unless he's on a call. What's wrong? D-Did I say something wrong?"

"No, no. Everything's fine." I push her aside and sprint to my truck.

I had thought the picture was a gift from Grandma. A message. I thought she wanted me to stay on Boyer's Bluff. To have this party! But no. The strains of "New York, New York" must have been a figment of my imagination, my desperation. Everything I thought was real. Not. Oh my God, I'm pitiful, pathetic. Maybe I need to be admitted to a psych ward? To think I had hope. I had believed. Grandma's not watching out for me at all.

2:42 P.M.

JEREMIAH'S PICKUP IS in the parking lot and so is the island police Ford Expedition. Inches before I hit the building, I slam on the breaks and ram the gear into PARK.

He greets me at the door, ushers me in with, "Just let me explain."

"Linnea called you."

"Sit down." Maybe Linnea wouldn't defy his authoritative stance, but I do. His tone softens considerably. "Please sit and hear me out."

I sit. Not because he asked, but because my rubbery legs can no longer hold me. Tears stream down my cheeks. Jeremiah walks behind his desk and sinks into his chair. His shoulders relax, but the tension doesn't leave his face, deepening those craggy lines on his forehead that never quite disappear.

I remove the photograph and wave it at him, tears pouring down my cheeks. "Do you know what I thought? I thought the picture was Grandma's way of saying she wanted me to stay. For me not to sell Boyer's Bluff. I thought it was a gift—from her! But you—It was you." I'm crying so hard, that my voice hitches with almost every word. "Why would you come into my house?"

Jeremiah leans forward across his desk. His eyes plead with me to calm down. "I knocked. You didn't answer. The door was unlocked, and I was worried."

Fury replaces tears. "Why?"

"Because the last time I saw you, I knew Brian had left and you didn't say anything."

Suddenly the photo feels too heavy to hold. I set it on top of a pile of papers. "You could have asked."

"Tricia." That tone again. "Brian's mom had insisted that everyone give you and Brian time to work things out. But that's not why I didn't say anything to you. I hoped you'd confide in me, that we had a relationship where you could. When you didn't, I—" He clears his throat. "I knew you painted the parlor."

It takes me a few moments to speak. When I do, my voice is raspy. "But, that doesn't explain why you went into Grandma's office and left the picture."

There's sorrow in his eyes, regret too. "The guns. I was glad that you gave them to me but... Well, I was still concerned. With Brian gone, you were isolated. When you didn't answer your door, I came in, did a standard check. Including the office."

"And the picture?" He leans back in his chair, rubs his forehead like a headache is coming on. Then he drops his hand, briefly scans the office like he's looking to see if someone's hiding somewhere. I grow impatient. "Jeremiah?"

Bracing his elbows on his desk, he says, "It was the strangest thing. I hadn't seen that photograph for years. But when I woke up this morning, it was on my nightstand. Beth and Linnea both insisted they didn't place it there. I thought—and I know this sounds crazy—that maybe your dad did? I stared at it for quite a while, wondering what I should do."

Like a crack of lightning, a shiver skitters down my spine. My head spins and I reach out, grab the handles of the chair to steady myself. *Was it Grandma?*

Jeremiah presses his palms together, almost in supplication, then laces his fingers into a tight grip. "Tricia, your parents were so happy, so in love with each other and life. They loved Boyer's Bluff and so did your grandma. Thinking about them, what they would want for you, I knew I had to give you the photograph."

He hesitates, then says, "Your dad always said he was the luckiest man alive until—" He clears his throat. "After the trial, your dad was still so angry, enraged over the unfairness of it all. He needed a place to put all that pain and rage. Re-enlisting seemed like the perfect answer, and after weeks of discussion, your grandma reluctantly agreed. You know he loved you. He loved Boyer's Bluff. And even though he had to get away for a while, it was still home. It's *your* home. Eventually, your dad realized that the memories didn't disappear, the pain didn't disappear. He had a lot of regrets, Tricia, and he missed you and your grandma fiercely. During his last tour he was ready to face his old demons and come home."

"Too late."

"It doesn't have to be too late for you." He picks up the photo, offers it to me. I take it. "You asked why I left that in your grandma's office." He shakes his head in wonder. "When I saw you asleep, safe, I decided not to wake you. I went back downstairs and was going to leave the picture on the hallway table. But then I thought maybe I should write you a note. I went into the office for some paper and a pen. For a few minutes, the family photographs on the wall distracted me. So many memories. And then I walked to the desk, set the picture down. I can't explain why I left it there or why I didn't write a note. But it felt right. I walked out, locked the door, and left."

He stands, moves in front of the desk, and sits on the edge. "I'm sorry, Tricia. I didn't mean any harm."

I take a long, shuddered breath, wipe my eyes with my sleeve. "It's okay," I answer. And I mean it.

4:17 P.M.

IN THE LAST twenty minutes I've swept the porch, replaced a burned-out light in the lamppost, and washed the outside of the first floor windows, all while waiting for Brenda to show up. The three o'clock ferry should have arrived fifty minutes ago, and I'm beginning to wonder if she missed this one too. Once again, she hasn't responded to my text messages. But just as I contemplate calling Brian, the hum of a truck engine sends me running into the circle drive.

I shield my eyes from the late afternoon sun. Brenda's SUV crests the hill and parks off to the side of the garage. She waves, smiling. She's not alone. Brian and Savanna hop out carrying pizza. Lots of pizza.

But that's not the only surprise.

Hunter and Linnea and Sarah and a whole crew pull up behind them. I walk from one pickup truck to the next, saying hello and hugging my friends. Almost everyone from our high school is here, and they're geared up to help.

"Thought I wasn't coming?" Brenda asks, poking at me.

I poke back. "I'm glad you're here. I'm glad everyone's here."

Her deeply shadowed eyes scrutinize me. "Even Brian?"

"Always," I say.

"Good."

Brenda quickly takes over as the general contractor. I'm the consultant. We choose a spot closer to the cliffs for the bonfire and fish boil, choose the grassy area for the tents, and decide the porch is the perfect place to serve food.

Because the garage has electricity, Brenda decides it's the perfect backdrop for the stage, and a crew starts to lug the pieces of plywood and two-by-fours from Hunter's truck bed. Others get out ladders and set them up all around the yard. Over the next several hours, paper globe lanterns in blue, turquoise, and pale green are hung from trees and the porch, and dangle from string after string of twinkle lights. More lights outline the garage and porch, spiral around the trees, and loop from one area to the next.

Music pumps through four speakers perched in the crook of a maple, an oak, and on the garage roof. Everyone takes a break to eat pizza and drink lemonade at the picnic tables some of the guys brought. A few tents get set up. We finish the bonfire pit, arrange the food tables on the porch, and reassemble the stage.

⌒

OUR ENTIRE CREW stands in the driveway to admire our handiwork. Boyer's Bluff transformed into a shimmering wonderland.

Brenda drapes an arm over my shoulder and says, "Well, what do you think?"

"Amazing. Thanks for all of this."

"It'll be even better tomorrow night. Can you picture this place packed with a couple hundred people, the band playing? No rain in the forecast and Saturday is supposed to warm up to seventy. Can you believe it? Someone's watching out for you."

My phone rings. It's a 920 number I don't recognize. A tingle of hope surges into my heart.

"Hello?"

TWENTY-SEVEN

"Make yourself necessary to somebody. Do not make life hard
to any."
Ralph Waldo Emerson

ANGIE

STURGEON BAY   THURSDAY, 7:09 P.M.

Called Brenda one, two,
three times in four hours.
Ignores texts, Facebook
messages. Haven't talked
since yesterday.
She   h

      u

        n

          g

up. Didn't let me explain
what I said to Emerson.

wallofsilencewallofsilencewallofsilencewallof
silencewallofsilencewallofsilencewallofsilence
wallofsilencewallofsilencewallofsilencewallof
silencewallofsilencewallofsilencewallofsilence
wallofsilencewallofsilencewallofsilencewallof

Not ~~one word.~~ I'm feeling...

abandoned   alone   bereaved   betrayed   broken
crushed   depressed   filthy   furious   guilt-ridden
lost   mortified   sickened   shamed   worried
unlovable

I need Brenda.
Does she need me?
BFF?

NERʀʀʀʀVOUS, will
I lose ~~her~~?

෴

7:22 P.M.

ISLAND PARTY INFO:
Brenda
posted Tricia Boyer's
phone number. Dial.
Ring. Answer.

"Hello?"

"Hi, is Brenda there?"

One beat. Two.

"Hello?"

"Brenda? I'm—"
Voice cuts out.

Hello?

"Angie?"

"I'm
so sorry.
Do you hate me?"

"We're fine."

"But...you hung up.
Twice."

"Bad cell reception.
You know how it is
on the island."

One beat. Two.

"But, earlier—
Emerson?"

"We talked."

"Okay, but—"

"Please Angie,
there's nothing
to say.
Leave it alone.
The past
is the past.
Move on. I am."

353

"We can't talk
about it?"

"Nope.
I'll see you
tomorrow night,
right?"

SLAM.
This door
won't open unless
Brenda unlocks it.

"You still want
me to come?"

"It won't be
a party without
my best friend."

Nothing's changed
between us.
Good? Bad? Same.

"So tell me,
what's
up
with you
and Jordan?"

Typical subject
change. I laugh,
eyes mist over.
Then I tell her
everything.

Even the lies.
Hating Jordan,
the biggest of all.

⌒⌒

Lying
side by side
on Jordan's bed
his finger traces
    the orange
      flames across
    the faded
Thrasher magazine
    T-shirt. His. I kept
      it since seventh
    grade. His touch feels so good,
a distraction for my dark,
miserable thoughts.

I can't stop thinking about
Brenda and what happened.

      Jordan says,
      "Talk to me."

Magic words.

Secrets locked
inside. Who
can hold

them in?

Brenda. My mother. Emerson?

I can't. I want, need
~~someone~~ Jordan
to know who
I am.
Clueless.
Still
so many
unanswered ??s.

Why did my mother marry the Demon?
(No clue.)
Who are her parents, my grandparents?
(No clue)
When Brenda moves to NYC, will we stay friends?
(No clue.)
What does the future hold for me?
(No clue.)

I talk
and talk.

Jordan listens
and listens.

I'm
open,
intimate,
more naked
than I've ever
been with Emerson.
And we're dressed.

Jordan carries
my burdens,
my secrets,
my hopes,
dreams.

Later,
an hour
later,
after I thank
Jordan
for listening.
he plants
a kiss
on my lips,
pulls
me into his side.

"I don't understand.
Why do you like me?"

He laughs,
fingers the edge
of my shirt, brushes
my stomach with a fingertip.

"I love...
your heart, your hope, your honesty."

Shhhhivvverr.

"I love...
that you're imperfect, but perfect for me."

"Why?"

"You're a work
in progress.
So am I."

Wonderful. Perfect. Words.

FRIDAY, 11:35 A.M.

Senior Skip Day:

Party! Party! Party!
StreSSssSed O—U—T.

Brush teeth, shower.
Underwear, makeup, hair.
Fashion emergency.
What top?
Which jeans?
Text Brenda for consult. She'll
know what I should wear.

Wait. Wait. Wait.
No text. No TEXT.
Wait. Wait. Wait.
No text. No TEXT.

Yes text.
☹ Not Brenda.
☺ From Jordan. *U ready?*

We'll stop 4 lunch b4 5 pm ferry.
Text to Jordan: *Not dressed yet.*
From Jordan: *Sexy underwear. Jeans. T-shirt. Done.*
Text to Jordan: *Dream on.*
From Jordan: *I am, babe. I am. 10 min I'm leaving.*

Arrrrrrrrrrrrrrrrrrrrrrrrrrrrrrrg.

Open drawers, closet, looking
for the perfect outfit. Which one?
Faded jeans, purple T-shirt, Converse?
Black jeans, pink blouse, belt, boots?
Skinny jeans, yellow tee, ballet slippers?

White tee.
Black zipped hoodie.
Faded, holey hip-hugger jeans.
Hiking boots. Check mirror. Cute? Sigh.

Pack for tomorrow. Toiletries, underwear, jeans, tee,
PJs. Sleep? Where will we sleep? In the same bed?
We've done it before. As friends. But now
we're more.
I've only thought about sex...with Emerson.

StreSSssSed O—U—T.

Worried
sick.
Sex with
Jordan?
Should I
ask if he
has a condom?

Relax. Breathe. Relax. Breathe.
Relax. Breathe. Relax. Breathe.

It will be okay. Please God, let it be okay?

Mom comes in carrying
Emily, bouncing excitedly,
cooing, whining, stretching
out arms until I take her.

Shhh, shhh, shhh, shhh.
Stops fussing, buurrp.
I kiss her rosy cheeks.

Oh Emily.
Sour milk
drips
o
w
n
my
white
shirt.

"Here, I'll take
her," Mom says.
Emmy clings like
a spider monkey.

She s-C-rrrreamS
     R   R
   Y   Y
   I   I
   N   N
   G   G

Text comes in
from Jordan.
Leaving!

I text Jordan:
5 min. plz!!!!

Dig
in closet.
Clean black tee.
Mirror check.
White
was better.
Sigh.

                           "You all set?"

"Yeah, I'll see you
tomorrow night."

                             11:58 A.M.

AHHHHHH!
NERrrrrVOUS.

Liza Wiemer

"Call me,"
Mom says
as I scurry
toward
the door.

"I'll try. You
know reception
on the
island."

࿔

2:22 P.M., FISH CREEK

Turkey club, fries,
iced tea, and one of
Jordan's
onion rings left my
stomach queasy.

Jordan's driving
isn't helping.
Matching JJ's,
Army green,
is not my
best color.

Hello?

Jordan reaches
for my hand.
"Hey, you okay?"

"Yeah," I say.

"You've been quiet
since we left.
Something
on your mind?"

Yes. I bite my lip. *SEX*.

Left turn signal.
Settlement Shops
in Fish Creek.
Parking lot.
Secluded
parking spot
beneath a tree.
Engine off.

"C'mere."

Jordan smiles
wickedly, pulls
me to his lap.

"That's better.
Now talk to me."

Scoot forward,
lips
brush his ear.

Liza Wiemer

"You're
sure you want
to talk?"

                                            "Yes."

One beat. Two.

Mouth to mouth,
teeth, tongues,
heat, chills.
Fingers brush.
Skin sings
a new melody.

Rock
of ages.

Reaching down,
caressing brings
a throaty moan.

"Jordan," I whisper.

His eyes fly open.
Looks around.
We're all alone.

Unzip. I continue
my spontaneous
plan. Doing...
this for him.

UNTIL...

364

Hello?

"Angie, I—ohhhhhh.
STOP!"

"Stop?"

"Yeah," he breathes. "Stop."
One beat. Two. "That...this...
Amazing, but—" Jordan lifts
me up, zips his jeans, winces.

"Don't you...?"

"I do!" he says.
"But not here.
Not now,
not this way.
Whatever you
had with Emerson,
I don't want for *us*."

"What?"

"Car. Sex. No rebound sex."

"Rebound sex?"
I push him   away.
Shift to
my seat, stunned
by his
verbal slap. I'd like
to slap him.
#*$%*@* I don't.

"Why are you upset?"

Liza Wiemer

"Upset?" Disgusted.
"Not all rumors
are true. We're both
still virgins. Are you?"

His mouth
d
r
o
p
s
to his knees.
Then he

G R I N S   W I D E !

It's contagious.

> He nods. "I am too."

BUT...doubts plague my mind.
What ~~did~~, does he think of me???

"If I had slept with
Emerson, would it
have bothered you?"

Sideward glance,
raised
brow. Smirk.

> "Angie, at ten
> I wanted
> to kiss you. At twelve,
> I wanted

to touch you,
and by fourteen discovering
all of you was the pursuit
of my deepest, blissful
dreams. Am I glad
you didn't sleep
with Emerson?
Hell ya. Would
it have changed
how I feel about you?
Heck no. We've shared
a lot of firsts. So
you can't blame me
for wanting this one, too.
And now...
we wait."

"We wait? Why?"

He laughs. "Because you're
not ready. And if you're
not ready, neither am I."

Indignant, I say,
"How do
you know?"

"I know every look
you have, and you can't fool
me. For a split second,
I saw it on your face
when I brought you
to my lap. You put
on a great
show. Definitely can't

complain. But Ang? With
everything we do,
I want it to be
all of us, not just
the physical, but this."

Jordan takes my hands,
places one on his heart,
places the other on mine.

Beat. Beat. - Beat. Beat. - Beat. Beat.

He skims two fingers up,
over my shoulder, neck,
cheek. Stops. Moves his
fingers to his lips. Plants
a kiss, then gently taps
them against my temple.

"And this."

"I'm nervous."

"That's good." He smiles.

"Why?"

"It means we matter."

He leans over,
pulls me close.
Runs his fingers
through my hair,
brushes kisses
from ear to ear,

chin to forehead,
and back again
until I'm flushed
for other reasons.

Jordan kisses
away my doubts.

❧

Key in ignition.
Engine grrrinds.

"C'mon JJ, start
for me."

Pats dash,
rubs steering wheel,
flicks sea shell.
He tries again.
Nothing.
Nada.
Dead.

"We have to get
to the island," I say.
"I promised Brenda."

"We're a half-hour
from Northport
Pier. Plenty of time to

catch the five o'clock."

"How?"

"Our friends
will pass this way.
We'll get a ride."

Text friend after friend
after friend after
friend after
friend.

No room.
Room for one
not for two.

"Austin texted.
No one's going with Travis."
Cringe.

"I'd hitchhike first,
walk and swim."

"Maybe your mom?"

"She can't leave the store."

Incoming text from Matt Busby:
Emerson's driving alone. Try him.

"Emerson has space."

Groan. "Anyone
but Emerson."

"Travis?" I grimace.

Shake steering wheel,
kiss the dash, Jordan
turns the key. No
resurrection of the dead.

"Fine. Call Emerson."

TWENTY-EIGHT

"Accept the place the divine providence has found for you, the society of your contemporaries, the connection of events."
Ralph Waldo Emerson

EMERSON

HWY 42 AND WASHINGTON ISLAND   FRIDAY, 3:11 P.M.

ANGIE'S PHONE NUMBER flashes on my screen. To answer or not to answer, that is the question. Voice mail wins.

I crank up the Violent Femmes, a '80s punkish country-rock band similar to the younger Red-Eyed Loons, and drive with the windows down toward Northport Pier. There is nothing like the smell of spring in Door County—the lake air, turned farm fields, cherry trees on the verge of blooming, damp limestone.

I left early for the five o'clock ferry. There's a stop I need to make on the route, one I've contemplated since my visit with Dr. Shale. I head along the west coast, north on Highway 42. A ghost to revisit. A ghost to free from earthly shackles chained to me. I'm not sure I can do it. But I promised myself I'd try.

Doubt creeps through my system like poison. Yet, I'm driven forward, the need to face the past and bury it for good the only antidote.

Five minutes later, I pull into the parking lot for the Settlement Shops in Fish Creek, park in the spot closest to the corner of Highway 42—Egg Harbor Road and Main Street—and get out. I'm not sure if it's the moisture coming off the water or if it's a reaction to being in this place, but suddenly my skin is clammy, chilled. I hesitate, look behind and up toward the top of the hill for any traffic that might barrel down before I cross Egg Harbor Road. Turning around, I face the rebuilt gift shop on the other side of Main.

For a few minutes I take in the scene.

Behind the shop's plate glass, fine glazed pottery, handmade leather goods, and jewelry are on display. A wooden bench presses up against another showcase window. It wasn't here thirteen years ago. I search for evidence of the past—a memorial perhaps?—but see none. An American flag flickers with the breeze and fish-shaped windsocks balloon out from the awning. Don't remember these, either.

As I examine the sight, a weird dip-and-drop sensation from the top of my skull to my feet makes me lightheaded and oddly disconnected from my body. Leaning against the stop-sign post, I concentrate on breathing—a deliberate, agonizing effort not to pass out. The environment shifts and transforms into my past, and I'm as dizzy and weak and helpless as I was over thirteen years ago. It's like I'm a part of an old home movie, shaky, grainy.

My five-year-old self is inside the gift shop, stir-crazy, claustrophobic from the innumerable knickknacks overstuffing the store. "Can I wait outside?" I beg Mom.

She appraises me. Takes pity on me. "Stay by the door where I can see you," she says.

I scamper outside before she can change her mind, relieved and revived by the cooler air. Something silver and shiny catches my attention, and I crouch down, pick it up. A quarter. When I stand, my eyes dart to the old-fashioned candy store a short distance down the street. In tall jars along the window, a sour-apple licorice rope calls my name. So does chewy taffy and caramel. My mouth puckers and waters. I turn around to go inside to ask Mom if I can spend my quarter in the candy store.

A high-pitched cry stops me cold, paralyzes me.

Time slows. A woman flails her arms frantically in front of her, shouting at me. I hear her, but don't understand. Run? Why? She knocks into me, pushing me out of the way as a tan truck jumps the curb, slams into her, misses me as I tumble. The truck smashes into the store with an explosion of noise. Shards of glass and metal rain onto the street. I inhale a plume of dirt. And cough.

Time speeds up again.

I see the woman under the truck bed. Her arm flings to the side. I crawl to her, kneel next to her, take her hand. Thick auburn hair fans over her shoulders and spills onto the concrete. Her eyes shine like green marbles with flecks of gold, and lock on mine. She tries to speak. I lower my head, but only a gurgle sound comes from her mouth. She blows spit bubbles. A red river flows from her nose, trickles toward her lips. Her legs twitch, and she stills.

I'm grabbed from behind and dragged away. The woman's dirty, scraped hand slips from mine. Sirens, screams fill the air. I cover my ears. Mom cradles my face, peers into my eyes, and I see her mouth move. She repeats herself again and again until I hear, "Are you hurt?"

I'm scraped, bruised, and there's an indescribable pressure squeezing my heart. I shake my head. She scoops me into her arms, says something to the saleswoman from the boutique, and carries me to the minivan only a few parking spaces away. Mom straps me into the car seat, leaves the rear passenger door open, and tells me she'll be right back.

Moments later, an EMT and police officer return with her. Carefully, I'm checked for injuries. Nothing that won't heal quickly. They ask questions I don't answer.

Some wounds slash so deep, they change you forever.

A day after the accident, I shut down. Snapped.

Didn't speak for a month. Series of CAT scans and an MRI showed no head injury, at least not the visible kind. For six weeks, I became the youngest patient in the children's mental ward, under the care of psychiatrists and psychologists. Acute mental psychosis brought on by PTSD, at least that's what I was told years later. I had no memory of being in the hospital until my sisters' and mother's voices pulled me out of the fog.

I became animated and, at times, anxious around my family, especially my mother, my sisters. I followed them, kept track of them, and even had my own phone to contact them when I became apprehensive. Their reassurance helped calm the panic that was always lurking, ready to surface. I watched them, fell asleep next to them at night. And I saw a psychologist two to three times a week for over a year. A lot of play therapy. I missed kindergarten because I couldn't leave my mother's side.

That was when the doctor suggested we leave Fish Creek and the accident scene behind. A fresh start. A few weeks before the new school year started we moved a half-hour away to Sturgeon Bay. We've avoided this corner ever since.

Maybe it helped.

My sisters were under strict orders not to discuss the accident with anyone in our new school. The accident was in the past and I would learn to move on with the help of Dr. Shale, whom I saw on a weekly basis, then twice a month, then on an "as needed basis" by the time I entered fourth grade.

In talking about the lady who died, I was told nothing could have been done to save her. There was nothing I could have done to help her. She had internal injuries, head trauma.

One psychologist told me she died instantly. Wrong. She squeezed my hand. I saw the light fade from her eyes. Death marked me as He took her away.

I was plagued with what ifs. What if I had run? If I had stayed inside with my mom? If I hadn't picked up the quarter? If she hadn't pushed me out of the way? Why her and not me?

I don't know who she was, and I never asked my parents if they knew. Only when I was in high school did I realize I could obtain the police report. But I haven't done it. Mostly because I've wanted life to move forward, but it's also because I'm afraid. She saved me and died because of me, and not knowing her name is a tiny barrier between us, the anonymity like a small gift of immunity for my tiny part in her death.

Until my conversation with Frankie and her talk of suicide, I thought I had successfully moved past the accident. Sure, on occasion when I'd see a woman with the same color hair or there was a loud noise, it would trigger the memory like a static electric shock.

And I admit, Thanksgiving and Christmas and birthdays—family times were the worst. I'd think about the woman and wonder about her. Where was she from? Was she married? A mother? Where did she work? Did she play a musical instrument? Sing? Was she buried? Cremated? At times, I could see her before me like she were flesh and blood.

Dr. Shale was right. I've done everything I could to control what was in my hands. School, sports, watching out for Angie. Being the DD. I wanted to make the woman's sacrifice worth something. For the past two years I've kept the horrors of that accident at bay. Until Frankie. And now...

I can only do my best. I know that's the answer. I can rationalize and explain and unburden myself of all responsibility. But when will my heart catch up? When will it let me off the hook, as Isabelle would say? I dig my palm into my scar hard against my ribs, but it does nothing to ease that band that tightens with every beat.

Beeeeeeep! I jump. A horn blasts again. I steady myself on the stop-sign post, glance over my shoulder.

"Emerson! EMERSON!" It's Angie, waving at me from the driver's side of my car. Without looking, she runs across the road. Halts in front of me.

Breathless, she says, "I've been calling and calling your name. What's the matter? Are you all right?"

I nod, as breathless as she is.

"You don't look all right. It's like you were in a trance. You scared me. You were so still. You didn't answer me."

"I'm fine."

Her eyes dash to the storefront on Main. "What were you staring at?"

"Nothing," I say. "Why are you here?"

Angie's expression shifts from concerned to deeply perplexed. "Aren't you here because of my message? I told you, Jordan's car won't start." She motions to the side and I scan the parking lot until I spot Jordan's heap.

My T-shirt feels tight against my throat and chest and I reach up, stretch out the neck. "Sorry. Didn't know."

"We need a ride to Northport and—"

"I can't, Ang. I need to be alone." I wipe the sweat from my forehead. Hair sticks to my skin and I peel it free with my fingers.

"But...we already put our stuff in your trunk."

I look toward my car. Jordan rests his forearms on the open passenger door. I pat my pockets and locate my keys. My body aches like I'm coming down with the flu. "No. I don't...think I'm going."

Once again, her gaze lingers on the storefront, then darts to me. Her expression deepens into the classic Angie frown. I've known her long enough to understand she's struggling with what to say, to ask me. We've been at this crossroad before—questions I refuse to answer about personal stuff. I'll shut her down again, and she knows it. In the past, whenever I came close to revealing this secret to her, something held me back. I didn't trust her, couldn't. Not with this. Her revelations the other day proved my instinct was right all along.

"Please, Emerson give us ride? I *promised* Brenda I'd come to the party. She *needs* me. We tried our entire class and everyone's cars are filled up."

Jordan walks over, drapes an arm over Angie. "Hey, we really appreciate you coming to get us. I'm pretty sure the starter's completely shot, but if you've got jumper cables, we could give it a try, see if we can get 'er running."

I shake my head. The flu-like symptoms punch my stomach and sweat pools on my neck, drips down my back.

Jordan says, "You don't look so good."

"I'll be right back." I sprint across Main and round the corner to the rear of the shops on the shore side of Fish Creek. I position myself far enough out of view to get sick without being noticed by a passing car or a pedestrian. My head throbs. I flip onto my back, knees up, arms out, chest heaving, and ignore the pebbles jabbing into my shoulder blades and spine.

I'm relieved Angie and Jordan didn't follow me. But of course that doesn't mean that they won't come in search of me soon. I really don't want to start coming up with excuses for my behavior, for getting sick. And even though I still feel sick, I force myself to move. I take it slow, push up onto all fours. My head droops close to the cracked asphalt. When I regain my equilibrium, I shift and balance onto my knees and toes. Finally I'm able to lift my head, then stand. I take a step, then two. My pace belongs to an old man.

From across the street, I spot Angie and Jordan sitting on the curb, focused on their phones. When I approach, they look up. Angie says, "It's okay, Emerson. We'll call a tow truck." Her face and tone radiates empathy and mild disappointment. I'm riddled with guilt.

"I'll take you," I say, without thinking it through.

"You will?"

I don't respond. *Idiot!* I'm furious with myself for giving in to rescue mode, for falling into old habits. Isabelle would have a field day. I have this mini-conversation with her in my head. *I know, I know,* I say. *I'm trying to stop. Cut me some slack, okay? You wouldn't leave them here, either.*

All at once it occurs to me that I'm the one who needs to give myself the break, to accept myself for who I am. Is it so bad to care? To be kind? Is there a balance between feeling burdened and doing something because you want to, because it's the right thing to do?

I pass my car and walk to the vending machine, pay for a ginger ale to settle my stomach. When I return, Jordan's sitting in front, Angie's in back. Nice choice of seating arrangements. I glance in the rearview mirror and meet Angie's eyes. There's gratitude, not an expression I'd normally see from her.

I start the car.

Blasting the Violent Femmes doesn't help my pounding head much, but it keeps Angie and Jordan from talking. There are numerous emotions lingering from my accident-scene reunion, and I'm trying to process them. I wish I had had more time without their invasion. Reliving the nightmare, and seeing the place as it is now, blend together. Past. Present. It's like overlaying one image on top of another, layer by layer by layer, until the past is painted over. Yet underneath, there's still a scar. Like my scar. My right hand brushes over my ribcage before I return it to the steering wheel.

Life moved on. I can move on.

It's such a basic thought, but it gives me comfort. The elastic band wrapped around my heart eases a fraction. When I inhale, it doesn't ache as much. Neither does my scar.

Jordan drums his fingers against his thigh, obviously liking the music. Strange coincidence Jordan's Jeep broke down at that very spot. Stranger still, that Angie called me. Is there some deeper meaning to it?

Divine Providence? Was I meant to help them? Thirty minutes later, I still don't have an answer as the road zigzags back and forth, back and forth again and again and again and again. And then, it straightens out and we arrive at Northport Pier.

The pier is packed with students from Southern Door, Sturgeon Bay, Sevastopol, Gibraltar. The party has started. I drop off Angie and Jordan near the ferry pay booth and drive to the parking area.

It would be so easy to turn around and go home. No one would miss me.

I park. Stay in the car with the doors locked. And think.

What am I doing? I had made Dr. Shale a promise I'd do something for myself without worrying about anyone else or looking for hidden danger. I'd have *fun*?! But I've already gone into rescue mode by bringing Jordan and Angie here and it seems to defeat the purpose. This party, all these people...

Once I'm on the island, if I don't catch the last ferry back at eight-thirty, I'm stuck until morning.

I just wish I'd get a sign. Is this where I'm supposed to be? I look behind to the zigzagging road cutting through the forest leading back to the site of the accident and home. I stare ahead. Throngs of people hang out, laugh, goof off. Some guys toss a football, others a Frisbee. So normal. No worries. They're having *fun*.

I could do it.

The late afternoon sun broils above. I open my window. A few girls I know from school walk by and wave. Amazing considering that less than a week ago they believed the worst of me, treated me like I wasn't worth the dirt under their shoes. Catalina saunters over. She braces her arms against my car roof, leans in, and smiles flirtatiously, a smile she's flashed my way on numerous occasions. Angie accused me of hooking up with her. Never. Her ego is bigger than Wisconsin, with breasts to match. In her low-cut top, I get an eyeful. She notices me noticing. The grin on her face spreads with satisfaction. "Hey, Emerson."

"Cat."

"I have a double sleeping bag. Come find me." Then she laughs, bounces away, catches up with the rest of her friends. The girls bump hips, giggle. Catalina flips her raven hair, turns around, sees me watching, and blows me a kiss.

No thank you. Catalina isn't my idea of fun. More like a warning sign of impending danger. *Go home.*

But then Colin Michaels, the lead singer of the Red-Eyed Loons, parks next to me. He rounds the hood to the passenger side, opens the door, slips on his guitar strap, and hooks a finger into the top loop on his pack. He dips down and says, "Hey."

I untie my tongue. "Hi." How two letters can sound so stupid—

"It's Emerson, right?"

"Impressive. You remember."

"I try," he says, smiling sheepishly. "But your shirt's kind of a giveaway."

I look down. I'm wearing a Red-Eyed Loons T-shirt signed "Rock hard, Emerson," with the band's signatures. "Oh." I let out an embarrassed chuckle.

"Whadda say, mate? You ready to cross Death's Door?" He motions toward the pier.

Death's Door is a notorious, turbulent section of water we have to cross to get to Washington Island—there's even vodka named after it. Hundreds of people lost their lives navigating those waters over the past hundred or so years. Bad sign?

Screw it.

"Yeah, I'm ready." I grab my camping equipment and backpack and join him.

❧

AT LEAST FIFTY of us are still waiting around for some of the island guys to shuttle us from Detroit Harbor to Boyer's Bluff in their pickups. With the sun going down and a brisk breeze blowing off the water, there's a nip in the air. I zip up my hoodie and sit off to the side to wait for a ride to the party.

Another ten minutes tick off the clock when a guy finally pulls up in a truck. He calls out to us, "Hey, I'm Brian. It's a short drive to the party, so cram in." Three girls squeeze into the cab with him. Six of us climb into the bed with our gear and coolers. He drives out of the harbor and it's not long before he makes a left onto Main Road. We pass the school, baseball field, farms, an old steepled church. I notice that each and every time another vehicle approaches from the opposite direction, both Brian and the other driver lift a hand in greeting, and I wonder if it's an island practice.

A few minutes and several waves later, including one from a couple walking their dog, Brian turns onto a rutty road covered in patchy areas of moss and dead leaves. The truck bounces as it climbs and winds to the top. Three-quarters of the way up, Brian pulls over because the last section of the driveway is blocked with other cars and trucks. We jump out. I swing the strap from my one-man tent and my backpack over my shoulder and hoof it to the top of the hill.

I take in the scene, wander along the fringe of the action. People are everywhere. I'm amazed at how much land surrounds the majestic limestone lighthouse with its large porch, numerous shuttered windows, and its lamp tower rising above the tree line. There's an expansive lawn filling with tents, a garden on the right side of the house with a small, old structure behind it—probably the original outhouse—and woods everywhere else.

Navigating through the crowd, I walk behind the lighthouse. The view from the cliffs is spectacular. The sun's rays bounce against the turquoise lake like God dropped glitter from the sky. Several islands dot the horizon with sandy beaches and spectrum of greens, blues, pinks, yellows. Despite the absent palm trees, it's hard to believe I'm in Wisconsin and not on some paradise island in the middle of the Pacific.

Even with all the background party noise, it's so... peaceful.

After I've had my fill, I move on, ready to explore more. A bonfire blazes in a stone pit on the left side of the house.

Matt comes up to me with a beer and says, "Hey, glad you made it. We claimed an area by that clump of trees." He points to a spot not far from us. "Want help setting up your tent?"

"That'd be great."

He takes the tent bag from my hand and, after tossing a stick aside, dumps out the pieces onto the grass. "This place is incredible, don't you think?" he asks.

"I'd live here," I say. "In a heartbeat."

"You and me both, my friend. From what I hear, the girl who owns this place is available. Maybe one of us will get lucky."

I laugh. "She's all yours. I need a break right now."

We're greeted by the rest of our varsity basketball teammates and some of their girlfriends. Forty-five minutes later, we have ten tents lined up in two rows.

With the sun melting into the horizon, the paper lanterns and thousands of twinkle lights draped in the trees illuminate the area in blue, green, and white. One of the girls calls for a group shot of us guys under a cluster of globes. She wrangles us in, but with all the goofing off and laughing, no one stays still for more than a second. Travis moons the camera, and I have to say, it's a good replacement for his face. I can only hope his pimply ass gets tagged with his name and put on every social network site imaginable.

The girls have their turn for pictures, which is much more subdued, and then collectively agree to being hungry and thirsty.

We make our way to the crowded porch. Tables line one side. There's an assortment of dips and chips, veggies, and baked goods. I wolf down a slice of the best cherry pie I've ever had, then polish it off with two chocolate chip cookies. Matt dunks his hand into a cooler and fishes out a beer. He offers it to me, and the look in his eye clearly shows he knows I won't take it. He's just being hospitable. I hesitate and take it from him anyway, almost like it's a dare, but it's my dare, not his. His expression is neutral. He gets himself one and takes a long gulp. I open the can, tip it into my mouth, and choke down froth.

Lifting my fingers to my neck, my pulse knocks, knocks, knocks against them. I wipe my mouth with my sweatshirt sleeve, desperate to spit. A girl who

I believe is from Gibraltar comes over to Matt and hugs him. He's just about to introduce us as I shuffle around a few people and get away. Tossing my beer, I maneuver around the masses with an end goal of solitude. I'm waylaid by the stage.

The Red-Eyed Loons begin "No Going Back."

You possessed my heart,
I claimed yours,
'Til you let me go.
Oh, you let me go.
Damn the marks you left,
Now ink across my chest.
I won't look back, no going back.

I allow the music to take me in, allow myself to relax, close my eyes. *No going back.*

After they finish the song, Randy Rane, the Red-Eyed Loon's electric guitar player, cranks out a kick-ass solo performance, shredding and wailing much to his fans' roaring approval.

When he finishes, Colin Michaels introduces the band, and I use the opportunity to take in the crowd. The moon peeks out from the clouds, illuminating the area. I spot Brenda at the edge of the mosh pit standing with her arm around that Brian guy. Just as I wonder about Brenda and Brian's relationship, the Red-Eyed Loons begin "Reaper." There's a loud cheer. Brian removes his arm from Brenda and fixes his hands to the waist of a petite, brown-haired girl in front of him. As the music ratchets up to a fever pitch, he pulls her into him. She spins around, pushes against his chest. He lets go of her, raising his hands in apology.

She moves away, dips and dives through the crowd, her hair swaying wildly across her back. I catch a quick

Hello?

glimpse of her face—clearly upset. In less than a beat, Brian starts after her. The protective instinct ingrained in me kicks into high gear, and I fight every twinge to go after her. "Not why I'm here," I remind myself.

My body missed the memo because I step forward and not so gracefully collide with Catalina, who spills beer on the guy grinding into her.

He arches back, lets out a few choice swearwords. The pale light dims to gray as the moon goes behind cloud cover.

"It was Emerson's fault," she says, flicking her thumb into my clavicle. *Thanks, Cat.* A friend of hers reaches in, yanks her out of the middle like sandwich meat. I'm evenly matched with this guy, give or take ten pounds, and I took taekwondo. Defending myself won't be a problem. That's all I need to put the cherry on top of this rotten week.

The guy strips off his soaked Wisconsin Badgers sweatshirt and throws it at my face. I'm hit with the smell of a brewery and the sight of his orangutan chest.

I unzip my hoodie and hold it out to him. "Can we call it even?" I ask. He shoots me a look that says I'm the biggest moron on this island. Right now, I agree. I'd love to kick myself for falling into old habits, one after another. Will I ever learn? That girl with Brian is not my problem. I'm my biggest problem.

Beer-belching orangutan takes my hoodie.

Problem solved, I turn around and move the opposite direction from where I saw that girl heading. As I make my way out of the crowd, I notice there are a lot of people older than us, mid- to upper-twenties, probably native islanders here to listen to the band.

I move toward my tent to pick up my extra sweatshirt. Moaning floats from inside a few zipped flaps and I hurry past them, ignoring it the best I can.

There are dozens and dozens more tents now, a few identical to mine. I look for the clump of trees, but there are lots of clumps of trees and I'm not exactly sure where we set up. After one miss, I see the blaze orange ribbon Matt attached to the top of his tent pole. Thank you, Matt.

Other than those few occupied tents, most people are by the bonfire, porch, band, the fish boil, or hanging out near the cliffs. I relish the relative quiet and allow it to wash over me. *This is good,* I think. *Not being responsible for anyone else.* And even though it's good, something inside longs for something more. It presses against my heart. My scar throbs and I pause for a moment to think about what's...missing.

Frankie. I almost say the name out loud when I spot a girl tying her hiking boot in front of my tent. When she notices me, she stands and slinks away like she wants to fade into the night. I don't move. Then I recognize her. She's the girl who shoved that guy, Brian, and bolted when he put his hands on her. "Are you okay?" I ask.

She shoots me a furious look, like I invaded her space, her privacy. Without answering, she turns on her heels and starts walking away. Under my breath, I say, "Nothing can bring you peace but yourself." Why did I quote Emerson? It's not something I do. Ever. Except during my conversation with Frankie, and if I recall correctly, she started it.

Suddenly, the girl stops. Whirls around. Stares at me.

I stare back.

Twinkle lights shine on her from above, dusting her with white. My eyes seem to sharpen and I notice small details. Like her glitter nail polish, the sparkle of her small hoop earrings. The one in her nose. She's beautiful, in an unpretentious way. I had said she was petite, but in this light she's seems frail, like fine crystal. There's something about her, perhaps it's the intensity of her eyes—dark orbs with rings of light—that mesmerizes me.

Her voice is distant, airy. "Emerson?"

Did she say my name? I glance down at my shirt and can barely read the inscription. There's no way she saw it. I have this weird sense of déjà vu, and a surge of energy whips through me. I murmur, "Yeah, it's me."

"Is it *really you*?"

It's the way she asks. Goose bumps burst onto my skin. My eyes sweep over her and I move toward her without rational thought. Purely reactionary. "Frankie?"

She laughs, and I remember that sweet laugh. I laugh too.

All at once I'm taken in and blown away. My mind empties of everything but her. Here, standing in front of me, looking at me with awe and wonder. Frankie is real, and I found her. We found each other.

"Yes. Frankie." She gives her head a tiny shake. "Well, not Frankie. I'm Tricia Boyer."

Staring at her, it's hard to believe this girl—this breathing, beaming, beautiful girl—could ever have thought about ending her life. I'm a million times grateful that I was the one who had her grandma's old phone number, that she called, and that I answered.

"You're here," she whispers. "You're really here?"

I take a step closer, and nod, not quite believing it, either.

It's as if our grins emit a force field, pulling us together. I gather her up in my arms, and in that second the band around my heart dissolves completely.

Liza Wiemer

She presses her cheek into my shirt and we're wrapped up in each other like a present. I breathe in her scent. Bonfire, lemon, and lavender? I inhale again. No lavender.

I say, "I-I've been thinking about you. A lot." I hold her closer, afraid if I let go, she may disappear.

Her arms tighten against my waist. "Same."

At this moment, there is no better four-letter word.

She steps back, rocks on her heels, angling away to look at me with her jade-colored eyes. "This is incredibly surreal. I needed some space, some quiet. My plan was to go inside." She draws her thumb over her shoulder. "This is my house, my party, and I wanted to hide out for a bit in my bedroom. But then, I don't know. I can't explain why I changed my mind. Something drew me to the tents. So I thought, why not? And here you are. With me."

"Tricia," I say, continuing to grin like a fool.

"Emerson." My name has never sounded better. Loud voices from a nearby tent momentarily draw our attention away from each other. "Do you...want to walk along the bluff? It should be quieter there."

"Sure."

She moves toward the lighthouse. I glance at my tent and decide to wait to get my sweatshirt. Matching her stride, I lower my voice, and say, "So, how have you been?"

Tricia's expression turns as serious as mine. "Good. Really good. A lot has happened since we talked. It's hard for me to believe I'm the same person who called you." Suddenly, her feet become her focus. "That was the lowest moment in my life, but I want you to know, that's not...me. It's not who I want to be."

"I could tell," I say. "And it's okay."

She throws me a sideward glance. "Is it?"

"Absolutely."

Strains of the Red-Eyed Loons's "Freedom," a song about individuality, floats over to us with the breeze. It's one of my favorites. I do my best to tune them out and give Tricia my full attention.

She says, "There are times I miss my grandma so much, it's hard to breathe."

My visit to the accident scene earlier today surfaces in my mind and how reliving that nightmare left me breathless. "It's understandable," I say.

"But for the first time in a long time, I'm not consumed by everything I've lost, you know? I'm doing my best to think about a future. To make plans." She twists a ring on her right ring finger.

I ask, "What kind of plans?"

She starts walking again, following the gentle downhill slope of the cliff, taking us farther away from the band and the bonfire. "Well, I'm thinking culinary school. My grandma was a phenomenal cook and an even better baker."

"Banana chocolate-chip cherry muffins?"

"You remembered?"

The surprise and joy in her voice strike at my heart. I want to say, *How could I forget? I've replayed every detail of our conversation over and over again. I even googled Ava Gardner.* But I nod instead.

"I made fourteen dozen for breakfast tomorrow," she says. "The house smelled so good and it reminded me of my grandma so much, that it got me thinking. She had at least a hundred recipes on scraps of paper and notecards, many her own invention, like the muffins. So I'm going to sort through them, and I just might create my own island cookbook. Who knows?" She shrugs. "I may even sell it at a local gift shop."

"Well, if you need someone to taste—I mean, I'm happy to taste your muffins." Heat skips along my neck to the tips of my ears. I shoot her a sheepish smile. "No innuendo intended." Her bright laugh is a worthy reward. "You can cook for me anytime. I'll shut up now."

"Innuendo forgotten. And we'll see about you trying my cooking after you eat my muffins." She gives me a playful shove. Her touch sears into my shoulder. This time I'm the one who laughs. I love that we can joke with one another.

After a short, comfortable silence, I say, "So, this is all yours?" I sweep my arm in front of me and motion toward the lighthouse.

"Thirty-five acres of bluff and forest. It's been in the family for at least a hundred years."

"It's magnificent here."

For a second, she frowns. "It is. But for the past five months I couldn't see it. Everything about Boyer's Bluff made me miserable. But since we talked, I fell in love with it all over again. It's hard to explain, but things happened after we hung up. Amazing things that changed everything."

"I'm glad. Really. You deserve only the best."

"Do I?"

She stumbles over a rock, and I reach out, snag her around the waist, and steady her. "Absolutely." My eyes lock on hers. Near the edge of her jeans, my fingertips brush skin. Her breath hitches, and she sucks in her bottom lip. I let my hands linger a beat longer, holding her in place, wanting so much to gather her into me. But I let go.

She turns and points to a spot in the distance I can't quite see in the dark. "C'mon. It's one of my favorite views of Lake Michigan." As we maneuver around a clump of birch trees, she asks, "So, what was your week like?"

I shiver.

"Are you cold? I have a sweatshirt in the house, if you'd like to borrow one."

"Actually, that's why I was by the tents." I cross my arms over my chest. "I was going to put one on. Somehow, I got distracted." I smile at her and she smiles back and I have this fleeting thought that if I could spend the rest of my life making her smile, I'd be happy. Except for the desire to touch Tricia again, being here with her, talking with her feels natural, comfortable, as easy as it was over the phone. It's not something I want to lose again. "Stop." I say.

She spins toward me. "What's the matter?"

"You made me another promise, remember?" I take out my cell. "Give me your number."

She laughs, and I want more of that, too. "I love your laugh," I tell her, and I'm rewarded again. I pass her my phone and point to the rectangle outlined in her jeans pocket. "Give me yours."

She does.

In my greatest fantasies, I didn't picture Frankie-Tricia like this—radiant, beautiful, real. It's overwhelming. Amazing. A *miracle*. And suddenly it takes all my effort to keep the floodgates shut. While I punch in my information and number, I let my hair fall over my eyes. Under the shield, I think about the fact that maybe if Angie and Jordan hadn't been at the accident scene, I may not have come. It's possible I would have turned around, gone home. I almost want to thank them.

We return our phones to each other.

The breeze picks up, carries a chill off the lake. "I could use my sweatshirt."

She leads the way back, and once we reach the tent city, I take over, keeping in sight the flag Matt tied to the pole. By the sound of things, a few more sleeping bags are occupied, and I really wish the Red-Eyed Loons weren't taking a break. I hum "Freedom" until... "This is my tent."

Tricia's expression turns weary as she scans the area like she's searching for someone. *Maybe she's thinking of that other guy? The one who put his paws on her in the mosh pit? Brian.*

A protective twinge hits my conscience, pounding in my head like a woodpecker's incessant pecking against a tree. The need to know why Tricia was hiding out earlier is as strong as the reproach telling me not to ask. Concern wins out. "I saw you before, listening to the band. Of course, I didn't know it was you. That guy, Brian? Do you know him? Was he...bothering you?"

She shakes her head, causing her hair to swing over her shoulders. "No. Brian's my ex."

Her answer feels like a slap. "Oh."

"We're—" She swipes her hand in front of her eyes like she wishes she could wipe out the memory. "It was...just a moment."

"Okay, as long as you're all right."

"Perfectly all right." Silence ripples between us, but it's not awkward. We're both lost in our own thoughts.

She taps her pocket, and says, "Hey, you changed your number."

"So you *did* call."

"I did. And as much as I really wanted you to answer, hoped that you would, it forced me to focus, to think about what I wanted to do with my life. But then again, I was also scared that I'd never talk to you again." She tilts her head up to take in the milky, black-blue sky.

"It was pretty much torture for me," I say, making her gaze snap to mine. "I couldn't stop thinking about you. I finally decided that I had to let the idea of meeting you go. To let *you* go. To forget about you." I don't like that her mouth turns down, so I quickly add, "Thankfully, that wasn't meant to be."

With a shy smile, she reaches for my hand. Her fingers lace with mine and it feels almost too good to be true. I rub my thumb over the ridges of her knuckles.

She says, "I prayed we'd meet. Maybe that's why I agreed to have this party? Do you know Brenda Alston? She's Brian's cousin. This whole thing was her idea."

I take a halting step sideways. *How did I forget that Brenda had a hand in this party?* "Yeah." That's all I can manage. Hard to believe I have Brenda, of all people, to thank for my reunion with Tricia. And maybe Angie and Jordan. Links in a weird cosmic chain?

After gathering my thoughts, I say, "From the moment we hung up, everything changed for me, too." I look at the sky. A few stars shine bright among the patches of clouds. The sound that escapes my mouth is part-laugh, part-groan. I refocus on Tricia. "Up until this moment, which is one of the best moments of my life, this has been one of the worst weeks of my life."

She shrinks away, but I step closer so our separation is exactly the same as it was before. "I'm sorry," she says.

"Don't be. It's not your fault."

"What happened? Y-you broke up with your girlfriend, right?"

"I did," I say quickly to reassure her. "In the end that turned out okay." Dread weighs on my shoulders. It's not easy to look at her, but the way she responds will have everything to do with how much I share about the accident and what happened after.

"I'd like to tell you something important. Something about today. Something I did before I came here—" I cut myself off. Not because of her expression, which is nothing but kind and concerned. It's because I'm unsure how to continue.

Tricia reaches out, briefly touches my arm. "Tell me."

"I don't know where to start."

"The beginning?"

I let out a long, ragged breath. "That was thirteen years ago, when I was five years old and living in—"

"Tricia?"

Startled, we jump apart.

"Brian?" He moves out of the shadows.

"Yeah." He eyes me with curiosity and distain, then completely zeros in on Tricia as if I'm not here. I'm half-tempted to introduce myself, but I step away, kneel, and unzip my tent. He says, "Am I...interrupting?"

"No, it's okay. What's going on?" she asks.

I yank my pack out and remove my extra sweatshirt.

"I need to talk to you for a minute. In private, please?"

Sliding my hood off the top of my head, I move over to Tricia. You'd think I could walk away, leave them to get on with it. But I can't. I don't.

Tricia tugs her sleeves over her fingers, buries her fists inside the cuffs, and glances at me. "Can we catch up in a bit?"

"Text me." I switch my focus to Brian. "I won't go anywhere."

That gets his attention. He extends his hand to me. "Brian."

His grip is killer, but I don't flinch. I match it. "Emerson." I don't see any indication that my name registers with him, so my guess is that Tricia must not have told him about our early morning phone call. Interesting. Disappointing?

He turns toward her, lays a possessive hand on her shoulder. She twists to the side. I smirk to myself, taking her evasive move as a small consolation.

I watch them disappear in the maze of tents and catch sight of them heading toward the lighthouse. If I had a hammer and nails, I'd consider banging them into the soles of my shoes. The urge to follow, to make sure she's safe, compels me forward. But the closer I get, the more I want to respect Tricia's space. That outweighs everything. *If she needs me, she'll text.*

Instead, I hang a right. Skirting the bonfire, I walk along the cliffs and contemplate how strange and incredible it is to have found Frankie—Tricia.

Tricia, who right now is having a serious conversation with her ex-boyfriend. Does he want her back? He doesn't seem to be able to keep his hands off her. And if she wants him?

I shudder at the idea. *We can be friends,* I tell myself. No, I don't want her to be with Brian. Why did I let her leave? The need to turn around and go to her builds. But once again, I ignore it and I force myself to keep going.

Surprisingly, the farther away from the lighthouse I get, the easier it is to relax. The sound of the waves crashing below almost lulls me into contentment. There's something about Boyer's Bluff's beauty. The lighthouse and the land. The mixture of cedar and earth and damp that's just a little sweeter than any other place I've been to on the peninsula. I feel a pull here, a tug that I undeniably attribute to Tricia.

The path veers west, dipping toward Lake Michigan, drawing me into the forest. Another smell mixes with the cedar and earth. *Lavender.* I examine the lichen-covered rocks and the forest floor. Does lavender grow in this climate? In the spring? It must, because the scent only grows stronger and stronger. Except I can't find the plant and its purple bloom anywhere.

I check my phone. 9:08 P.M. No calls. No texts.

I've been gone long enough. Once I'm on the edge of the action, I search for Tricia and Brian among small clusters of people. Boiling fish and potatoes and onions and carrots waft into the air, replacing the lingering smell of lavender. My stomach grumbles.

The bonfire's yellow, red, and white flames crackle and shoot into the night sky. All around the stone pit, people roast marshmallows, hot dogs, and venison brats. My mouth waters. I spear a hot dog onto a discarded stick and approach the flames. It only takes a minute for the skin to bubble and brown. Off to the side, there's a table filled with baskets of chips and several open bags of buns. I grab one, slide my hot dog inside, and top it off with mustard, ketchup, and relish.

Angie catches my attention with a wave. Jordan, who's at her side, has his hand in her back pocket. He lifts his chin like he's giving me permission to join them. I bite into my hot dog and stroll over. Seeing them together, you'd think I'd feel something, even a twinge of regret or envy. But nothing.

Jordan says, "What a place, huh? Did you see inside the lighthouse?"

"Not yet." I take another bite, lick the mustard from my bottom lip.

"Brenda gave us a tour," Angie says. "You should see the antiques. My mom would flip to have them in her shop. The view from the lantern room is spectacular.

Maybe if you ask, Brenda'll take you inside, show you around?"

I shrug, keep my face neutral. Jordan tucks Angie under his chin and wraps his arms around her from behind. I almost laugh at how he's claiming her. Which is a stabbing reminder that Tricia is with Brian.

Angie gestures with her head, directing me to look left. "See Brenda?"

It's not just Brenda I notice. Some guy has his arms around her like he's trying to teach her how to cast a fishing pole. She's beaming like a stage spotlight.

Without detaching from her, the guy slides four marshmallows onto a stick and spins it like a rotisserie over the flames. Angie and Jordan and I watch the two of them. And when they simultaneously give mouth-to-mouth resuscitation to the same marshmallow, Angie whispers something to Jordan. He shakes his head and they start arguing about Brenda.

That's my exit. Lesson learned with nosing into Brenda's business.

My phone vibrates.

A text from Tricia. *"Meet me in front of the lighthouse?"*

Every muscle in my back and shoulders uncoils. Just as I hit SEND to tell her I'm on my way, Brian approaches Brenda. "I'm leaving," he says. Our eyes lock for a moment and I can't even begin to figure out the look he gives me—not hatred or resentment or even curiosity. It's almost like he expects me to sprout another head or glow florescent green. His gaze flickers back to Brenda. "If you see my sister, let her know she can find me in my studio."

I turn and jog to the lighthouse.

TWENTY-NINE

"The secret of the world is, the tie between person and event.
Person makes event, event person."
Ralph Waldo Emerson

TRICIA

AFTER LEAVING EMERSON standing by his tent, Brian and I made our way into the lighthouse. I chose the kitchen because it's private but still open enough for anyone to pop in. Earlier, he had put his hands on my waist while we listened to the Red-Eyed Loons, but I pulled away, not at all appreciating the boyfriend move. He apologized. Said it was habit. I walked away. Now I hoped we weren't going to get into another discussion about it. He was deep-sea diving with my emotions, and my oxygen tank was near empty. Time to surface and climb out of the water.

I leaned against the kitchen counter and waited for him to say whatever was so important that we needed to be alone. He opened a cupboard, removed a coffee mug, and poured himself the last ounces from the pot.

"The guy by the tents, who was he?"

"Emerson," I answered.

"Yeah, I know. How do you know him?" I'm not sure I liked his protective tone. Concerned friend? Or jealous ex?

"He's a friend, Brian. Only a friend."

"Then why have I never met him before?"

So I explained what happened in the early hours of the morning he broke up with me, my need for a sign from my grandmother, my desperate phone call, and Emerson picking up. I told him about our conversation. Brian listened with patience and interest. "Emerson saved my life," I said.

"So basically you told your life story to a complete stranger who had your grandma's old phone number, and that was a sign from her? How?"

I explained that it was validation of her presence. "But, why would your grandma send you a sign through a stranger?"

"It was what he said. Things he could never have known like how my grandma used to call me Ava Gardner."

"Okay?" He shot me a skeptical look.

"It meant *everything* to me."

"You could have called me instead."

"No. I couldn't."

His eyes blazed, then dimmed with resignation. "You're right. Sorry."

He turned to the sink and washed out his mug. Talking over the rush of water, I'm pretty sure he said, "I'm glad Emerson picked up. I'm glad he was there for you when you needed someone." After wiping his hands on a paper towel and drying the mug, he returned it to the cupboard.

"What did you want to tell me?" I asked.

"I put your father's comic book collection in your bedroom. I would have put it in your grandma's office, but the door's locked."

"But I wanted you—"

He cut me off. "I can't keep it. There's some valuable ones and you should hold on to them." He cleared his throat. "All right?"

I nodded.

"I also wanted to tell you I'm not gonna stay. I started some sketches for a new pottery series and I'm anxious to finish them. Besides, I think we both need to forge ahead with a little more space between us."

I nodded again.

He took a sketch out of his large cargo-pants pocket, walked to the refrigerator, and secured it with a magnet.

In awe, I said, "Oh Brian, it's beautiful."

"You always said you wanted me to draw the lighthouse. I was gonna use it in my series, but—" He shrugged.

"Thank you. I love it."

As he moved past me, I reached out and touched his shoulder. He stopped and drew me into him, and I inhaled his familiar smell, clay included. He released me and walked away.

For a short time, I stood quietly, then I was ready to move on. As I made my way to the door, I texted Emerson to meet me in front of the lighthouse.

9:36 P.M.

STANDING AT THE bottom of the porch steps, I hear Emerson before I see him. "Tricia!" I squint toward the bonfire and catch sight of him sprinting toward me, dodging around people. He calls my name again, a thread of concern in his voice.

In a few short moments, Emerson engulfs me into his arms, the same way he did when we first met. I'm amazed at how natural it feels to be right here, close to him. How is it possible to experience such familiarity with a stranger?

He gathers my hair, reverses our spots to prevent the wind from blowing strands into my eyes. "Everything all right? Brian—"

"I'm fine. We're good."

"Yeah? You sure?"

There's a world of tenderness in Emerson's touch, his voice, his eyes. I've missed being...precious like this. Like I was to my family, and it dawns on me Jeremiah also perceives, cherishes me like this. Had I felt treasured with Brian? He *loved* me. I loved him. But not enough. Or not in the way either one of us needed. Rehashing our failures again seems pointless. I close my eyes, let him go, and open them to Emerson ducking down to see me better.

"You're shivering. Are you cold?" He runs his fingers through my disheveled hair. Laughter draws our attention away from each other. I glance around, notice the eavesdroppers closest to us. The noise level dips to a low buzz instead of the constant thrum of conversation, music. "Let's go inside," I whisper.

Side by side, we climb the porch stairs. A couple exits the house, and at this moment I wish I could clear everyone out, not just from the house but from Boyer's Bluff.

The lighthouse was supposed to be off-limits, but that hasn't happened. I locked my grandma's office and her bedroom. Put away a few valuables. Other than the short stint to hear the Red-Eyed Loons, my detour into the tent area where I met Emerson, and my walk along the cliffs with him, I haven't been ten feet from the lighthouse. Brenda played docent to her two best friends from Sturg. I've given a few tours, and several dozen ignored the "Do Not Enter" sign for a self-guided expedition. At least they treated the house with respect.

But now, with Emerson at my side, I want to shut everyone else out. I glance back at him. His pace has slowed as he takes in the details of the lighthouse.

"Love your home," he says.

"Thanks. Me too."

I lead him to my grandma's office. Slipping the key from my pocket, I unlock the door, wait for Emerson to step inside. The room is dark. I walk over to my grandma's desk and switch on the antique lamp.

It emits a warm glow amidst the dim moonlight filtering in through the window. Having Emerson in the room that stores some of my best memories of my grandmother seems so right, cozy.

I expect Emerson's curiosity about the house to continue, perhaps admire some of my grandmother's Depression glass collection or the family photos, but he only gives it a cursory view and returns his attention to me. His back is pressed against the door. He looks completely wiped. Exhausted. He confirms it when he slides to the floor, sits with his legs extended into the room.

I sit next to him, our fingers almost touching.

Neither one of us says anything for quite a long time. And then...

"Thank you," he says quietly.

"For what?"

"For being here. For having this party. For recognizing Emerson. *Me.*" He pauses, then says, "As I said before, it's been...a tough day. A tough week."

I wait for him to continue. The outside din grows louder as the band starts up again. I don't mind being away from the action. I'm exactly where I want to be. Emerson's dark hair falls over his closed eyes and meets his five o'clock shadow. I become aware of the change in his breathing. Shallow, rapid, strained.

Maybe it's something he's thinking about? I want to ask him, but I'm not sure how much I should invade.

"Emerson?"

"Hmm?"

"Remember when you said, 'Trust me, you can tell me anything?'"

He stares at me, guarded with his expression.

"That goes for you too."

His head clunks against the door. "You really want to hear this?"

"Only if you want to tell me."

He hesitates, then says, "Would you think I'm crazy if I told you how many pretend conversations I've already had with you?"

"That depends."

"On?"

"Well, if you're crazy then I'm crazy, because I've had numerous pretend conversations with you, even imagined what it would be like meeting you years from now. It wasn't...this. Not even close. This is a thousand times better."

He leans in, brushes his lips against my forehead, sending an arrow of happiness right down to my toes. "Without a doubt, not crazy."

"So?"

His fingers inch toward mine, and I reach out, lace ours together. I squeeze his hand, giving strength, giving reassurance.

"So, it happened a long time ago. When I was five. There was this woman, and she saved my life..." Air hisses out between his teeth. "But by saving my life, she gave up hers. I haven't been back to the accident scene for thirteen years. But today, of all days, I went to the spot."

His eyes shut. Agony distorts his features as he struggles for control. A single tear traces the contour of his nose. He lets go of my hand, glances up.

Emerson's eyes dart across the room. We start to speak at the same time. "Emerson—"

"Tricia—" He inhales, exhales deeply again. "Do you have lavender potpourri?"

What? No. Why?" The air seems to crackle and spark with light. I can't rationally explain it with any of my senses.

"Because I keep smelling it." He stands. "It's—" He cuts himself off, opens the office door, steps into the hallway, then comes back in. "It's much stronger in here."

"My gr-grandma's scent was lavender."

He circles the room, lifts the lid on a small pot, and peers inside. His search continues until his gaze falls upon the family photos. In a blink, he's inches from the picture of my father, my mother, and me taken the day they brought me home to Boyer's Bluff.

His eyes dart to another photo—one of my mother, glamorous like Ava Gardner, a lot more than I'll ever be. I cautiously move next to him.

"W-Who is this?" His tone is demanding, unfamiliar, almost frightening. He pivots, searches my eyes with his frantic, stormy ones. "Green with a hint of gold," he mutters. "No."

"That was m-my *mom*."

I look at Emerson. I look at the picture.

He shakes his head violently. "Your mom," he repeats. Another tear trickles down his white cheek, and all of sudden his entire body begins to tremble.

I blink to clear my vision. I'm beyond any comprehension of what's happening. Can only brace myself against the wall.

He mumbles incoherently, "It can't be. It can't be," and then he removes the photo, slides to the floor, and stares at my mom.

I sink next to him.

He continues to stare at the picture. He touches her face with his fingertip, then his hand drops to his side wide open. He looks at his hand like it's the most fascinating thing he's ever seen. His fingers curl into a tight fist and unravel again as if to show that it's empty. Once again, his eyes focus on my mother and several silent tears trickle down Emerson's cheeks.

The pieces begin to lock into place. Oh my God. I'm almost certain I know what this is about, but I need him to say it. "Emerson, what's going on?"

He's so grief-stricken, it takes everything I have not to burst into tears. "God, Tricia. This is beyond—" His eyes plead with me. "There is no intellectual explanation for this. No logical, rational explanation." He sucks in a breath, lets it out. "Your mother saved my life. Pushed me out of the truck's path. But if I—" His voice cuts out. He shakes his head. "I'm sorry. Truly sorry. God, why? Why, when she's been through so much? I don't understand this. I don't understand why I'm here." His gaze bounces from me to my mom and back again. "Why did it have to be *you*?"

I shift closer, needing his comfort as much as to comfort him. His arm sweeps around me and he gathers me onto his lap, cradling me into his chest. I cling to him, hold him like I'll never let go, the way he holds me. He leans forward, buries his face into the crook of my neck.

I begin to construct a timeline based on what I know. Thirteen years ago my mother was killed by a drunk driver. His blood-alcohol level was two and a half times over the .08 Wisconsin legal limit. He blew the stop sign, jumped the curb, plowed into my mother. I vaguely remember Grandma mentioning a little boy, but I never, ever gave it much thought. I definitely don't remember her or Dad or anyone else telling me that Mom saved his life. *Emerson's life.* Nine and a half months after the accident, the guy who killed my mom was sentenced to twenty-five years for homicide by intoxicated use of a vehicle. Before this accident, he had three previous OWIs.

And then thirteen years later, give or take some months, I called my grandma's old phone number. Emerson's phone number, and he answered. If he hadn't...I might have—Oh God, it's so horrible, I can't even imagine it. But I'm here because of Emerson. He's alive because of my mom. And now he's *here* with me.

He pulls away, sets his hands on either side of my face, and looks at me with tenderness and a plea. "I never knew the name of the woman who saved me. But I've always wondered about her, about her family." He glances at the wall of photographs. "Thinking about her life was always in the abstract. Now there's you."

"Tell me everything," I say. "I want to know all the details of what happened."

So he does. He tells me about the quarter he picked up, he explains how my mother shouted at him to get out of the way, but it was too late. And he tells me how she saved him and how she died. I'm not sure how it's possible to be numb and ache at the same time, but I am. Numb for me, aching for Emerson. So much of this I didn't know.

"My mother, my family actually, did everything they could to shield me. A year after the accident, we moved to Sturgeon Bay and I did my best to put the crash behind me. I know it's not my fault. But still, in here—" He presses his hand over his heart. "Can you... forgive me?" His voice chokes out.

"Oh God. Emerson, I could never blame you. Even a raindrop of guilt is too much. It's wrong. And to know my mother saved your life, then you saved mine. Who are we to understand life's mysteries? Miracles?" My heart surges with a powerful, protective love, and I'm possessed with a desperate need to melt away—no, obliterate—his years of unfair torture with everything I have to offer.

Red light. The sudden need to be closer to him, to press my lips against his surges through me, and I'm worried that it would be too much between us after all this. I slam on the brakes.

Emerson kneels in front of me, cradles my hand in his like it's a cherished treasure. There's something in his piercing gaze that suspends time, shoots straight through my soul, and holds us in place for an eternity.

I breathe.

Yellow light. I'm cautious and wavering over the direction we may be heading and if it's the right one.

He sets his thumb against my wrist. Nerves leap into my throat, rob me of rational thought. My racing pulse stomps against the pad of his thumb as it strums along the sensitive skin. He continues to search my eyes, looking for something. Whatever it is, I hope he gets the message that I need this, need *him*.

Green light. With my free hand, I reach up and tangle my fingers in his wavy black hair. His arm hooks around my waist, holding me in place like a safety harness, tethering us before we jump off this bridge together. I pull him to me as he pulls me to him. We leap. Our lips brush against each other's, gentle, so incredibly gentle, and sweet. The kiss deepens, his tongue parts my lips. I'm lost in him.

And found.

I slide my hands under his sweatshirt and T-shirt. He hikes them over his head, tosses them aside, and kisses me again—a thunderstorm for a parched desert. My palms race over his skin until my fingertips brush against a hard ridge, quivering along with his heart. Emerson breaks our kiss and grabs my wrist.

I look down and see a long raised scar, a white slash against his solid chest.

I stare, wondering if he had open-heart surgery or... "Was...this from the crash?" I trace the mark.

He jerks away, and I lose my balance, catch myself with a braced arm against the carpet. His eyes turn to midnight, then close. Seconds later, he regains composure and opens them. "I had a heart defect. At least...that's what I tell everyone outside of family. It's not even a lie, depending on perspective. It's just not... everything." He reaches for his shirt, but I get to it first.

"I want to know."

He laughs. It's filled with so much grief. "And I guess I want to tell you." For what seems like the hundredth time tonight, Emerson observes me. He's made an art form out of reading people's body language. He pays attention. I move closer. Place my hand over the scar.

Sighing, he says, "It's self-inflicted. The day after the accident, I-I went into the kitchen, pulled a chair up to the counter, and took a butcher knife to cut out the pain."

I cover my mouth, horrified by the image formed in my mind of that wounded little boy.

"Obviously, I didn't know what I was doing. Except I'm pretty sure I got the idea from a neighbor kid who actually did have a heart defect that was surgically repaired. After the accident—After I watched your mom—" His Adam's apple bobs against his throat. "My heart felt like a ticking bomb ready to explode out of my chest. This—" He strokes the tips of our fingers against the scar. "—is what I did to to try and stop it."

"Oh Emerson."

"Honestly, it's okay. I don't have a conscious memory of doing it. I won't go into the gory details, but I was lucky. My mother found me before I bled out.

I went into shock, was hospitalized for a few weeks. Part of that first year, I stayed in a children's mental ward, then therapy. Lots and lots of therapy."

Leaning in, I trail my fingertips over the scar. When I've touched every inch, I place a kiss on top of it, then cover the scar with my palm. I have never been more grateful for two beating hearts.

He takes my hand, sets it on my lap. His eyes glaze over as if he's miles away.

"What are you thinking?"

He looks at me. "When we talked on the phone and I said, 'I'm an answer, Frankie. Maybe you're an answer for me, too.' Do you remember that?"

"Yes."

"You are my answer, Tricia. I just didn't know I needed one until you called."

"My grandma," I say. "I think she knew all along what we both needed."

⌒

11:58 P.M.

WE MAKE IT outside just in time for the Red-Eyed Loons's last set of the night. I don't have a second to protest when Emerson picks me up as if I weigh no more than a pebble and hoists me up onto his shoulders in one fluid movement. His hands run along my legs until they settle on my ankles. Soon there are dozens of other girls with the same bird's-eye view. We're dancing and singing and clapping and high-fiving as the guys keep us balanced. A few girls get into a playful chicken fight.

Emerson climbs onto a picnic table and I squeal, afraid he'll drop me. "I've got you," he says, laughing.

From this height, I scan the crowd and realize young and older from the island have joined us, twice as many people as earlier—a sea of islanders coming together to celebrate on Boyer's Bluff. *Grandma would have loved this.* I tell myself.

While Emerson and I were inside, the clouds cleared, leaving a spectacular black sky filled with winking stars and a brilliant almost-full moon. With the sparkling lights, the thrum of the guitar and bass, and the beat of the drums, the air shimmers and vibrates. I inhale a breath of beauty. It penetrates into my very being, making me—all of us—a part of something so much bigger than this small slice of heaven.

Colin Michaels calls out for a last request. Emerson shouts out "One Night." More people join in and it becomes a chant. Michaels proclaims "'One Night' it is," and the crowd roars its approval. Then Michaels waves to Brenda and everyone else in the mosh pit to come on stage. Soon, people pack every free inch. The band begins to play.

With extended instrumentation and repetition and an incredible mash-up, the music continues for a good fifteen minutes. The best fifteen minutes outside our time together in the lighthouse. Emerson sways gently beneath me and sings along:

> *If I had one night, I'd hold you in my arms,*
> *Find redemption, no more contention,*
> *Keeping you close. Too long, years gone,*
> *Wasted away. One night, our night,*
> *Remember this, I won't forget you.*
> *No, I won't forget you.*

∽

EMERSON STAYED AND helped clean up and tear down, then caught the last ferry at 4 P.M. His parents expect him for some family function at seven. I drove him to Detroit Harbor and couldn't bring myself to leave until the boat's ropes were untethered from the dock and the motors roared to life. I can't think about our good-bye without getting emotional. We talked about seeing each other, but didn't make any definite plans. My solace is that he's only a phone call away. It'll have to do.

Now, as I sit alone on the bottom porch step and look over Boyer's Bluff—the land worn with the memories of our magical night—I wish more than anything that I could go back in time. If Grandma were here, we'd play the Memory Game and capture the details and store them into a mental scrapbook. I close my eyes. Choose one favorite memory out of a dozen favorite memories from the party.

Right before dawn, Emerson and I stood outside the lighthouse shivering in the damp air. Most people had retreated to their tents. Islanders had gone home, and some of the Mainlanders had made it inside and crashed wherever they could find a soft surface. My bedroom was occupied by Brenda's best friends from Sturgeon Bay. At least a dozen people lingered by the bonfire talking, kissing, drinking, sleeping. Brenda and Christian, a friend of mine from school, seemed to have mastered three out of the four.

Emerson stepped closer to me, his hands deep in his pockets. Not wanting our time together to end, I tried to cover my exhaustion, biting back a yawn that parted my pursed lips with a sharp inhalation.

"Do you have a sleeping bag?" he asked.

Slightly apprehensive, I nodded.

I wasn't ready for more between us, but I also wasn't ready to say goodnight. Even though we had only kissed, the intensity of it electrified me in a way I'd never felt before. What we shared was more intimate, raw, and revealing than I could ever have imagined. And it frightened me.

Emerson sensed it.

"I'll get my sleeping bag from my tent. Let's go find a spot on the bluff and sleep under the stars, okay?"

"Yeah," I said. "That would be perfect."

We found a secluded area in a small clearing and zipped our sleeping bags together. Tucked in, we shared my pillow and stared up at the endless sky dotted with flecks of yellow, brightening as black slowly washed away into a soft light. Legs, hips, shoulders touched. But I couldn't relax. Emerson rolled onto his side, facing me. He whispered, "We've been a part of each other's lives for over thirteen years and didn't know it. We're linked. For now, let's not analyze it or question it. Let's just appreciate it."

"Okay," I whispered back, awed by the fact he somehow knew I'd been questioning, analyzing.

I placed my hand over his scarred heart, hoping that it finally had healed.

Our breathing slowed. Our eyes closed.

And we slept.

WE WOKE TO the sounds of voices, people gathering to watch the sunrise. Emerson and I climbed out of our combined sleeping bag, shook it out, smoothed it down, and sat facing the lake. Others joined us, some obviously nursing hangovers. Sitting in a line, we wrapped our arms around each other, shoulder to shoulder or waist to waist, as much for warmth as in friendship. From the water's blues and greens, a thick, gray cloud hovered against the horizon, then cleared. The rising sun burst out with a palette of orange and yellow rays as far as our eyes could see.

A light breeze kissed my face. I can't explain how or why, but I sensed it was good-bye. I looked out over Boyer's Bluff to the lighthouse and to Emerson, who held me just a bit closer, almost like he knew. I took a deep breath and caught the last wisps of lavender.

4:28 PM

MY PHONE PLAYS "Call Me." A Frank Sinatra song.

It's Emerson.

A photo of the two of us making silly faces blinks onto my screen. I smile until I'm all-out beaming like a high-powered, rechargeable flashlight. Yeah, definitely recharged.

The plink plink of rocks skidding across packed dirt draws my attention toward the crest of the driveway. Emerson stands there. Like he never left. I'm caught in a freeze-frame that shrinks until there's just Emerson.

His phone is cradled against his ear and he's wearing the most irresistible grin.

Boyer's Bluff springs to life.

Rising to my feet, I hit TALK, and press the phone to my ear. As I walk toward him, my steps quicken. When we're almost close enough to touch, my hand reaches out for his. We move together. Our fingers meet, and I say, "Hello."

DEAR READERS,

THOUGH THE CIRCUMSTANCES In *HELLO?* are not my circumstances, I definitely drew upon what I can only say was an extremely difficult childhood, especially from grade school through my freshman year of high school. Sophomore year changed everything. I ended up joining a fantastic youth group run by teens from my and other local high schools. I went from a sad introvert to a vivacious extrovert. Who knew that could happen? Although circumstances didn't change much at home, life outside became a million times better.

During my darkest days, I thank God there were people who were there to protect or help me, even if they weren't necessarily aware of what I endured. For example, my fifth grade teacher Mr. Cienian, took a sobbing little girl bullied by mean girls, sat me down, handed me a Baby Ruth candy bar, which melted all over my fingers, and introduced me to the wondrous world of books.

Before that moment, I was a horrible reader. The introvert me had been traumatized by my second grade teacher, who forced me to stand in front of the class and read out loud. I choked every time. I was in the lowest reading group. The teacher was a bully who pinched cheeks hard, turned over desks, and humiliated students. School wasn't a safe place for me. My fear of school didn't leave until Mr. Cienian's kindness and belief in me transformed my life.

If you have a friend who might be like any of the characters in this book, the best thing you can do is to be a friend. It means *everything.*

For Tricia's relationship with her grandma, I drew upon my own with my grandparents, Lena and Jack. There were many times—though I don't think my grandparents consciously knew it—that they were my salvation. Simply put—they just loved me for me, unconditionally.

I know what it means to be a victim of abuse. I know what it means to survive. Most importantly, it's been many years since I've thought of myself as a survivor. Instead, I am a **thriver.**

If you're suffering, please know I'm sending you a virtual hug. Take positive, healthy action. There were so many things I couldn't control, especially when it came to abuse I suffered at the hands of adults. But one of the biggest lessons I learned as a teen was that I could choose who I wanted to be as a person. I didn't want to repeat history. Kindness and compassion became my mantra. Every day, I wake up with the prayer to be the best Liza I can be. Be the best you. That is your greatest defense against darkness.

Liza Wiemer

Suicidal thoughts:

No doubt, there were moments growing up when I felt like Tricia, so much despair that I wanted to end it all. Perhaps you have felt this way too? Even at this moment? Don't! Please don't. There is light in darkness. There are people who care! It may not feel that way now, but there are. If there is no one for you to reach out to, then please, I ask you to call 1-800-SUICIDE or go to http://www.suicide.org for local listings. Call. You matter. You really, really do.

Though Tricia reached out to a stranger, please call the number above. I have no doubt there are Emersons out there, but it's **always** best to reach out to experts.

If you have been a victim of sexual assault, PLEASE DO NOT SUFFER ALONE.

As of July 1, 2015, the RAINN (Rape, Abuse & Incest National Network: http:/www.rainn.org) website statistic page states: "Approximately 4/5 of assaults are committed by someone known to the victim. 47% of rapists are a friend or acquaintance."

RAINN's National Sexual Assault Hotline: 1-800-656-HOPE (4673)

Additional places for help:

NSVRC (National Sexual Violence Resource Center): http://www.nsvrc.org

Trans Lifeline: Hotlines: USA 1-877-565-8866, Canada 1-877-330-6366 http://www.translifeline.org

The Trevor Project (Crisis & Suicide Prevention for LGBTQ Youth) Hotline: 1-866-488-7386 http://www.thetrevorproject.org

SOAR (Speaking Out Against Rape): http://www.soar99.org

WOAR (Women Organized Against Rape) Hotline: 1-215-985-3333

ACKNOWLEDGEMENTS

OVER THE COURSE of several months, I've thought about, typed, and deleted many versions of what I wanted to say in my acknowledgements. I came to one very important conclusion—words cannot accurately capture the depth of gratitude to the people who have contributed to bringing this novel to publication. Words are a dim reflection of what's in my heart.

Know this, without those mentioned below, *Hello?* wouldn't be what it is today. I wouldn't be who I am today. Without question, each and every one of you is an important link, connecting us to each other and to every reader. I am deeply, deeply, humbly grateful.

If I inadvertently forgot to include you on this list, I ask for your forgiveness.

My thanks to:

God.

Stuart Krichevsky.
Shana Cohen. Ross Harris. Elizabeth Law.

E. Carrie Howland.

Patricia Riley.

Danielle Ellison. Kelly Hager. Karen Hughes. Kate Kaynak. Asja Parrish. Jessica Porteous. Richard Storrs. Cindy Thomas. Megan Trank. Jenny Zemanek. The Spencer Hill Contemporary Team.

Martina Boone. Benay Browne Katz. Laura Harrington. Jillian Heise. Kathryne Squilla. Justin Wiemer. Lynn Wiese Sneyd. Heidi Zweidel.

Erin Arkin. Jaime Arkin. Miri Berger Katz. Jen Cooke Fisher. Barry Doft. Nili Doft. Shirlee Doft. Andye Epps. Barbara Goldberg. Don Goldberg. Peter Goldberg. Daniel Goldin. Eileen Graves. Glenn Graves. Mike Hunt. Betsy Kaplan. Aryeh Katz. Avital Katz. Jeff Katz. Sarah Kealy. Rachel Kinnard. Maureen Komisar. Mitch Lechter, Sharon Lerman. David Luddy. Hannah McBride. LouAnne Occhiogrosso. Peter Occhiogrosso. Gary Richter. Jerry Richter. Lucy Richter. Barbara Weiss. Sarah Weiss. Stan Weiss. Nancy Wiese.

Rob Carr. Marleen Erlich Johnson. Trisha Hansen. Randy Holm. Ann Lennon. Tyler McGrane. Richard Purinton. Timothy Raymond. Renee Rudolph. Gary Schultz. Lydia Schultz. Sarah Schultz. Sarah Waldron. Steve Waldron. Melody Walsh. The staff, teachers, and all the 2011-2012 students at Washington Island School. The community of Washington Island, who made me feel so welcome!

Robert Nickel. Linnea Schmelzer, Savanna Townsend. The group of 2011-2012 junior Sturgeon Bay High School girls who spent their lunch hour talking with me. Kelly Hellmann and Deb McDonald at the Inn at Cedar Crossing, Sturgeon Bay.

The incredible YA community of authors, bloggers, teachers, librarians, booksellers, and readers.

My Wiemer, Ruminski, Katz, Doft, and Goldberg family. My grandparents Jack and Lena. Dad and Cathy. The lights of my life: Jim. Justin. Ezra.

> "Do not be too timid and squeamish about your actions. All life is an experiment. The more experiments you make the better."
> Ralph Waldo Emerson

My gratitude to Ralph Waldo Emerson, whose wisdom permeates this novel.

Author note: Door County, Wisconsin—specifically Sturgeon Bay and Washington Island—is a huge part of this novel. If you're thinking about taking a vacation, I encourage you to consider visiting. The beaches, parks, Mann's, the Red Cup Coffee House, and other places mentioned in this novel, exist. Door County's beauty is so much better than I could ever describe. The people I met epitomize friendly hospitality.

The Red-Eyed Loons are a figment of my imagination. Although I used authentic island and student names from both high schools, every person is fictional. Any resemblance is purely coincidental. The general portrayal for the Sturgeon Bay bed and breakfast mentioned in *Hello?* came from my stay at the Inn at Cedar Crossing. The only major liberty I took in this novel was placing the nearby Pottawatomie Lighthouse on Rock Island—the inspiration for Tricia's home—onto Washington Island's Boyer's Bluff. The cover design includes a photo illustration of the lighthouse and a magnificent sunrise taken at Jackson Harbor, Washington Island by Steve Waldron.

Websites to check out:
http://www.sturgeonbay.net
http://www.washingtonisland.com
http://doorcounty.com

DISCUSSION QUESTIONS

Brian broke up with and walked out on Tricia in her time of great despair. Do you think he handled Tricia's loss the best way he knew how? Did he make you angry? Frustrated? In what way can you sympathize with him?

Do you think Tricia made a good choice by keeping her real name a secret and asking Emerson to change his phone number? If you had been Emerson, would you have done it?

Throughout the novel, Jeremiah Johansson attempts to be a father figure for Tricia, but allowing him to take that role is very difficult for her. Why do you think that is, and how do you think that might change in the future?

Breakups are, at the very least, unpleasant. Emerson's breakup with Angie was disastrous. What do you think is the best way for one person to break up with another?

The only person Angie really ever revealed herself to completely was Jordan. What qualities did Jordan possess that you believe made Angie feel safe and comfortable enough to share her vulnerabilities?

Why do you think Angie expressed herself through poetry? What did it reveal about her?

Brenda threw herself into acting and writing screenplays. Why do you think she chose this outlet? How did it help her to cope with her trauma?

Though Brenda and Angie were best friends, they also had a disconnect in their relationship. There were many reasons for that, some more obvious, some more subtle. What were those reasons? Do you think they'll be able to maintain their friendship after Brenda moves to New York?

Brenda rarely went through her OCD routine of locking and unlocking and locking and unlocking doors and windows in front of other people. Why do you think she did that? Why did she dismiss Angie's concern, and then later Tricia's questioning look?

Brenda tells her father that she doesn't need to continue to see a therapist. What do you think of her decision? Why might continuing be beneficial for her?

Brenda said to Brian, "The past is a lonely, depressing place to live, and I'm done." What do you think she meant by this? How had she been stuck in the past? How would you apply that to the other characters?

Brian initiated sex with Tricia to soothe her in a moment of great despair. Why do you think he failed? Are there circumstances when sex could be a way to comfort another person?

Did you think that Brenda's text to Brian was a good way to get him to drive over to Tricia's? Did the end justify the means? What else could she have done?

While Tricia's life improved after her call to Emerson, Emerson's life began to fall apart. He experienced flashbacks and fell into moments of despair. Why do you think that happened?

After Emerson broke up with Angie, he faced a nightmare situation because of the gif. He deleted his social media and, once he said he was innocent, refused to continue to defend himself. Why do you think that was? Did he handle it the best way he could? Do you think his actions would have been different if he wasn't graduating in seven weeks?

Do you have any sympathy for Travis in the gif incident? In what way should he be responsible for his actions?

Emerson asks Dr. Shale if he had paid back the universe by saving Frankie's life. Why do you think Emerson felt like he owed a life in the first place? What did you think of Dr. Shale's response? Did you agree with his answer?

Tricia's perception of Washington Island and Boyer's Bluff changed dramatically. Some of that took place in the narrative, but there were other things that happened behind the scenes. What do you think enabled her to see the community, the people, the land in a different light?

Emerson is often caught in the crossfire of Brenda's anger. In what ways do you agree or disagree with how she treated him?

Brian starts a new pottery series titled, "Island Beauty." In what way do you think it kept him connected to Tricia? How do you think it helped him cope with their breakup?

The party has a huge impact on each one of these characters. How does it change them? What do you think happened behind the scenes with Tricia and Emerson before they went outside to listen to the Red-Eyed Loons? Brenda and Christian? Angie and Jordan? Brian after he returns to his studio?

There were many serendipitous moments in this novel. Have you ever experienced any? What were they?

How did the interlinking story and multiple points of view impact your perceptions of these characters?

One character who is "off-camera" throughout this entire novel is the grandma. How did her role impact this story?

Saying "Hello," even to a stranger, can have a powerful and positive impact. Why do you think that is? Why do you think the author chose to end the novel with that word?

What do you hope will happen for each of these characters in the future?

Often times we don't see how our lives interconnect with others, but our actions can clearly affect other people. Can you think of anything you have done that has had a positive and profound impact on someone else?

ABOUT THE AUTHOR

Liza married the guy who literally swept her off her feet at a Spyro Gyra concert. Their love story can be found on Liza's "About" page on her website, LizaWiemer. com. Besides being a die-hard Packer fan, Liza is also a readaholic, a romantic, and a lover of crazy socks and rooftops. *Hello?* is her debut YA novel. She also has had two adult non-fiction books published, as well as stories and articles in various publications. She's a graduate of UW-Madison with a degree in Education and the mother of two sons. Say HELLO to Liza on Twitter: @LizaWiemer

CPSIA information can be obtained
at www.ICGtesting.com
Printed in the USA
LVOW04s1138180316
479747LV00002B/2/P